CHANGING

LIFELINES

Hugh McLeave

ROBERT HALE · LONDON

© Hugh McLeave 2008
First published in Great Britain 2008

ISBN 978-0-7090-8679-6

Robert Hale Limited
Clerkenwell House
Clerkenwell Green
London EC1R 0HT

www.halebooks.com

2 4 6 8 10 9 7 5 3 1

Typeset in 10/14pt Century Schoolbook
Printed and bound in Great Britain by
Biddles Limited, King's Lynn

chapter I

Gascoyne's key stuck in the lock and in his exasperation he nearly broke it before realizing he had erred by inserting the street door key. He still cursed, murmuring under his breath about days like this when nothing went right and even inanimate matter seemed hostile. Entering the flat, he tossed his briefcase on the coffee table, knocking over an ashtray. He opened the drinks cupboard and built himself a triple vodka and tonic, downed it in one then poured himself a second, which he sipped sitting down, hoping it would burn off his bleak mood.

He had decisions to make.

All that day he had felt depressed. Before he left for his chambers, he and Nancy had quarrelled, a real up-and-downer which had left him with a tension headache and an urge to take it out on anything. Now he couldn't remember what had triggered their row; a bad sign when they broke like thunderstorms out of a blue sky.

In the law courts he had sat through three hours of a divorce case before Judge Grantland, a prurient old sadist with a keyhole psyche who treated every divorce like a duel to the death in the eternal war of the sexes. No speck of smut was left undredged. That session reminded Gascoyne only too painfully of his own marital troubles before Grantland threw out his case for lack of evidence of adultery.

To cheer himself up during the adjournment, Gascoyne had rung his mistress, Anne Howells, to invite her to join him for lunch at the Wig and Pen opposite the law courts. When he told her about the row that morning, Anne said, 'Admit it, Bob, your marriage is a write-off. Nancy wouldn't miss you any more than you'd miss her.' She leaned over to whisper in his ear, 'Why don't you pack your bags and move in with me? I've got plenty of room, money – everything.' She dwelt on the last word, injecting it with the right lewd resonance.

Gascoyne looked at her, smiling. Anne was chic, nubile, worldly, almost everything Nancy was not; yet somehow the social polish and the haute-couture clothes could never disguise the fact that deep down she was a whore. Though that might have been why they had found each other.

'Let me think about it.'

'Don't think about it for too long,' Anne murmured, her hand seeking his under the table to run painted and pointed nails over his palm, sending anticipation tingling through him.

When Judge Grantland adjourned his next divorce case early that afternoon, Gascoyne thought first of ringing Anne and meeting her at her flat, but then he felt this was tantamount to accepting her offer, and he did need time to think and at least make the split with Nancy decently.

In the cab taking him home he reflected that Anne was probably right. His marriage was finished after six years; Nancy and he had no children, nothing to tie them. And they were squabbling much of the time.

Now he remembered how the row had started. On the previous evening, he had stopped off for a few drinks with some barrister colleagues and arrived late and well lit for dinner with the five people she had invited. Hell, couldn't a man have a few drinks after a hard day's work?

Nancy hadn't seen it that way. At breakfast she had glowered at him while he was taking cover behind *The Times* sports page.

'Do you remember anything of the dinner last night?'

'Only that it wasn't memorable.'

'You mean what you ate and drank wasn't memorable, or was it the company and the conversation?'

'Everybody looked pissed and the repartee was lousy – with one exception.'

Nancy did not give him the chance of explaining that he was the exception, but said, 'You don't remember insulting Jack Dobson, then?'

Dobson? Dobson? After several tries, Gascoyne finally nailed him: the stoop-shouldered accountant with weepy eyes, a boomerang snout and dirty fingernails. 'No,' he said, 'but insulting him is one thing I'd like to have remembered.'

'And the wine you spilled over his wife?'

'Our best wine, was it?'

Again, she ignored the sarcasm. 'You should also know, in case you run into Neil Johnstone, that you tried to chat up his wife, Pam, and it was all I could do to stop Neil from clouting you.'

'Thanks for that.' He meant it. Johnstone was a megalith, built like the massive nineteenth-century safe in Tyndall's chambers where Gascoyne worked; he had played as a front-row forward for London Scottish and would have eaten him whole. 'Anything else?' he said.

'Yes. You called Simon Cranston a poof.'

'Your publisher? Well, he talks in a high soprano and he's at least hermaphrodite and he must have done something to deserve the epithet ... Now I remember, he put a hand on my crotch.'

'But he wasn't sitting anywhere near you.'

'Then he has arms like a chimp.'

Nancy cleared the table and stalked out. From the banging and clattering as she slotted the dishes into the washing-up machine, he could hear that she was still seething. They kept out of each other's feet until he left for his chambers and a day in the law courts with Judge Grantland.

Now in the flat as he sipped his second vodka and tonic, he flicked the switch on his CD player to find some music and stared at the machine when it failed to respond. It was then he noticed the note in block letters Nancy had propped up on the mantelpieces: MY WORD-SPINNER'S SEIZED UP. PLEASE FIX.

Peremptory! No Bob or Bup, his diminutives. So she was still fuming about their grisly dinner and morning spat.

Gascoyne took his drink through to the study, which he shared with Nancy, and examined the computer and printer. Both plug and flex seemed all right, but when he tried the plug on a table lamp it did not light up. It must be the five-amp plug fuse, he thought, and headed for the kitchen and the mains box where he kept the fuses. He swore when he discovered he had run out of five-amp fuses; it meant walking to Halford's electrical store on the corner of Earl's Court to buy half a dozen fuses.

Back in the flat, he replaced the blown fuse, and sure enough the printer rumbled and the computer came to life. To his surprise, the printer began to vomit paper. Nancy had obviously instructed the printer to deal with what she had written at the moment the fuse blew. There were a good dozen pages. Nancy had evidently done a lot of work that morning for it was the best part of a whole chapter.

Idly, he cast his eye over those pages then began to backtrack through the script. Nothing here to blow even a one-amp fuse, he reflected. It was in Nancy's usual quiet, laid-back style, consistent with her character. It would probably do no better in the bookshops and kiosks than her three previous romantic novels, which stood on the shelves above the word processor.

She had published them all under the pseudonym Dorothy Armour at his behest, for he did not want his fellow barristers sniggering behind their hands, fancying that these books reflected his marriage or, worse still, that his own hand might lie behind some of the trite or mawkish sentiments in Nancy's books.

However, if none of them had made a splash, they still earned Nancy and the Aphrodite Press, which published her, a few thousand pounds from the 5,000 or so hardback and 30,000 paperback copies they sold.

Gascoyne had to admit the money came in handy. He wondered if she would have written the books had he earned more at the bar and didn't look like ending his career as a junior who could never aspire to becoming a Silk, a Queen's Counsel pulling in fat fees for civil and divorce cases. He realized, too, that these books were, after a fashion, Nancy's secret garden; she rarely mentioned them and hardly ever hinted at what she was writing, or asked his opinion.

Nevertheless, Gascoyne reckoned he knew what Nancy's books lacked. He had once told her that if she wanted to set the bookshops alight, she should forget about moonlight and magnolias and love among the asphodels; there were always more cads than Galahads, more Messalinas than vestal virgins. And all but the most trite romances finished as burnt-out cases.

If she needed proof, she could read the divorce briefs he handled every day, and there were enough of those cases to make a fortune for Geoffrey Tyndall, the QC he served as a junior, and a hundred other lawyers like him. Those fine romances ended as sordid wrangling over money and possessions whether it was the contents of the kitchen cupboard, the clapped-out car or a brace of kids.

Nancy had listened to this indictment in silence, but her blue-grey eyes were sparking and he felt she might have thrown something had there been anything handy.

Take this book he was looking at. *The Heart's Reason* she had called it. Who among the little secretaries and shop girls who read Aphrodite Press stuff knew about Blaise Pascal, let alone his dictum, 'The heart has its reasons that reason knows not of'? He knew the simple plot, though what did plots matter? They were like life on earth, all spawned from two or three basic seeds; everything depended on what you did with them.

Nancy had imagined a young Scottish farmer, Malcolm Forsyth (she had a way with names), who meets Jane Sutherland, a girl of good class, during the agricultural show in Edinburgh. They fall in love at first sight and get married before the show finishes. Jane has a shock when Malcolm takes her home to the isolated sheep farm in the Scottish border country south of the Tweed. Everything seems hostile – the land, the weather, Malcolm's collies, and especially the stern, Presbyterian mother who scorns her ignorance of farming, housework, making meals and even life. Jane sees her husband only at night when he is exhausted from hard work in all weathers. All this eats into their love for one another.

At this point, Malcolm's younger brother, Iain, arrives from Oxford for his long vacation. He has no time for the farm or for helping his brother. Money is the name of his game, big money made out of buying and selling property or stock exchange speculation. His mother dotes on him. Soon, Jane falls under his spell, impressed with his patter, his knowledge of the world. Malcolm knows about their attraction for each other but says nothing. He feels that beside Iain he has no learning, no culture and no attraction for Jane.

Iain seduces Jane and persuades her to run away with him, although he does not love her and is only interested in her body. They are running away when their car crashes. Iain is killed and Jane is picked up seriously injured. Malcolm comes for her and takes her home.

Gascoyne put down the script. No wonder the printer had seized up, for so had her story. It lacked punch and the characters moved along too well-trodden paths. Why hadn't she made Jane more of a tart, somebody who'd have set her cap at the well-heeled farmer for his money and inveigled him into marriage? That would have heightened the conflict with the mother, who would see her for what she was worth. And why a sheep farmer? Sheep had no sex appeal – they sent people to sleep, didn't they? Bulls had a different sexual image. And horses, especially stallions. They exuded sex as anybody was aware who had sat on a horse or been around horses. So, why couldn't Malcolm run a stud, breeding race horses or even shire horses?

And why couldn't the younger son, Iain, have known Jane and her background from having picked her up in a bar or even met her in a brothel. He would obviously blackmail her into having sex with him. Malcolm finds out and they have a fight in one of the stables and the younger brother dies from being felled then kicked in the head by one of the horses which had panicked.

Gascoyne could see the whole thing unreeling like a film. Malcolm on trial and the girl returning to take the stand to save him with her testimony ... then discovering she loved him and she was determined to convince him of this and seek his forgiveness. Well, he could probably beef up the ending if it were left to him.

Gascoyne picked up Nancy's script and began to read it again, trying to transpose some of his thoughts and ideas into her pages. There were some fine scenes and excellent pages in the book as it stood. Nancy was good on quarrels, something he knew from personal experience. He realized, too, from the way she made love, that she might have written the love scenes with more feeling.

But, in a curious way, those scenes recalled his first years with Nancy. Those things they shared like the pub meals around the law courts where she would wait for him to finish a case, or the crowded Soho and Covent Garden restaurants or a sandwich in the Temple gardens; they reminded him of the theatres and concerts or the jazz clubs they took in. They even shared their reading.

Now why could those feelings, those shared experiences, not have lasted? They were as near love as Gascoyne thought anybody could get. Where had things gone sour? Where? He could not put a finger on the time or place.

His divorce court work told him that even what couples had taken for true love only had a limited run. The fifth, sixth, seventh, eighth years proved the tricky ones in which most of his divorce cases fell. He himself was having a touch of the seven-year itch to change partners. Could he blame himself? He had a mistress who looked like a bra-and-panty ad, was artful in the sheets, was rolling in money, agreed with most everything he said, and wanted him to move in with her.

What was he waiting for? Sometimes, like today, he wished he knew the answer to that one.

Gascoyne returned to the script. There, anybody could see that Nancy's homework on the Scottish borders and their sheep farmers showed through too much. All right, perhaps nobody had given *Lady Chatterley's Lover* points for pheasant roaring or fox trapping, perhaps those who read romantic novels hardly expected them to reflect real life; but the book also lacked the sort of characters and incidents that people could identify with.

Gascoyne primed the word processor to print another full version of Nancy's script while he went to fetch a packet of cigarettes.

He had often used her machine to write divorce and other briefs. Now, with a new disk in it, he began to rewrite Nancy's story as he saw it.

He started by juggling with Nancy's text, injecting muscle into it here and there and adding bits as they occurred to him. But he also saw ways of linking the narrative passages and interspersing new scenes. It gave him a kick composing scenes, for when he thought about it, that was what divorce was all about – scenes from married life.

Odd, that what he thought and felt went into the machine so effortlessly, almost as though the text put itself together. There was that French literary egghead who said novels wrote themselves. Well, he had something, whoever he was.

Time went through him painlessly. When he finally lifted his head to look at his watch, four hours had gone by like so many minutes. His vodka and tonic lay untouched and his ashtray had one stub in it. His bleak mood had evaporated and Anne Howells and her offer had not even entered his head.

When he had printed out what was on the disk and read over what he had written, the result pleased him. He had three chapters and a rough outline of where the story was headed, and the bones of several more scenes.

Oh, it was rough, unpolished prose, and where he had borrowed tracts of Nancy's original script and revised them, the seams showed. But he could correct all this later. Gascoyne found himself looking forward to Nancy's return from her group practice. She would be tickled when she read his version of her fine romance.

chapter II

For Nancy the morning had gone sour. First there was the terrible spat with Robert because she had forgotten to fetch his dinner jacket from the cleaners. Damn his barrister's talent for cutting, insulting repartee which always left her speechless! How would he react, she wondered, when she revealed what the cleaners had found in his pockets?

She would soon find out when they had their next bust-up, for nowadays they slagged each other off about everything from her burnt toast to what he spent on vodka. How much longer, she asked herself, could they endure bickering and points-scoring and living within the glass walls they had built round themselves?

She must have transmitted her simmering temper to the word processor, which had hiccupped twice then given up. Even Umberto, her Fiat 500, seemed to be playing her up. What next?

Now waiting for the lift in the basement car park, she turned and spotted something that did not improve her mood – the sleek, Savile Row outline of Dr Bernard Mason approaching her. One of the four partners in the group practice, Mason appeared to go out of his way to annoy and harass her.

She disliked almost everything about the man: his slicked, dark hair which she was sure he tinted, the way he smiled by retracting his thin lips to show his six front crowns, the Svengali effect he tried to create in women with that husky, drawling voice of his, and his halitosis, at least a yard long.

But most of all, she hated those cold, green snake eyes which never stopped inching over her from top to bottom, mentally seeing her do a strip-tease garment by garment.

With his lecherous look, he had a lecherous line of patter.

What was such a smoothie with his Oxford drawl doing in a rather shabby suburban group practice in Shepherd's Bush? It mystified her. Mason dressed in style, Savile Row or Armani, and drove a vintage Bentley which must have cost two years' income from his small health-service list and few private patients at this practice. What was his racket? Drugs, abortion or some other fiddle? She prayed for the day the General Medical Council would put its official pencil through his name on the medical register and bar him from practice.

His Bentley parked, Mason arrived smoothing his Garrick Club tie and Gieves mohair suit. He shot Nancy a warped smile then, true to form, thrust his face forward to whisper in her ear: 'Nice to roll you over in the lift in a power cut.'

Nancy recoiled then glared at him. 'What was that you said?'

Mason looked surprised, indignant even. 'I merely said, "Nasty little Rover left in my parking lot."' He paused to observe her reaction, then added, 'Whatever did you think I said?' and gazed at her accusingly as though her lewd mind had traduced his words and thoughts.

'You know what you said and you know I know what you said.'

Mason shrugged his incomprehension then smiled. 'How can I help it if I speak faster than most people think,' he said.

'Does that "most people" include yourself?' Nancy came back and noticed that for once she had hit him between those snake eyes.

She turned and left him the lift, swearing under her breath at this Jekyll-and-Hyde quack. Even if she wired herself up with a tape machine, it would be difficult to separate the words of those suggestive phrases he spat out so quickly. Obviously he rehearsed them over and over again before letting them loose on her. She ran up the stairs to the first floor where the practice was housed. Mason was leaving the lift, walking towards his consulting room.

Patricia Williams, who did the morning stint, greeted Nancy then nodded at Mason's back.

'Didn't feel like sharing a lift with Mr Hyde, then?'

'Like I would a rattlesnake.'

'What was it – more aural sex?'

Nancy nodded. She repeated what Mason had said and his get-out phrase, and Pat laughed. 'You've got to hand it to him, it's a good line.' She put on her quirky little smile and said, dreamily, 'I wonder what he'd be like.'

'I'll leave you to find out.'

Together they went over the cards for the patients their doctors had seen that morning, and for those people still in the waiting room. 'They're all regulars,' Pat said. She pointed to the consulting-room door of Dr Philip Fothergill, doyen of the group practice. 'He's running half an hour late and he's got a batch of afternoon visits to do. Hurry him up.'

When Pat had picked up her hat and coat and said goodbye, Nancy checked the cards and filed those for patients who had been seen. She confirmed their names and their treatment on the master computer, which was linked with those in each consulting room, in case Pat had missed something.

She was just finishing when she spotted Dr Fothergill's code-word appear on the computer followed by four letters spaced out with several points between them: S ... T ... R ... O...

As she gazed at the screen, puzzled, Dr Fothergill's patient came running out. 'It's the doctor, I think he's ill,' she said.

Fothergill was sitting at his desk staring straight ahead as though wondering where he was; he was trying desperately to move his lips but succeeded only in fluttering his eyelids.

'It's all right, Dr Fothergill,' Nancy said in his ear. 'Don't try to move.'

She lifted his phone and punched out Peter Clarke's extension number. As the senior partner after Fothergill, he would have to take charge. When the phone had rung half a dozen times, she assumed Clarke was elsewhere or busy and decided to go and tell him direct.

Nancy still had to knock and wait until he had called on her to enter before she dared open the door. Not long after she started in the practice, she had been faced with a patient who had fainted. She had barged through Clarke's door to find the doctor lying on the floor on his back; his knees were flexed and he was moving his buttocks and back rhythmically.

It stopped Nancy in her tracks, for her first impression was that Peter Clarke was simulating the sexual act and trying to work up an orgasm.

It turned out to be something much less interesting. Nancy discovered later that Clarke suffered from disc trouble and low back pain and did exercises and adopted a certain posture to prevent trouble. It had often mystified her that the doctor had a man-ape-size effigy of the Neanderthal Man in his consulting room. When she asked why, Clarke explained that he had once worked for an orthopaedic specialist who had evolved a treatment of spinal and joint maladies based on the posture of the first erect primates. She now knew why Clarke stood with his weight on the outside edges of his feet, his legs slightly bowed, his knees flexed, his buttocks compressed, his shoulders slightly hunched and his arms dangling. At first sight, he looked as though he had perhaps had a bowel spasm and had been going but had not quite got there before events overtook him. She had told Pat who shrugged, grinned and said, 'That's nothing. I once found him hanging upside-down like a bat from a bar he'd fixed over the door between his office and the cubicle where he examined his patients. He said it was yoga.'

Now, when Nancy entered Clarke's room, she found he had been carrying out a detailed examination on a child whom he brought to the door with her mother.

'Excuse me, Doctor, but Dr Fothergill's had a stroke, I think.'

'Go and wait with him and I'll be there in a minute,' Clarke said. 'Oh, and call an ambulance – from Hammersmith Hospital.'

Nancy realized that Clarke would have to go and fetch his wife, for he did nothing without her say-so. When they arrived a few minutes later, Marcia Clarke explained that she would take over Dr Fothergill's list that afternoon. Peter Clarke gave Fothergill an injection and accompanied him to the hospital when the ambulance arrived. Like Fothergill, the Clarkes were founder members of the group practice. From what Nancy gathered, they had met each other at St Thomas's Hospital medical school. She could never imagine how they had ever become physically compatible. Peter was small and wiry with quick, darting movements, intelligent eyes and a mobile face which he had spoiled by growing a stubbly moustache that bristled like magnetized iron filings. Marcia could have made two of him; she was broad-beamed, big-bosomed and as spry in her movements as a lame hippo and as slow in thought as a meatless day. From her neat chignon through her spatulate, unvarnished nails to her flat-heeled shoes, she looked the most practical of women. But Nancy had found her hopelessly unorganized. For instance, computers terrified her. A 'blip' on their circuit and Nancy knew it was six-fingered Marcia.

Now she had to take Marcia in hand, alternating her patients with Fothergill's. It would have been easier to transfer the information from the sick doctor's computer to Marcia's, but this would have ended in chaos and errors, maybe even a fatal one, in treating patients. Fortunately, Nancy could have handled Fothergill's list herself and therefore kept Marcia from making any serious mistakes.

There was Mr Stimson who turned up every three months to have his blood pressure checked and a supply of beta blockers; Mrs Sandra Braithwaite came with her usual shopping list of everything from anti-inflammatory pills for her rheumatism to tranquillizers because she was worried about an incipient ulcer caused by the painkillers, antacids and a sleeping pill to bomb her into oblivion between midnight and breakfast TV; Margery Butler arrived with one of those migraines that occurred every time her husband disappeared on a drink-and-sex binge. After her they had Patrick Robinson, who had mild diabetes, and Matt Benson for his steroids to treat his asthma. They had one serious case, and Marcia had to tell Leonard Browning that his tests had revealed an undifferentiated lung tumour, in fact a cancer, which required surgery.

Within an hour, Clarke had returned from the hospital to report that Fothergill would be away for at least four months.

'What do we do – split his patients up among the others?'

'We'll have to, until I find a locum.'

Somehow, Nancy steered Marcia Clarke through the rest of Fothergill's list without endangering any of his patients. However, she had to hint diplomatically that she should reduce Mrs Gorman's Valium dosage, for the elderly lady was already walking with a sort of soft-shoe shuffle and Nancy had feared for some time that Fothergill's heavy hand with the drug would turn her into a zombie or stop her in her tracks altogether.

At the end of a tiring four hours, she was packing up and logging the records in her computer when Mason appeared from his consulting room. He leaned over to whisper: 'You'd be a whiz in the nude in the sack.'

She glared at him, but he smiled back.

'Don't you like compliments, Mrs Gascoyne?' he said. 'I repeat – you always look good from the back.'

Clapping his hat over his slicked hair, he tipped it to her, grinned and went on his way.

When Nancy finally locked up the surgery and made certain Fothergill's calls were re-routed to the Clarkes' home number, she picked up her shoulder bag and took the lift to the basement car park. She was relieved Mason's Bentley had gone.

She eased Umberto out of the bay and up the ramp. He was old, drank too much gasoline, ate too much oil and wheezed and hiccupped now and again, but she had grown attached to him; he was air-cooled, easy to handle in traffic and park in congested streets. Mason had a quip about her car, too. Anti-social, he said, a car where your legs stuck out the window when you were laid flat on the back seat.

One day she would get even with him, she thought, pulling in at her café in Church Street where they made old-fashioned strong coffee and she could wind down with a cigarette while she made her shopping list.

Her shopping required little time or imagination. Supermarkets might be a battleground for some women, but she bulldozed her metal cart along the trenches at the double, throwing meat, vegetables, fruit and tins and boxes of this and that into it. At one point she would have read the fine print on labels and assessed the best buy in terms of quality and price, but that was in the first years of her marriage when she had great ideas about cuisine and diet and devoured *Larousse Gastronomique* and other kitchen bibles and spent hours preparing meals.

If Robert had encouraged her … But he hardly noticed the

difference between deep-fried cod and chips bought from the local café and Sole Bonne Femme served with Pommes de Terre Dauphine; he liked his meat boiled, braised or stewed, knew only Cheddar and Stilton among cheeses and had a penchant for ice cream, chocolate cake and other sweet-tooth items. His palate had not survived eight years of Brown Windsor, charred meat, over-boiled cabbage and mash, bread-and-butter pudding and mouldy cheese at boarding and public schools.

For him, food meant fuel like coal for a steam engine or petrol for his Rover. Except that he seemed more concerned about its octane rating and brand than whether his own intake was protein, fat or starch. Their wine, too, came from supermarkets, for Robert drank plonk and scorned those who could tell the year, region, vineyard and whether the grapes were pulped by hand or foot, dismissing them as charlatans who were merely hyping and hiking the prices of the so-called Grands Crus.

At the supermarket, she filled her trolley, emptied it into the small boot of her Fiat 500 then drove home to their flat in an old building behind Barkers in Kensington. Although she had left Robert a note, she hardly expected to see him until late that evening. If her word processor was still playing up, she would forget writing a few more pages, fix herself an omelette and eat it in front of some mindless TV show before bedding early.

chapter III

When Nancy opened the door, she spotted his briefcase on the coffee table and wondered why he had come home so early. Her eye went to the half-empty glass of vodka and tonic, which puzzled her, for Robert hardly ever left anything drinkable in a liquor glass. A ratcheting sound reached her from the study. Her old printer. So he was evidently tracing the fault on her computer.

Nancy decided to leave him to it and carried her plastic bags of shopping into the kitchen and started to unload and pack it away. She had her head in the fridge when she heard a sound behind her. Robert was standing at the kitchen door, smiling at something.

'Anything the matter?' she asked.

'Noooh, nothing. Everything's tickety-boo.'

She caught him eyeing her, a bit like Mason, and wondered about that unaccustomed light in his eye. That used to spell a kiss, a clinch and some heavy petting which ended in the bedroom on the counterpane. But Nancy refused to rise to the hint; she felt too tired to care.

Gascoyne was, in fact, looking at her with a new eye. He was realizing that, without thinking, without being conscious of the fact, he had built Nancy's features, her body language and bits of her personality into his version of the character of Jane, the heroine of the novel. They did say (didn't they?) that you had to paint or draw somebody to know his or her face and body. In a sense, he had done this unconsciously – and wondered why.

His heroine had Nancy's froth of blonde hair cut to the shape and tilt of her head; she had the same fluid way of moving, same trick of finger-combing her hair, same low, mellifluous voice; even her eyes were blue-grey and had Nancy's alert way of scanning your face or looking straight into the other person's eyes – as she was doing now with him.

If they'd asked him to paint a word portrait of Anne Howells, he might have found it hard to describe precisely her eyes or the flare of her nostrils or the voice timbre and inflection, or any of her gestures.

Why did he now notice things in Nancy that he had missed, or had gone stale? Was it because he had just written those love scenes that had aroused him and sent a sexual tingling through him he had not felt for a long time? No, not even with Anne. Was it seeing Nancy in a new pose that had fired his blood?

Nancy was gazing at him, a puzzled frown on her face. 'Well ...' she prompted.

'Well what?'

'I asked you what you wanted for dinner. You have a choice. An entrecôte steak and chips, salad, cheese and/or ice cream. Or a three-egg omelette where the steak would be.'

'You mean to say I missed all that!'

'You looked as though you were very elsewhere, about a million light years elsewhere.'

Gascoyne pointed to the remainder of her shopping on the table. 'Throw that stuff in the fridge and the larder and let's go out to dinner. There's a new Italian restaurant at Notting Hill which they say does your favourite osso bucco like no one else.'

'Have you won a case?' Nancy asked. 'Or what are we celebrating?'

'Do I have to win a case? Do we have to celebrate something? It's a long time since we had dinner out.'

'Don't I know it?' Nancy murmured. 'But some other night.' She explained what had happened that day at the practice, the chaos it had caused and the extra work it entailed.

In his turn, Gascoyne told her about his day, pleading before Judge Grantland who was making his usual contribution to the juicier pages of the *Sun, Mirror, News of the World* et al. 'I felt homicidal. He's the sort of judge that wouldn't last five minutes if they waived their rules about no side arms or machine guns being introduced into the law courts.' Nancy could perceive that he was only half joking.

'Did you manage to fix the computer?' she threw over her shoulder as she packed the shopping in the larder.

'Hmmm!'

'What was wrong with it?'

'If you want my opinion, you probably weren't feeding it the right stuff and it reacted by blowing a fuse.'

'You fixed it, then?'

Something in his attitude, and his slight hesitation, roused her suspicions. 'What happened? You haven't rubbed out what's on the disk, have you?'

'No, that's all right.' Again, he hesitated before adding, 'I read what you've done when it fell out of the printer.'

Nancy stopped packing her shopping away and rounded on him. 'And I suppose you want me to know what you think of it, is that it?'

'If you insist, yes. I think you should scrub the lot and start again.'

Nancy banged the larder door shut. 'You've been up to something with my script,' she said, pushing past him and marching towards the study. He followed her.

Her eye first went to the sheets left in the printer then took in the pile of paper by the side of the computer; she picked it up and stared at the scribbling in the margin and the blue pencil on the text.

'What's all this?' she cried.

'Don't worry, I haven't touched your disk. I just printed another copy of what you'd done and was playing around with it.'

Her gaze tracked more slowly over the pages he had edited and rewritten. Watching her, Gascoyne saw the flush spreading over her features to the roots of her blonde hair. When had he ever seen her so angry? He began to realize he had struck some painfully sensitive spot he had never touched before.

After reading a dozen of his pages, she turned. Her eyes had gone a deeper shade of grey-blue and were sparking; her nostrils were quivering. 'So that's what you think of my story,' she got out.

'Oh, it's all right,' he said, trying to temporize. 'I just thought it needed more muscle, a bit more testosterone and other hormones and beefing up a bit. Don't you think this is the way it should go?'

'No, I don't. I like my own version and I'd like you to keep your hands off it.'

'Only trying to help.' Gascoyne shrugged, smiled at her, then pointed to her original script, which he had piled up by the computer. 'That stuff will never win the Bleeding Heart award or make you rich.'

'It's the Golden Heart, and I don't give a damn if it doesn't.'

'All right, darling, don't get worked up.'

'Don't darling me.' Nancy was shouting now. She stabbed a finger at her own script. 'I've spent months on that – and you've spent how long messing it around?'

Gascoyne looked at his watch. 'Five, six hours – but it's not the time that matters.'

'Oh no! It's the talent, of course. It's the genius you've got and I haven't.'

Slowly, deliberately, Gascoyne lit a cigarette. Not because he needed to satisfy his nicotine hunger, but because it acted as a circuit-breaker. As a barrister, he knew that in the adversarial system there was almost always an incident or a moment where the case tilted one way or another. At such tricky moments in court anything and everything served to distract a witness, the opposing counsel and even the judge. Wig-straightening, nose-blowing, gown-flapping. Gascoyne pulled on his cigarette, excused himself and offered Nancy one, which she waved away.

'Why don't you have a better look at it and you might find something you can use?' he suggested, though he could see his offer had no effect on her temper.

Nancy looked at the sheets in her hand then shredded them and threw the tattered pages at him. 'I've read your divorce briefs before and I don't want one of your revamped divorce triangles in my story.' She glared at him. 'You don't realize it, but you've been listening so long to divorce cases you no longer understand ordinary people.'

'Meaning you?'

'If you like.'

'Listen, Nancy, I've only written what I think happens in real life, and what people want to read.' He indicated her script. 'You can do better than that romantic guff. Leave all that to the frowsy spinsters who've never had any, or the candy-floss countesses who've had just enough to frustrate them into churning out books about ethereal love while secretly yearning for Lady Chatterley's game-keeper or a caravan of passing gypsies.'

'You mean Barbara Cortland?'

'No, but scrape off the Max Factor and strip off the Hardy Amies organza and she'd fit my theory. Where do you think we'd find her heroines? Virgins who won't open their legs to anybody under the rank of marquis? And the other school is no better – the one that's rubber-stamped by the Vatican and has only one conception of the novel, no fucking without issue.'

'Cut out the four-letter words.'

'Love's a four-letter word – and so's life.'

Gascoyne was warming to his subject, perhaps overheating. He was forgetting the injunction of his first legal mentor, old Mansfield-Brown. 'Never take your eyes off the witness, laddie. Read his thoughts and emotions. Watch for anxiety, fear, arrogance, temper – and don't needle them too much or you'll lose the judge and jury.'

Now he did not realize that to Nancy he sounded as though he was making his closing speech to the judge and jury.

'You see, Nancy, love's an animal thing. If it wasn't, why does it start with a tingling in the groin and a rush of blood to the head swamping all lucid reflection. Love's nothing more than chemistry, molecular biology, nothing more than a reflexive response of the brain and the ductless glands to natural stimuli, a pure physiological reaction.

'If people only admitted that the romantic dream was all in the mind, that it went no further than the altar or the registry office, they would avoid a lot of pain and strife and tragedy. Have you ever asked yourself why all the great love stories finish in tears, blood and the grave? Cleopatra does herself in with an asp, her lover, Marc Antony, commits hara-kiri, Romeo and Juliet use poison and the knife, Anna Karenina throws herself under a train ...'

Had Gascoyne looked hard, he might have read something like anguish in Nancy's face at this diatribe against love. Even her voice had a rough edge when she broke in to say, 'Doesn't all that prove how powerful love is when they died for it?'

'It doesn't prove a thing. Heloise's old man didn't drive a stake through Abelard's heart to stop him making love to his daughter – he castrated him because he knew the real epicentre of love.'

Nancy pointed to the typescript fragments lying on the study floor. 'So I suppose your Scottish Casanova of Kirk Mains stud farm knows all the answers. What about the real Casanova – didn't he finish a ravaged, disillusioned wreck? Or Don Juan, who was eaten away by his own lust and wound up in the hell of his own creation? Where do they finish in your cynical universe?'

'Casanova and Don Juan were whopping liars and only women would believe their exploits. Anyway, they were both making a hopeless quest for the woman of their fantasies – and she exists only here.' Gascoyne planted an index finger on his right temple.

'And there,' he added, aiming the same finger at her script by the computer.

'It's all in the head. Nobody ever lives the romantic dream and all romantic novels are written out of the head, not the heart.' He grinned at Nancy. 'Be truthful, you've got to fake it because the girl next door doesn't want to read about the girl next door. Unless, that is, she's made it with a sheikh who has a hundred oil wells and is living it up in Malibu or Marrakesh.'

'She doesn't want to read about people having kinky sex in all its biological detail, or fighting like cat and dog, or jumping into bed with whoever's handy.'

'Oh, I know, if they go to the picture palace it's to see the Dame aux Camélias sacrificing herself for love, if it's opera it's Tosca diving into the void for her lost lover.'

Gascoyne paused to stub out his cigarette. 'Where's the reality? Why don't they say Cleopatra had weepy eyes, a runny nose and halitosis to stop a camel stampede and Caesar was no great lay?

And why don't they dare tell us Helen of Troy was just a whore and a nympho?'

'Why do you want to twist and soil everything?' Nancy shouted.

'Me twist everything? I just want things the way they are,' Gascoyne came back.

'Your romantic dream ends in the divorce court one in every three marriages with couples grabbing the credit cards and squabbling about everything else.'

'Yes, urged on by divorce lawyers on each side who are so case-hardened they think there's no such thing as love, and if they admitted there was it might lose them their share of the carve-up.'

'Meaning me?'

'If the wig and gown fit.'

Gascoyne had never seen Nancy so angry, so bitter. What had he done to ignite her temper? He wondered what had happened that day. Had she heard something – an inkling about Anne Howells? An intuition that he was thinking of leaving her?

He should pull back, temporize, try to defuse the situation with a joke or a soft word as he so often counselled his divorce and civil clients. He might have drawn the line there and held out an olive branch had he not lost his case and his temper with Judge Grantland earlier that day. And had he not met Anne Howells for lunch.

Now watching Nancy pick up her own typescript then scan it as though to ensure he had not soiled it with corrections and additions, Gascoyne wondered what had needled her. Normally, she was sweet-tempered and it took a great deal of provocation to muse her. Unlike most women, she cared little for possessions. When he had broken her favourite Dresden ornament and smashed up the Mini she had driven for years, she shrugged them off.

But now he had wounded her, had touched something that went deeper than possessions or the fame and money her manuscript might bring.

It suddenly struck him that Nancy might be in love with somebody. Was this Scottish border farmer the disguised portrait of somebody she had met and fallen for? Funny, he had never imagined Nancy being unfaithful to him. Oh, he realized she was very attractive and appealed to men. He'd only had to listen to some of his men friends extolling her charms. A sudden twinge of jealousy ran through him, though momentary. Finally, he pointed to the script in her hand and his torn version on the floor. 'All that argy-bargy over a few bits of paper.'

'They're not just bits of paper,' she said, looking straight at him.

'Well, I suppose they've got words and thoughts and emotions on them ...' Gascoyne stopped. 'You mean, they show how far we are apart in our ideas and everything else?'

'Maybe something like that.'

As if to keep her hands occupied, Nancy got down on her knees and began to retrieve the torn pages, rearranging them in some sort of order. Turning to the table where the computer sat, she picked up her printed script, checked the pages then put them in a folder. To his surprise, she removed the floppy disk from the machine and thrust it into her folder. She had her back to him as she spoke, slowly and deliberately.

'What does the marriage guidance oracle say to couples like us before they make tracks for the divorce court – don't they suggest a cooling-off period, or perhaps a trial separation so that both parties can review their positions in the calm?'

'Is that what you want – a trial separation?'

'Let's say, I find it difficult to go on living with someone who doesn't love me, or even believe in love.'

Gascoyne took a step towards her but she halted him by holding up both hand palms facing him. 'Come no closer,' she said through her teeth.

'But I said romantic love,' he protested, amazed at the reversal of the situation. He had come home more or less determined to pack his things and move in with Anne Howells, yet here he was trying to persuade Nancy to give their marriage another chance.

'If I argued against you, it was only because of the way I saw your story develop, that's all. I didn't realize you'd take it so much to heart.'

'If it was the only thing.' He noticed Nancy had conjured two ticket stubs into her hand. She passed them to him. 'The cleaners found them in the pocket of your dinner jacket,' she said. 'The date on them is the night you were having one of your dinners in the Inner Temple.'

Gascoyne looked at the tickets, his eyes blurring with confusion. 'All right, I was given two opera tickets and skipped the dinner and went to Covent Garden that night.'

'*Der Rosenkavalier*?' Nancy murmured. 'It must have been a long night for you, sitting through Strauss's most romantic opera. But I presume your companion must have liked romantic music and love stories.'

'I suppose he did.'

'Oh!' Nancy exclaimed. 'Then he wasn't the lady you took to Wimbledon.'

'Wimbledon?' Gascoyne was doing his best to disguise his unease.

'Number One Court in line with the net and about three rows back. Kafelnikov v Costa if my memory serves me.'

Gascoyne looked surprised, puzzled. 'Yes, I saw that match – but at Wimbledon who's to tell whom you'll be sitting beside. A lady, you say?'

'I can't swear to the lady bit, though I know you had your left arm round her.'

Nancy fixed him with those blue-grey eyes. 'You weren't to know it, but a TV camera just happened to back into you both.' She paused to let that statement sink in and give him time to answer. When he did not, she went on. 'She was pretty. Looked Welsh. What's the male scuttlebutt about Welsh girls among your slap-and-tickle colleagues in the Inner Temple? The three Fs – faithful in love, fervent in chapel and frantic in bed.'

Gascoyne drew a deep breath. 'All right, I took a lady out a couple of times, but it was nothing more than a minor flirtation.'

'That lasted at least three months between *Der Rosenkavalier* and Number One Court. Quite a flirtation.'

'It didn't mean anything.'

'You mean to you?'

'It wasn't serious, I assure you.'

'Who is she?'

'Nobody you'd know. She runs a secretarial agency. I handled a civil case for her and when we won she took me to the opera. Then someone gave her two tickets for Wimbledon and we had lunch a couple of times.' He threw his hands open to signify how little it had meant. 'There was nothing more to it than that.'

'Well, I know you're not in love with her since you don't believe in that guff – but don't tell me you haven't slept with her.'

In any cross-examination there was invariably one question around which the whole case could pivot, one question where, depending on the answer, you could win or lose. And here it was. Nancy knew he had lied about the Inner Temple dinner when he was with Anne Howells at Covent Garden. Did he face her with another lie, which she would find hard to swallow, or tell the truth? Thinking rapidly on his feet, he decided on a half-truth.

'All right, I admit I slept with her – but only once,' he said. 'And we haven't seen each other since.'

From her face, he could see that Nancy did not even buy his half-truth. 'What went wrong? Your chemistry, your hormones, your molecular biology weren't in phase, was that it?'

She was taunting him, like one of those fly witnesses who knew most of the answers and kept a jump ahead of counsel, jury and judge. What else did she know about Anne Howells and him?

'Look, Nancy, it's finished and done with.'

'Now who are you talking about? You and your girlfriend, or you and me?'

'You're not going to let a peccadillo come between us,' Gascoyne said, a law-court quaver in his voice. 'How can I make it up to you? How can I make you believe it will never happen again?'

Nancy did not answer. Instead, she pulled her briefcase out of the cupboard and put her typescript in it, then her pencils and pens from the desk. Gascoyne watched her, puzzled.

'What are you going to do?' he asked.

'Me? I'm going to find myself a private billet somewhere and write my book in my spare time without having a cynical eye looking over my shoulder.'

Nancy shrugged. 'It's your flat. I've loaded your fridge and larder, you have a cleaning woman who'll do your washing and ironing and you can invite your girlfriend to do the cooking. And if you want a divorce I won't be too greedy about alimony. We're lucky.'

'What do you mean, lucky?'

'We haven't got kids to quarrel about.'

Gascoyne stood there, stunned. For once he was at a loss for words, bewildered by the turn of events. He regarded Nancy pick up her loaded briefcase and make to leave; he felt powerless to stop her. It was she who halted suddenly as though hit by an after-thought. She stooped to gather the bundle of torn pages on which he had toiled so hard and handed them to him.

'Sorry I lost my temper and tore these up,' she said.

Gascoyne took them mechanically. 'They weren't worth much,' he murmured.

'I don't agree,' she said. Witnessing his surprise, she went on, 'What I read wasn't badly written and your version of the story is as good if not better than mine. So why don't you go ahead and finish it?' She smiled. 'It might even win the Golden Heart award.'

As he digested that compliment, Nancy did something that shocked and stunned him. She picked up the computer, held it shoulder high then dropped it face down on the floor, shattering its screen. She threw the keyboard on top and, for good measure, followed this with the printer.

'Why?' he gasped.

'So that if there's anything left of mine in there you can't pinch that as well,' she said.

He stood there clutching his script, listening to her moving around their bedroom, evidently packing a case.

Only when the front door banged behind her did he realize she had gone.

chapter IV

Gascoyne stood for a moment, immobile. He gazed at the tattered fragments of his version of Nancy's story. What did those bits of paper symbolize? Something he did not begin to understand. He looked at the mangled wreckage of their computer and wondered about Nancy's real motive for savaging her favourite toy. She who never broke anything and rarely threw things.

Not like Howells with her Welsh temper; she could have given a baseball pitcher points for throwing cups, plates, bottles, anything that came to hand. Often for his pains he failed to field them. But hard-headed Anne took care never to hurl anything rare or costly at his head when they had their lovers' quarrels.

Gascoyne could not take his eyes off the remains of the computer. Why had she destroyed it? Did she believe the machine might somehow hold traces of her thought processes? Was it possible? He had often wondered himself if these microchips and printed circuits had some secret memory function and retained traces of the material the machine had processed. Her action symbolized something but he did not know what. He could not bring himself to believe that Nancy had walked out on him. How had it happened? A quotation from Samuel Johnson spun round in his head. 'There are people whom one should like to drop, but would not wish to be dropped by.'

It fitted this case. Nancy had beaten him to the punch.

If he had really wanted to drop her.

Why had she done it? For these bits of paper, an unfinished story? No, he was sure it was something more. This row had been building for months, perhaps for more than a year, building into a critical mass just waiting for the slightest jolt or collision to provoke the explosion. It might have been anything – a broken glass, a drink too many, a grisly dinner party as well as the rough draft of her novel.

Gascoyne pulled himself up. He walked through to the living room to pour himself another vodka and tonic and toss it over his throat. Another followed, then a third, though he took this one more slowly. It might be an idea to get drunk, he thought, looking at the half-full bottle. Suddenly he seized it and shoved it to the back of the drinks cupboard and slammed the door shut. That way lay paralysis, mental and physical. He had to think straight.

He sat down to wonder where things had gone wrong and what to do about them. But his concentration wobbled. Those three large vodkas were already beginning to lap through his system and had obviously done something to his mental chemistry, for his mind started to throw up a whole series of flashbacks. All of them about Nancy. The evening they met. It stood out in his mind now, diamond-clear.

He was then working for Mansfield-Brown, one of the most affluent chambers. A client of theirs, a big West End ad firm, had given a party to thank them for winning a case against them of misleading advertising, abuse of confidence, false pretences. As a junior who had worked on the case, he went along.

During the introductions he had noticed the girl, even catching and remembering her name, Nancy Elliott, and the fact that she belonged to the ad firm's public relations offshoot. He did not know why she impressed him, for she was not the prettiest girl in the room. Maybe it was the curve of her breasts or thighs or her frank way of looking at him when they were introduced. Across the room, he took stock of her. Blonde hair cut short to frame her oval face and with a fringe over her forehead, striking blue-grey eyes, good figure under her silk blouse and skirt, and well turned calves. He liked the way she stood tall and relaxed. She had a champagne glass in her right hand with a smouldering cigarette sticking out between her fingers. He noticed she had a quirky little gesture (she still did) of smoothing a lock of hair behind her left ear with her middle finger.

Somehow, she exuded sex. At least for him. He wanted to get to know her. Who was he fooling? He wanted to sleep with her.

Gascoyne had meant to cut in on the person she was talking to and introduce himself. But one of his colleagues had the same idea and got there first. George Congden, who else? It was his style in chambers, too, grabbing the easy, sure-fire, headline-catching cases and leaving juniors like him the long legal wrangles that often finished with them and the client defeated. Congden was next in line to take silk and set up as a Queen's Counsel in his own chambers.

Congden made no secret of his triumphs in the law courts or his long line of conquests outside it. He wasted no time wining and dining or chatting up potential bedmates but put the leading question, did she or didn't she?, he boasted that nine out of ten times, the answer was yes.

Gascoyne watched, intrigued, out of the corner of his eye. Congden did take time to call for two fresh glasses of champagne and offered Nancy Elliott a cigarette, talking all the time. He seemed to have caught her attention and Gascoyne saw her smiling.

He was dismayed. Would she be one of the nine who said yes, or the tenth who said no? He held his breath as Congden's snub nose and jowly face edged closer to the girl who stood her ground even when the lawyer rammed his ample paunch against her.

Now Congden had an eye-lock on her; he abruptly thrust his face forward, placing his lips an inch from the girl's left ear and whispering something. Nancy Elliott recoiled a little. She gazed down at the stubby figure with a half-smile on her face. She pulled at her cigarette while Congden watched her, waiting for her yes or no. She sipped a little of her champagne then, surprisingly, handed him her champagne glass.

Standing with a glass in either hand, Congden was immobilized, powerless to prevent what happened. Nancy Elliott seized the band of his pin-striped trousers and tugged it free of his full belly a few inches. Into this space she dropped her lit cigarette then released the trouser band, which snapped back into place.

Congden's yell stopped the crowded room in its tracks. Heads turned to see the lawyer clapping two glasses of champagne to his crotch and pouring the fizzy liquor over it.

Dropping both champagne glasses, which splintered on the marble floor, he rushed for the toilets, unbuttoning his fly with everyone staring after him.

Gascoyne did not wait to see how Congden put out the fire in his groin but followed the girl as she headed for the lifts with a quick stride. She had already pressed the button and when the cage arrived he stepped inside with her.

'What did he do – proposition you?' he asked.

He noticed her blue-grey eyes were shot through with dark brown flecks and they looked at him through narrowed lids in a way that disturbed him. He could see Congden's point. She had sex written all over, even if he could not put a finger on why.

'What is it to you what he did?' Her voice had a faint north-country tinge, but was low and husky. Mellifluous was the word he sought. 'Are you a lawyer?' she asked.

'Yes I am, but ...'

She punched a button, stopping the lift at the next floor, then opened the doors and strode through. 'In that case I'll walk the rest of the way,' she called over her shoulder.

Gascoyne waited in the foyer and buttonholed her as she emerged from the staircase. 'I'm a lawyer but I'm no friend of Congden, the man who harassed you.'

'He had snake eyes and a face like an orangutan and an obscene tongue – even for a lawyer,' she said. 'And since you're from the same stable, what do you want with me?'

'I just wanted to tell you they'll sack you for what you did to a prominent lawyer who handles their legal work.'

'They won't get the chance, I'm resigning.'

'Let me buy you a coffee and explain why that would not only be foolish, legally speaking, but could cost you several thousand pounds.'

Those blue-grey eyes looked into his then inched over his face as though the mind behind them was trying to analyze his thoughts. Finally she nodded her head and followed him to a small café he knew off Oxford Street. When he had ordered coffee, he told her he worked for Mansfield-Brown QC, and was a junior like Congden.

'That one a junior? He's no junior and neither are you.'

'It's merely a trade term,' he said, explaining that Queen's Counsel had juniors to assist them or even handle cases and they might stay juniors all their lives if they did not have the where-withal or courage or talent to turn QC.

Nancy Elliott was a good listener and sat sipping her coffee and smoking while he told her that Congden could sue her for assault and had fifty witnesses to prove his case while she could only oppose her word against his that he had provoked her assault by making an indecent proposition. However, it would probably never come to that. Congden had too much to lose and advertising agencies knew the penalties of adverse publicity.

So, they would let the whole matter drop and content themselves by sacking her to appease Congden. She must report for work normally and let them sack her, though she should not accept the two weeks' or one month's pay in lieu of notice. Gascoyne wrote on his card the name of a firm of solicitors he knew and the name of a young barrister who specialized in unfair dismissal cases. 'Go and see these people when you're sacked. I'll ring and fill them in about the affair.'

Nancy Elliott had a question. 'Why are you doing this for me?'

'You mean, do I have an ulterior motive?' She nodded and he paused for a moment. 'I don't like Congden and never have.'

'Nothing else?' Those eyes fixed on him and he could see their flecks like orbiting electrons.

'Yes, there is,' he said. 'I'm attracted to you.'

That seemed to satisfy her and quash her doubts.

Nancy had complied with everything he had suggested. Her company settled her suit for unfair dismissal out of court to avoid publicity, paid her £5,000 and met her legal costs. She was able to move out of the bedsitter she rented off Chiswick Green and into a two-roomed flat in Notting Hill.

That incident transformed Gascoyne's prospects, too. Suspicion fell on him for befriending Nancy and under pressure from Congden, the head of his chambers, Mansfield-Brown, whispered that he'd do well to find another legal firm. A few doors away in the Middle Temple, Geoffrey Tyndall, a new QC, was looking for a junior and took him on to deal with civil and divorce cases.

By then Nancy and he had become friends. She was in her early twenties and had been engaged to an architect who had jilted her for a rich client, and she had also had another lover. But she still let him court her for more than three months before she would allow him to make love to her. When it happened, he discovered she had the sexual temperament to go with her figure. She moved into his Kensington flat and six months later they were married.

That church wedding? Gascoyne smiled at the reminiscence. Nancy insisted on being married in a Kensington church with all the trimmings; she had chosen the music, some lively tripping thing by Grieg – Wedding Day in some fjord or other, Trondheim wasn't it? – but the organist got it round her ankles and played something between the Dead March in Saul and Ellington's Mood Indigo, they never found out exactly what. Then a couple of his barrister colleagues got slewed at the reception and had a punch-up over Nancy's bridesmaid, and one of them landed in St Mary Abbot's casualty ward with a broken nose.

Where and when did it start to go wrong?

They had a reasonable relationship. They made mutual decisions such as postponing having children until their mortgage was paid off; Nancy would work to help bring that day nearer. In any case, she said, housework, shopping, cooking and washing would drive her up the wall. So she found a job with a small publishing house doing publicity and helping with the editing and marketing of books.

That bloody mortgage was a ball and chain. He was not making enough at the bar to pay it off in a reasonable time, so Nancy sacrificed her publishing job and went to work for the four doctors in the group practice. Gradually they stopped talking about having a family or making plans beyond a month, then a week. Nancy compensated for losing her publishing job by writing books, which did boost their income. He seemed to get through a bit more liquor each week.

Gascoyne could not put his finger on where things went awry. Their excursions to restaurants, to the cinema, to the odd show, tailed off. Even their conversation began to restrict itself to things that went no deeper than newspaper gossip or that day's menu or the film or serial on the box that evening.

'Robert, I never know what you're thinking or feeling,' Nancy would say. Did anybody ever?

People spent years building barricades and even castles of incomprehension, they sat on volcanoes of inhibitions and repressed feelings until these erupted without warning and for no apparent reasons. Like their row.

But didn't he know this from his divorce court briefs and those hundreds of family wrangles that landed in chancery or elsewhere in the law courts? As a lawyer, he discovered more about couples in weeks than they had let on to each other in thirty years of marriage. Hatred, venom – yes, and sometimes affection – spilled out of them as though pent up over a lifetime, as though they had never dared admit such feelings to themselves, let alone to their marriage partners.

Gascoyne supposed that somehow all those cases had soured him, convinced him that happiness and marriage were incompatible, bound to end either in divorce or a life of quiet desperation.

Was that what had happened to Nancy and himself? Locked into their own private worlds?

He remembered trying to teach her to appreciate the jazz he liked – Ellington, Basie, Coleman Hawkins, Louis, Cootie Williams, Lionel Hampton, Charlie Shavers. Who could listen, unmoved, to Lester Young's great solo on Basie's Lady Be Good, and to his obbligato to Buck Clayton's muted trumpet solo on the same record? Nancy did.

But could you share that emotion with anybody? It was as personal and unique as a fingerprint.

Nancy had a predilection for things like Schubert's lieder and Chopin, which turned him off as much as her predilection for nymphs and shepherds paintings.

But none of this seemed to explain what turned a simple spat into a full-blown row that tore people apart. He had often faced that same question when studying the evidence of both parties to a divorce. In most cases it was nothing; the spat was merely the flint spark that ignited the tinder already piled there, and this set the house ablaze. Nancy might have passed his revision of her book off as a joke, torn it up, tossed it into her waste basket. But she had chosen to make an issue of it. Why? Did she see her romantic story as a metaphor for life, for her own life? Had he failed her and forced her to take refuge in the sort of romantic fiction that she created?

Gascoyne rose and walked through to the bedroom. Nancy's wardrobe lay empty of her clothes; she had removed her toilet articles from the bathroom and her brushes and make-up things from the bedroom dressing table. He could still smell the musky perfume she used.

From the bedroom he went into the study. He got down on his knees and began to gather up the fragments of the computer. As he packed them into a plastic refuse bag to put them out for the dustmen, he came across the disk, which was undamaged. To his surprise, he realized it was not the new disk he had written his version on, but the old one which contained Nancy's original text. She would get a shock when she discovered her error and printed out the version he had created of her novel.

From the study bookshelves he took down the three novels she had published and took these and the disk through to the living room, where he sat down to read them. He had already skimmed all three books, his mind taking in only the story and something of the style. Now, he read them to analyze what might lie behind the stories.

By the time twilight had filtered into the room and filled its corners and forced him to pause in his reading, he had got through the first book, *The Heart's Reason* and half the second, *Blue Horizon*.

Nancy was on almost every page of these two books; he could see it now as plainly as he had failed to see it before. He had lived with the woman who wrote these books for six years, they had shared everything; they had made love more times than he could count.

Yet, sitting there in the twilight with her book open on his knee, Gascoyne realized that he did not know Nancy at all.

chapter V

Nancy took three days off to find herself a one-room studio in Shepherd's Bush. When she knew Gascoyne was either working in his chambers or at the law courts, she collected the rest of her belongings, including her books, from the flat. Pat Williams had done her afternoon stints at the practice and had informed her that Gascoyne had called her twice on the phone and left a message for her to ring him. He had asked for her address, which Pat refused to give him.

When Nancy arrived on the third day, Pat was pummelling data from that morning's surgery into their main computer. 'How's freedom?' she said over her shoulder.

She, too, had husband trouble, though nothing more serious than the occasional drink binge and a permanent love affair with Chelsea football club.

'Freedom,' Nancy said. 'Freedom's six square yards, a cupboard kitchen, a sitz bath and a backyard view on half a dozen other blocks and one stunted urban cherry tree with carbon monoxide poisoning.'

'You mean back to square one?' Pat looked at her quizzically over the half-moon glasses she wore for close work.

'That's about it,' Nancy said. 'Oh! And a second-hand bike as well. I've sold the Fiat.'

'You've sold Umberto!'

'Hmm. He had to go. It was a wrench, but I needed the money and the dealer assured me he'd find him a good home.'

'What are you going to do about Robert?'

'Leave him to his girlfriend.'

'You mean divorce.'

'It'll probably come to that. He's good at divorces and we'll get it cheap.'

Pat looked at her, wondering if she was really cynical or whether it was bravado.

'What was the row about?' she asked, 'to put it in our trade jargon, what was the precipitating factor?'

'We had half a hundred of those,' Nancy said, dismissively. 'Never mind about me – what's happening here?'

She listened while Pat explained that morning's surgery and the various patients they had sent to hospital in-patient and out-patient departments. They sat down and went through the paperwork together.

'Who's the new locum?' Nancy asked.

'Wait till you see him,' Pat whispered. 'He's a whiz. He's on house calls this afternoon.' She said his name was Edward Monclar and he was a psychiatry registrar at the Royal Free, but had already worked in general practice as a locum. 'He knows his stuff,' she whispered. 'He's already put Marcia in her place about Mrs Badham, sent her off for a gall-bladder check and she's down for keyhole surgery in a fortnight.'

Nancy gazed at her, incredulous. Marcia had been through the book with Janet Badham, a comely blonde housewife who had been complaining for months about agonizing stomach pains. Marcia had made a dozen guesses including ulcer, pancreas, hiatus hernia, without touching the pain.

'And that's not all,' Pat went on. 'Mrs Ward said nobody was going to tell her she was using her bad back as an alibi for staying off work. Seems our locum had her touching her toes lying down before she could twig what he was up to.'

'I'd like to have seen that old faker's face,' Nancy said, grinning at the idea of Marjery Ward exposed.

'You'd better know that our favourite rock 'n' roll raver, Jamie Sands, left without his weekly fix and a letter to the Granton Clinic where they do aversion therapy.'

'You mean the drugs and vomit therapy? It'll kill him.'

'So will the drugs, Dr Monclar said, and he even convinced Jamie to give the treatment a try.'

It appeared he had also signed their tame malingerer, Michael O'Riordan, off the sick list a week earlier than usual and blasted the ear of some social security clerk who had kept a patient's records for two weeks.

'He sounds a handful, this locum.'

'He'll liven up this place, you'll see.' Pat finished logging the data and filed the patients' cards in the steel cabinet. 'Wonder why nobody's grabbed him?' she murmured almost to herself. 'Wait until you look each other in the eyes and you'll see what I mean.'

'Pat, you haven't fallen for him, have you?'

'Of course I haven't – yet. He hasn't given me the chance.'

She picked up her shoulder bag, verified she had her car and house keys, and the shopping she had bought that morning, said goodbye and left.

Looking after her, Nancy wished she had her casual, philosophical outlook on life.

She had told Pat about her split with Gascoyne, but not the real reasons. No one at the practice, nor indeed any of her few friends, knew she wrote romantic novels under the name, Dorothy Armour.

Practical Pat would have considered it a flimsy motive for walking out on someone like Gascoyne, who might not be a prominent QC but was often quoted and complimented in the press reports on his divorce cases.

Pat would also have sniggered if Nancy had confessed that she had risen at five that morning and cycled to Putney Common to watch the sun come up, a first in ten years. She hardly knew herself what that act symbolized or represented. Perhaps the urge to start anew, to shed the old habits and routines.

For years she had trekked from the flat to the practice to the supermarket to the flat; she had left her spoor on pavement slabs between the flat and the local pub and local restaurant and local café and local cinema; she had grooved tracks on the floor from the kitchen to the dining table and back; and all these tracks must have imprinted themselves on the synapses of her brain. Now, she felt like breaking out of such petrified habits. No use explaining all this to Pat; she would never have understood.

If she had changed somewhat, things at the practice had not. Mason's sleeked head popped round the office door.

'Been away for a few days, Mrs Gascoyne?' His voice held on to the last two words. Nancy said nothing, 'Not sick, I hope.'

'No.'

'Good job. But you'd know better to come anywhere near this lot if you were.'

'I'm busy, Dr Mason,' she said pointedly.

At that, he crept closer to her and said in his slurred, quick-fire style: 'Stripped you'd be a helluva sight in the buff.' She turned to glare at him, but before she could get a word out, he gave a sick grin, held his side with his right hand and said, 'I said I tripped and fell over on my side in the bath.'

'You said nothing of the sort,' she snapped. 'You have a filthy mind and a filthy tongue and one day I shall report you for sexual harassment.'

'Mrs Gascoyne, isn't it your curious mind that twists what I say into what you'd like me to say? It's a well-known form of sexual paranoia.'

'Go away and leave me alone,' Nancy shouted so loudly that patients in the waiting room stared at each other. 'One of these days you'll go a bit too far.'

'If you mean with you, I can't wait,' Mason came back then stood there smirking, waiting for her to reply.

Nancy did not gratify him by replying, though she would have dearly liked to throw a few questions at him. In fact, she and Pat never stopped speculating about the mysterious Dr Mason, who would have looked more at home in Harley Street in his Savile Row suit, Garrick tie and Lobb shoes.

Nobody who dealt with health-service patients in a group practice and relied on a yearly capitation fee for each person on his list could afford such style. Did he have a rich wife? Neither secretary had heard of one, though they knew he took calls on his private number from several women. Had he won the lottery or the pools, or perhaps inherited from a wealthy parent?

'I think he's in some racket,' Pat said, 'Probably abortion.'

'No, if he was doing legal or illegal abortions he'd have set himself up in some backstreet clinic. I think it's drugs or maybe some sexual skullduggery.'

Nancy watched Mason turn, open the front door then nearly collide with someone coming through it.

'Ah! Dr Monclar, good afternoon. Met Mrs Gascoyne, have you?' He nodded at Nancy. 'She keeps us all in our place here.'

Nancy looked up. She had expected to discover somebody representing Pat's ideal, but Dr Monclar stood not much taller than herself and looked slightly built; he had reddish-fair hair and blue eyes. His hand closed over hers in a dry, firm grasp and she felt his eyes inch over her face. To Nancy, he appeared nothing extraordinary, though something about his attitude and his face struck her as different A sort of smouldering tension and a look that was at once aggressive and defensive.

When Mason had gone, Monclar turned to Nancy. 'Mr Carruthers who came this morning. Did Dr Fothergill ever consider sending him for a brain scan?'

'Not that I know of.' As she spoke, Nancy was entering the name on her computer and printing the data on Carruthers as it appeared on the screen.

'I've seen all this,' Monclar said. He put a finger on the first item of the printed data. 'Do these headaches go back further than this?'

'I remember – he's had them for about eighteen months. If you like I'll find the previous record.'

'No, it's not necessary.' Monclar produced a prescription pad and scribbled a note to the neurology department of Charing Cross Hospital asking them to run a brain scan and query a cerebral meningioma (olfactory groove). Handing the note to Nancy, he requested her to ring Carruthers and instruct him to collect the note and take it to the hospital.

'If he asks why ...'

'Say it's a routine check.' He hesitated. 'But for your information, he probably has a benign brain tumour which might have been spotted six months ago. He's lucky and it's probably slow-growing and they can excise it.'

He was turning to go when she called: 'Dr Monclar, perhaps I shouldn't ask – how did we miss it?'

Monclar shrugged. 'It's not too easy to spot – but when there's a progressive loss of vision, smell and touch it's on the cards that we have what they call a meningioma.'

Later, he did not even mention the fact that Charing Cross confirmed his diagnosis and carried out the brain operation successfully.

Monclar intrigued her. Over the days that followed, Pat and she constructed theories about everything from his background to his love life. What was someone with a bit of a Cockney accent doing with a French name? Why wasn't somebody with his medical qualifications and professional flair in Harley Street earning big money? Monclar gave nothing away; they had the phone number of his flat in Gray's Inn Road, uncharted territory between St Pancras and King's Cross stations for both of them.

He seemed to live alone with an answerphone, and in a fortnight he took only one personal call from a woman who sounded either very tired or tipsy. They noticed his Cockney accent grew more pronounced when confronted with Mason's Oxford drawl and he had no money to throw around, for he usually lunched off a sandwich and coffee in the local café on Shepherd's Bush Green.

No need to speculate about his work. He memorized the cards of those patients waiting to see him, and sent the regulars packing so that he could spend more time with genuinely sick patients.

Jane Barford, for instance. This young mother in her thirties had been complaining for years about breathlessness, attributed to asthma, and tiredness which was treated with vitamins and tonics. Monclar found a blowing heart murmur over her right ventricle, and sent her for an ECG which revealed she had a stenosis of the tricuspid valve needing surgery.

He discovered that another woman patient, middle-aged, had falling hair, constant cramp and general fatigue and turned her into a new woman by treating her for thyroid gland failure.

It became embarrassing when Monclar found a dozen other chronic illnesses that Fothergill had overlooked or misdiagnosed; within a fortnight both Nancy and Pat were receiving requests,

45

especially from Marcia Clarke's patients, to see the new doctor. It exercised all their diplomatic skills to avoid friction between the practice doctors, but a row blew up just the same.

Dr Mason had taken a week off to attend a conference on sexually transmitted diseases in Paris and some of his patients were seen by Monclar, who arranged for an eighty-year-old woman to have an operation to dilate a coronary artery and an eighty-two-year-old man to have a cataract operation.

When Mason returned, he walked into Monclar's surgery and challenged those decisions, claiming the patients were too old for such surgery. Nancy could not help overhearing the quarrel.

'The patients didn't think they were too old when I asked them,' Monclar countered. 'And neither did I.'

'It's a waste of time, money and medical services,' Mason shouted.

'Would it be a waste of resources if you were eighty-five and had a cataract or a stroke or pneumonia? Would you like your doctor to tell you it wasn't worthwhile treating you on the grounds of old age?'

'They were my patients.'

'But they came to me for treatment and I treated them,' Monclar came back. 'And if you don't want the over seventies on your list I'll be only too willing to relieve you of them.'

Mason went red with fury and shouted even louder. 'Look, I know you, Monclar, and you're a trouble-maker. I know why you left the Queen's and why other hospitals have shut their doors on you.'

'I don't know you, Mason, but I know some of your friends so don't high-hand me.'

'Just leave my patients to me in future,' Mason said and banged the door shut behind him.

When nine of Mason's patients applied formally to transfer to Monclar's list, the two secretaries had to argue them out of it, saying the new doctor was overburdened and could not accept them. Another score of patients informed Nancy bluntly they were not looking forward to Fothergill's return to the practice and she had to use all her tact to keep them on the books.

In fact, it seemed from the hospital prognosis that the senior partner would be away for six months at least, and Peter Clarke hinted that Fothergill was considering retirement.

'I hope they ask Dr Monclar to stay on,' Pat whispered to Nancy.

'I don't know that he'd want to stay in a practice like this. He's too well qualified.'

Monclar had, indeed, more qualifications than anyone in the practice, including Mason. Apart from his basic medical degrees, he had done a Diploma of Psychological Medicine, was a Fellow of the Royal College of Physicians and had a doctorate of medicine from Edinburgh.

Nancy had looked him up in the medical directories and had discovered that he was the author of several papers on the management of Down's Syndrome, the genetic aspects of haemophilia and muscular dystrophy, and psychiatric counselling in general practice. Far and away the most conscientious doctor in the practice, he was always at his desk ten minutes before the doors opened at 8.30, and he was invariably last to leave at night. Nancy sometimes swore at him under her breath, for she had to finish the filing and lock up after him, which made her late.

But she respected him. She noticed he kept himself to himself, wasting no time in small-talk with the other doctors, giving all his time and attention to his patients. That was the difference between Monclar and the others: they did a job, while he looked on medicine as a sort of priestly vocation and even went after hours to visit his patients who were in hospital.

With all the problems at the practice, the upheaval of settling into a new flat and fording new bearings, Nancy had not even looked at the script of her novel since leaving Gascoyne. After a couple of weeks, she stayed late one night at the practice and used her main computer to print out the material on the disk she had kept. To her annoyance, she discovered she had picked up the disk Gascoyne had worked on. Fortunately she had her own version, the first draft of the novel.

She could not help comparing them, though now with much more composure than when confronting Robert.

As she ran her eye over his script, she realized he had written in some good scenes and made quite a few improvements to her text. In fact, some of the love play between the stud farm owner and his new wife were too strong for her taste; reading them even brought a flush to her cheeks. How had Robert imagined the physical contortions he had put them through, and the new bride's erotic reveries before their sexual tussles in bed, in the stable in open country and even in the back of his station wagon?

She wondered that he had never revealed this side of himself to her, mentally or physically. Where had it come from? Probably from his contact with divorcing couples and their testimony. Or perhaps gossip in the banisters' robing room. Or – she hated to think it – from his Covent Garden girlfriend. As he put it during their joust, he had tried to beef up her story. And he undoubtedly had.

Nancy put down his script, pensively. They said all writing was self-portraiture in one form or another. Didn't Flaubert insist, 'Madame Bovary – *c'est moi*? If this were so, then there were large tracts of Robert Gascoyne left uncharted as far as she was concerned.

Flaubert's confession applied to her, too. But Robert did not seem to understand her compulsion to write, why she wrote what she did and how it might mirror something of herself.

She had felt the edge of his sarcasm about her writing so that she could never reveal how she lost herself in her own books, how she sometimes had the notion she had slipped into a time warp and was creating her own microcosm or at least a sort of metaphor of what she knew about life and people.

Robert had never understood this; no more than he understood he was tampering with her creations. However, it might have stopped short of a quarrel and a split in their marriage had they not come from very different backgrounds.

Robert was from a family that had law connections from two centuries back as solicitors and barristers; one branch of his family had even thrown up a law lord, an appeal judge. Robert had the stamp of whole generations of professional people, had gone to Harrow and from there to Oxford and the Inner Temple.

How did she compare? Her father, son of a Liverpool docker, had dragged himself up through night school and correspondence courses to become a bank clerk in a Liverpool suburb; her mother had been a mill girl and was honoured to marry a bank clerk who handled thousands of pounds a day for clients. Her mother deferred to him as a superior intelligence and even now, ten years after his death, sought his advice through prayer when hit by some crisis.

Mary Elliott knew her niche in society and believed in remaining there. When Nancy revealed that she had left Robert, her mother had put on her I-told-you-so voice, declaring it served her right for stepping out of her class and breaking every social taboo. For once, she felt like telling her mother to shut up or punching the cut-off button and silencing her whingeing.

Though maybe her mother had something and their marriage had tumbled into the social abyss between them. Yet, she had never known Robert to show any social or racial bias one way or the other. Anyway, it was he who had courted her and not she who had lured him into the usual sex trap; she might never have married him had she not, when they met, been feeling low and footloose after an affair with an executive in a rival ad agency had gone sour on her.

And she had to admit it, Robert was more interesting than most. He had intelligence and imagination, he was witty, he had a huge fund of amusing law-court stories and a talent for taking off judges like Grantland and that old war horse of a Lord Chief Justice with a hanging mania whose name she had forgotten.

When they met, Gascoyne was up and coming as a divorce lawyer and was spoken of as a future Silk; she never ceased wondering why they had not exploited his gifts as an advocate. It was like their sex life: it was fulfilling, it was fun, it was something they shared exclusively, it had great promise, but that, too, had mouldered and died somewhere, probably in Gascoyne's vodka bottle. When she discovered his affair with his former client, it did not surprise her.

Nancy put down Gascoyne's script and looked at her own, a pile of typed pages telling a story in which she no longer really believed in words that rang leaden. Anyway, it had now been purloined by somebody else so, as far as she was concerned, it was going nowhere. Like herself.

What would her mother have thought had she realized her daughter wrote romantic novels under the name of Dorothy Armour? She would have been embarrassed, perhaps ashamed – even though, ironically, she had probably borrowed them from her local public library and lapped up every gilded word, every sham sentiment in those improbable stories.

One reason Nancy had used a pen-name was to avoid an awkward cross-examination of her mother at her local Methodist meeting hall and her sewing circle. But she had her own reasons for creating this cover. She had never worn her heart on her sleeve or given away too much about herself to anyone. Not even to Gascoyne. Dorothy Armour permitted her to fantasize a little out loud.

She began to leaf through the pages of her own script, wondering what to do about it. Perhaps it was worth some effort. She had no longer her computer, but had recovered her old manual typewriter from the flat. On it, she started to rough out the contin- uation of her original draft.

It was slow-going. Whereas in the past when she had schemed a book, she knew exactly where each chapter began and ended and how the story proceeded, now she felt uncertain. Somehow her script had developed a whole series of knots which she had to find and unravel.

But as she worked, she discovered that despite herself she was injecting some of Gascoyne's ideas into her story.

Almost as though he had contaminated it!

However, she kept at it, writing and rewriting, crumpling and shredding page after page until she looked at the clock and saw it was past midnight and she had finished no more than two pages which would have to be revised.

She had eaten nothing, though she did not feel hungry; she made herself a cup of sweet tea then undressed and flopped into bed.

In those moments of flickering images between waking and sleeping, she wondered if Gascoyne had taken up her challenge to write his version of the story, and if he was butting up against the same sort of problems.

chapter VI

Anne Howells noticed the bloodshot eyes and the hungover look when Gascoyne opened the flat door to her and realized he had drunk too much and slept too little the night before and perhaps for longer. Although they were nearly through Sunday morning, he wore a knee-length dressing gown in towelling material and had an electric shaver in his right hand. He beckoned her inside and pointed to the bathroom. 'I'm in there and I'll be with you as soon as I've shaved and had a shower. Make yourself some coffee or something stronger if you fancy it.'

When he had disappeared, Anne glanced round. She had never set foot in the flat before but could guess that Nancy had kept it in better order. 'Mind if I have a look?' she shouted at the bathroom door, then wandered round without waiting for his response. In the bedroom, he had made the double bed after a fashion, but the place smelled stale, unaired. She edged the window open a couple of inches and picked up a shirt, socks and pants off the floor and put them on a chair. A glass on the bedside table had the dregs of something smelling of vodka and tonic and a cigarette butt doused in them. She took the glass through to the kitchen and put it in the dishwasher, which he had half filled. On the table lay the remains of his toast-and-coffee breakfast.

Anne went round the flat collecting four empty glasses and two full ashtrays, picking up newspapers and bits of typing paper.

'Don't you have a cleaning woman?' she shouted.

His razor stopped. 'No, Nancy found one of them going through our papers and another went through my whisky bottle, so we gave them up.'

Anne moved beyond the kitchen to the study and gazed at the new computer and printer on the table. Around it, papers were scattered, among them two parchment folders tied with red ribbon, which looked as though they contained legal documents. She thought perhaps Gascoyne had been working late on some divorce or civil case until she spotted a green file with the words LIFE LINES in flaring red marking ink across it. She listened. His electric shaver was still buzzing so she felt safe to open the file and have a look.

A book? At least in embryo. Anne's eye took in the chapter headings, the corrections in Gascoyne's hand, the numbered additions, the fragments with afterthoughts stuck to the text and even a few pencilled faces and doodles drawn in the margins. On a blank page he had doodled in ballpoint a life-size right-hand palm with the life, heart and head lines marked in red ink.

Lifelines ... not a bad title, she thought.

Scanning the first twenty-odd pages, she realized this was a side of Gascoyne she had never suspected. Oh, he was a good lawyer. That she knew from the time he had handled her law suit. But here, he showed a sentimental streak she had never encountered in him; and a flair for descriptive writing that compelled her to keep turning the pages. He also had a flair for sexual by-play, but that she knew already.

Anne smiled as a thought struck her. 'He's Barbara Cartland without the organza but with orgasms.'

Her gaze went to the bookshelf above the computer. Somebody must like Dorothy Armour, she thought. Although the name triggered some memory, she had never read any of her books. Yet here were three titles: *Blue Horizon*, *The Heart's Reason* and *Dreamland*. To her surprise, she noticed the first book had been translated into French, and the second into Italian.

Dorothy Armour? Good cover name ... sounded like a Hollywood star of the black-and-white era. What a laugh if Gascoyne was writing schmaltzy novels in secret under a woman's pen-name! However, it seemed to have rung the changes on the usual love triangles of romantic novelettes. Here, a prostitute sews strife between the husband, his brother and their mother in the bucolic setting of the Scottish borders stud farm. Although skimming the pages rapidly, Anne was aware that all four characters were well portrayed – the prostitute looking for real love, the old mother who hated her, the elder brother who loved her and the younger one who wanted to use her body.

Her eye lighted on a scene where the elder brother is making his night round of the stud farm:

As he came towards the house with the two collies, Malcolm heard one of the horses, the stallion Grampian, whinny – a high-pitched, nervous note which he repeated several times. Shushing the dogs, he approached the stable cautiously thinking it might be a burglar, a horse thief or perhaps someone bent on injuring one of his best stallions.

He lifted the stable door latch, stepped inside and groped for Grampian's head, stroking it several times to reassure the animal.

Malcolm froze when he heard the movement that had disturbed the stallion. It came from the hay loft above the stable.

He kept stroking the horse and whispering in its ear and, when he had quietened him, he felt his way step by step up the ladder to the loft. Now, as he climbed, he heard a rhythmic beat against the loft floor and a low, moaning sound.

Level with the floor, he shone his torch in the direction of the sound.

Suddenly, the swinging beam caught his wife's face in its circle. A wide-eyed, frightened face. At that moment, the man astride her turned and Malcolm found himself looking at his brother's face.

Malcolm saw nothing of shame or contrition in that face as he held it in the torchlight.

Instead, Richard bawled at him. 'She's a whore, didn't you realize it? Your wife's a whore!'

Malcolm leapt on to the loft floor and flung himself at his brother without heeding his wife's cry. As Richard got to his feet, Malcolm punched him in the face knocking him back into the hay. But Richard bounced back on his feet and the brothers began to wrestle on the loft edge while Jane looked on, rigid with fear.

Below in the stall, Grampian was now rearing and whinnying and kicked out with both front and rear legs.

To her horror, Jane saw that both men were now on the loft floor near the edge. Richard looked as though he was gaining the upper hand and had pinned his brother on the floor and was now picking him up by the shoulders and bashing his head on the floorboards. As Malcolm tried desperately to push his brother off and lever himself up, he only succeeded in sliding even nearer the edge of the loft and over the rearing stallion.

Richard was punching his face with such fury that Jane could hear bone crunch on bone and the grunts of pain bursting out of her husband. She could stand it no longer. Against the wall stood a hay fork; she picked this up by the head and ran over to ram it at Richard's body, striking him hard on the shoulder and head with the handle.

Richard twisted round. 'You rotten little bastard!' he shouted, getting to his feet and grabbing the hay fork handle.

Without thinking, Jane put all her weight behind the implement, sending the handle into Richard's chest and knocking him off balance. For a moment he teetered on the loft edge then plunged down into the stable.

Grampian was now bellowing with fear and panic and rearing and stamping at what lay under his feet. Richard let out a terrible scream, then another, and another.

After that silence but for Grampian's hooves drumming on the stable floor and banging on the body lying there.

Malcolm was on his feet. He jumped the nine feet to the stable floor, caught Grampian's halter and held on to it until the horse ceased to buck and rear.

Opening the stable door, he led the stallion outside and tethered it then went back to the stable.

Jane was crouched over the inert body. 'I think he's dead,' she whispered.

Malcolm retrieved his torch and shone it on his brother's face and head. His skull had been smashed and his face was a pulpy mass from Grampian's hooves.

For a moment they looked at each other, stunned. Jane turned and blundered towards the door. Malcolm caught her by the arm. 'Where are you going?' he said.

'Away from here … away.'

'No, you can't do that … they'll think you're guilty.'

'But I am … I killed him.'

'It was an accident.'

'Even if it was … They might believe you. But not me.'

'Why shouldn't they believe you?'

'Because they'll find out what I couldn't tell you. I'm a prostitute, a call-girl. I sold my body for money. That's why they'll never believe me.'

They saw a light fill his mother's bedroom window and realized that in a few minutes she would come to find out what the fracas was. His two collies, Rab and Tam, had already run towards the house to meet her and were barking their heads off.

Jane pulled herself free of his grasp, pushed the door open and began running towards the drive.

'Jane, don't go!' he shouted. 'Jane, I love you.'

But when he ran after her she had vanished into the woods, flanking the track leading from the stud farm to the highway. He stumbled around, shining his torch under the elms and birches, calling her name. But she had gone.

He stood leaning against a tree to regain his composure. He could not believe what had happened. Back there, his brother was dead and he should think of his mother and him. But all he could see was Jane's image.

She might have gone, but he could still see her in his mind's eye. Her blonde hair, her oval face, blue-grey eyes, full mouth. Those eyes and that mouth did not lie, he knew that. Maybe she had secrets … who didn't? But he knew she loved him, for

if her mind held back, her heart and body did not. Like his, it
had yielded everything.

He heard his mother calling from the stables, then yelling
her grief ...

Anne read parts of that scene over again, slowly, line by line, impressed with the way Gascoyne had put it together.

She had not noticed him turn on the shower, but now she heard him turn it off. She shut the green folder and replaced it on the table.

As an afterthought, she reopened the folder and removed a couple of pages out of sequence from the first chapter and the second; these she took through to the kitchen where she put them on a tray while she filled and switched on the electric kettle and found a jar of Nescafé.

When she had brewed the coffee and brought it through to the living room on a tray, she noticed Gascoyne had dressed in slacks and a T-shirt. A signal that he wasn't in the mood to make love. Even after his shower, he still looked hungover. For her part, Anne did not think the moment right to jump into bed with him; in fact, she thought he seemed slightly shell-shocked more than a week after Nancy's departure.

She realized she had to tread warily, for even with her lover in disarray and footloose, it might not be too easy to walk in and set up house with him. She was also too wily to quiz him about why he had not called her in the past week or why he had switched over to his answerphone and failed to pick up and reply to her half-dozen messages.

However, she was surprised that his ego appeared so dented by Nancy's walk-out. Perhaps it was the manner of her going that had shaken him.

Anne decided to play it cool. 'Well, how's bachelorhood these days?' she said, pouring him a coffee and handing it to him.

Gascoyne shrugged. 'It's like everything else. Wives don't know it but they're becoming victims of the hi-tech revolution.' He waved his arms at the flat then pointed to the kitchen. 'I've a fitted kitchen with microwave, mixer, automated cooker, dishwasher, I've a choice of Chinese, Italian, Spanish and Indonesian takeaways, I have a handy supermarket where I grab-buy with the best of your sex, where everything's processed and painless from sliced bread and frozen chips to plastic salads and instant coffee.'

'Not very good with the feather duster, the Hoover or at bed-making,' Anne said, glancing round.

'Touché, but my feather duster moulted on me, my Hoover has run out of bags and I only make that side of the bed on which I lay my weary head.' Gascoyne swigged his coffee and looked resigned. 'One has to learn survival techniques these days.'

'And the social side. How's that changed?'

'If you mean I don't have to share a bathroom ...'

'Robert, I can see you don't want to talk about it.'

'What's to talk about? We had a spat, then she produced unassailable evidence about you because I left the opera ticket stubs in my pocket and she or somebody else spotted us on TV as the only unswivelling heads and eyes at Wimbledon.'

'And you admitted it,' Anne said, hopefully.

'Only as much as I couldn't help but admit.'

'What are you going to do? Try and make things up?'

'I don't know. I think we've both decided to cool it for a while.'

'Why, when you're on solid ground? Didn't she fly out of the conjugal nest?'

Gascoyne nodded. 'But only when she discovered the cuckoo. And with a good divorce lawyer and a few witnesses Nancy could wash, scrub and spin-dry me.' He gave her a hard look. 'Divorce lawyers don't like being at the sharp end of their business and there's a certain judge who'd love to write me into the *News of the World* headlines for them.'

He refilled his coffee cup then balanced a sugar cube on a spoon, which he doused in the sepia liquor and watched until it dissolved as though seeing it as a metaphor of his career destroyed by divorce. He raised his eyes to glance at her. 'You might have to answer a few tricky questions from Nancy's lawyer yourself.'

They both understood each other. After all, they had been lovers for eighteen months, ever since he had handled a law suit brought by one of the girls Anne employed. She ran a secretarial agency providing multilingual girls with commercial training for businessmen of all nationalities who needed short-term secretaries.

Her girls she handpicked for their good looks, good figures and compliant natures as well as their competence. To most girls she hardly needed to spell it out that their clients might want to wine, dine and bed them as well.

When one of the girls sued Anne for breach of trust and using her as a form of call girl, Gascoyne was assigned by Mansfield-Brown to defend the agency. He convinced her that to let the case go to court would destroy her reputation and her business whether they won or lost; he also affirmed they could not possibly win and their best tactic was to agree terms and settle out of court.

Anne concurred. She needed little persuading, for her own call girl past would have surfaced in court and ruined her. She also had an eye on Gascoyne, who had impressed her with his casual public-school charm as well as his legal savoir-faire. On the night of the settlement, she invited him to a sumptuous dinner at her West End flat, and they became lovers.

Now, sitting opposite him in his flat, Anne saw him not as an occasional lover but a future husband. Gascoyne she had always considered was one of those men who sold themselves short because they were unaware of their own talents.

She meant to enlighten him on how to make the most use of them and especially how to convert them into cash and other valuable material. Her money would set him up as a QC and there were enough friends of friends to ensure that he pleaded the best and most remunerative cases.

But Anne was too wily to dangle such bait before him or even to quiz him about why he had not called her or moved in with her, the more so after Nancy walked out. She realized she had to play a waiting game until the dent in his ego had filled and healed. She picked up the pages she had placed on the tray. 'These were lying between the kitchen and the door beyond ... What is it?'

Gascoyne looked at the two pages in her hand. A guilty look, she thought.

'Oh, it's a sort of study,' he said.

'I couldn't resist reading them,' she said. 'Know what I thought? You were writing a novel.'

'A novel!' He laughed. 'Nooh, I was just amusing myself.'

'But this is well written. Why don't you go on?'

Gascoyne shrugged and said nothing. In fact, he had spent hours on that script but had come to a dead halt. Mental block or writer's block – he didn't know which he was suffering from. Just that his story about the two brothers fighting over the new wife seemed no longer to inspire him.

Yet, in the week since Nancy quit he had written thousands of words. At first he thought it would be easy translating his divorce stories into scenes for the novel. But that hadn't worked. Instead, he found himself projecting himself into the novel, remembering boyhood events, bringing in the girls he had a crush on at school and in his first year at Oxford: Joan Dempster, the passionate redhead, Mala Hughson, a blonde with her Russian mother's Slav face and a nubile body, Myra Levison, the dark, possessive Jew with the millionaire father.

Gascoyne had seized on bits of them and welded these into a composite of the girl in his story. But he kept returning to Nancy, finding her character, personality and even traces of her physical appearance intruding into the narrative, wrecking the image of the call girl who had seduced and married the elder brother.

Finally, he had concluded that it was perhaps because he had worked from Nancy's original story that he had developed word block. If he were to continue, he must shake off her ideas and characters, which were contaminating his own.

'Well, why don't you go on?' Anne insisted.

'Why? Perhaps I'll think about it.'

Gascoyne looked at her. She was leaning back on the sofa, her breasts pushing against her shirt, her silk-sheathed legs crossed and showing enough knee and thigh to excite him; her dark eyes had that questioning glint that needed no words.

What would it be like to live permanently with a woman like this? Oh, she'd probably run him like her secretarial agency, fixing this and that contact, rubbing his shoulders against the right people, throwing dinner parties for the wealthy and influential to further his career as a Silk. He had a niggling doubt. Marrying a mistress might be like turning a pleasurable pastime into a commerce that became a drudge.

They'd have no quarrels about love-making, which for them was untainted by any romantic notions; in both their lexicons it meant no more than the physical act of sex, a chemical exchange of reproductive material and a release of kinetic energy between two superheated bodies in a controlled if violent collision. For both of them, sexual gratification was measured by an increased heart rate, raised blood pressure, higher temperature and work rate from the sweat glands and the reproductive glands. Orgasm was the culmination of all those factors and was the end in itself rather than species reproduction.

Gascoyne wondered if just looking at Anne had lifted his spirits, or if it was the two cups of coffee and the aspirin he had swallowed before taking his shower. His hangover had lifted and he felt better able to face things.

'You feel like lunch?' he said, then added quickly, 'Not here. I meant round the corner in the Trois Frères.'

Anne looked at the fob watch on her breast. 'It's a bit early and I'd say they're just clearing away after last night.' She fixed him with those dark eyes. 'We've got lots of time....'

'Do you mean what I think you mean?'

Anne nodded, smiling. 'I'll even make the bed – on both sides.'

'I meant an appetizer,' Gascoyne said.

'That's what I thought you meant.'

Anne rose and came to put her arms round him and tug him gently towards the bedroom, undoing the top button of his slacks as she went.

Gascoyne was suddenly eager for it, and he could see and feel that she was, too.

They had performed faultlessly so many times that he sometimes thought they acted like two well-rehearsed all-in wrestlers. So, why did it happen? What went wrong? Perhaps it was the wrong moment, or perhaps he had drunk too much the previous evening and that morning and still felt the effects.

Their love play went without a hitch. But at the moment she

was guiding him into her and he should have penetrated her, he went soft and none of the tricks she was so skilled at using could bring him to anything like a climax.

Anne laughed it off, saying that was what a hard week did even to the best of lovers.

But she wondered.

And so did Gascoyne.

chapter VII

It had been a long and wearying afternoon and Nancy could hardly wait to see the last patient out, close the practice doors, cycle to the supermarket before it shut, do her shopping and go home. Both Clarkes had left half an hour ago, but the other two doctors were still consulting. Monclar had tarried over an elderly man he suspected had some form of cerebral ischemia which was affecting his right limb. On the other side of the building, Mason had spent an eternity with his last two patients, one a Pakistani woman with two children, the other a slip of a Hindu girl, Shanta Mehta, who was with him now. Normally Mason wasted no time on most of his patients, giving them quarter of an hour at the most, yet he had devoted at least half an hour to the two Pakistani children, who were suffering from no more than sore throats and runny noses judging by what he prescribed. Nancy could only think he was chatting up their mother, a pretty creature with sly, dark eyes, a Gioconda smile which might spell come-on to a Casanova like Mason, and a nubile figure under her Punjabi silk shirt and baggy pants.

She looked at her watch and found he had been with the Hindu girl for thirty-five minutes. As though to answer her prayer, Shanta appeared. She looked so beautiful in an emerald-green sari trimmed with gold brocade that Nancy complimented her on her looks, then whispered, 'You must have a heavy date tonight, Shanta.'

'Why are you saying that, Mrs Gascoyne?' Shanta replied, turning her large sloe eyes on Nancy, as though offended at the suggestion.

'Well ... I mean that must be your best sari you're wearing and it suits you so well.'

'No, it is not my best sari, and I have no date. In fact, I am going home.'

Something in the girl's attitude and voice caused Nancy to wonder what she had said to offend her. She had a good rapport with the younger girl patients, especially the Indians, Pakistanis and Jamaicans, many of whom were on Mason's list. She liked joking and chit-chatting with them, listening to their bookish English in their quaint accents. Sometimes they brought their problems with boyfriends to her rather than discuss them with their parents. Quite a few of these girls were trapped between two cultures; they were naturally attracted to the free-and-easy lifestyle in Britain and this often brought them into conflict with parents who wanted them to hold to the old ways of their Moslem or Hindu culture.

Nancy saw girls like Shanta, and her friends Moora Numar and the Jamaican Violet Robinson, rebel against parents who would hardly let them go out alone. Moora's parents had, in fact, already arranged her marriage with an Indian boy she had never even met, and this so troubled the girl that she had to ask Mason for tranquillizers.

As Nancy watched Shanta leave, she heard Mason's footfall and turned to see him close his consulting-room door, then approach carrying his hat and coat and the girl's records, which he handed her. When she turned to file them, she heard him say: 'How'd you feel about a sex binge?'

She whirled round to find Mason digging the knuckles of his right hand into his back.

'Ah, I said I'd a bit of a reflex twinge.' He grimaced. 'That slip in the bath, you know.'

Pity you didn't fall on your head and drown, Nancy thought, glowering at him. To counter her look, Mason made a little head bow and left.

Nancy glanced at her watch. Nearly seven o'clock. These days she rarely quit the surgery before that hour, for Monclar took twice as much time as the others to see patients and was invariably the last to hand over his file cards and bid her good night.

Finally she heard him bidding his patient good night and rose, ready to receive him and take the card. She glanced through the window to check what the weather was doing and saw something that stopped her in her tracks.

On the pavement outside, a woman was falling, clutching at her left arm and doubling up with pain; her handbag and shopping in a plastic bag had dropped from her hand and Nancy could see that she hit the pavement with a heavy thud and lay still. Several people ran to assist and one person headed for their surgery entrance.

Nancy hurried to Monclar's room, opened the door and called, 'Doctor, there's a bad accident outside. Can you help?'

Monclar ushered the elderly patient out then came to the window where he observed the scene on the pavement.

'I'll call an ambulance,' Nancy said.

'No, it'll take half an hour in this traffic and whoever she is might be dead by then.'

He handed her his car keys and told her to drive round to where the woman had fallen. He fetched his bag and their portable oxygen equipment and took this with a blanket downstairs.

When Nancy got there with the car, he had moved the crowd back and placed the woman face up on the blanket; he was thumping her chest rhythmically with the heel of both hands.

Without stopping, he said, 'She's had a heart attack ... hold her head back and down and put your hand over her mouth and breathe into her nostrils.'

Nancy complied, holding the heavy, relaxed head in her hands and filling the woman's lungs; she tried to keep in phase with Monclar's cardiac massage. It gave her a strange sense of power, the idea of breathing life, her life, into someone who seemed dead.

Suddenly, she felt a change in the woman, a resistance when she breathed into her lungs.

'It's picked up ... it's going,' she heard Monclar say. 'Here, hold this over her mouth and nose.'

Nancy took the oxygen mask and held it over the woman's face as Monclar lifted and carried her to his car. He sat with her in the back seat, instructing Nancy to drive to Charing Cross Hospital, his own hospital, on the other side of Hammersmith. There, they handed her over to the intensive care unit and when they had given the hospital details of the cardiac accident, Monclar asked if she had anything to do at the surgery. Nancy shook her head, saying she had locked everything up, including her bike. He led them to the lift and pressed the button, then looked at her. 'You look as if you could do with a shot of something ... I mean medicinal whisky or brandy. I'm going to have one myself if you'd like to join me.'

She nodded and fell into step with him outside the teaching hospital. He led her into a pub called Three Tuns, where they greeted him like a long-lost friend, refusing the money for the two large whiskies and bottle of soda he ordered. At the corner table where he had seated her, he poured a measure of soda water into her glass at her request and clinked glasses with her.

Nancy was grateful for the liquor, which helped calm her nerves after the shock of seeing the woman dead then helping to resuscitate her.

'You did well on your first case of cardiac arrest, Mrs Gascoyne.'

'You very nearly had to resuscitate me, Dr Monclar.'

'My name's Ted.'

'Mine's Nancy.' She sipped her whisky. 'Do you think she'll live?'

'Fifty-fifty, I'd say. I'll ring in half an hour and find out how she is, but they'll keep her there for forty-eight hours at least.'

'Doesn't it get you down dealing with the sick all the time? It would me.'

'It's a job,' Monclar said as though not wishing to be drawn.

'Yes, but a life-and-death job,' Nancy insisted, then dared another question. 'What brought you into medicine in the first place?'

'Difficult to say. Maybe I just had a yen to help people.'

From his cagey attitude, she realized he did not want to protract this line of talk. For several minutes they drank in silence. Nancy noted his fine, long fingers wrapped round the glass; they looked scrubbed until the flesh glowed, the nails were cut short and clean, unlike Marcia Clarke's and even Peter's.

One patient had told her with astonishment that Dr Monclar

went to wash his hands in hot water before examining her and even warmed the metal end-piece of his stethoscope before placing it on her chest.

He had reddish-fair hair which contrasted with his blue eyes, an aquamarine blue in this light; his hair sprouted at the temples as though unwilling to lie flat, but it grew thick on top where he back-combed it.

Nancy was so intent on registering her impressions of him close up that she failed to realize for several minutes that he was also studying her with a quizzical smile on his face.

'I'm sorry,' she murmured, embarrassed. 'You must think I'm very inquisitive.'

Monclar shook his head. 'No, it's only natural that you should want to know somebody you have to work with. I'm an unknown quantity.'

'Not for everybody in the practice.'

Monclar hesitated for a moment, putting his glass on the table and spinning it round, watching the soda bubbles break and surface. 'You mean the mysterious Doctor Mason?'

Nancy nodded. 'I couldn't help overhearing your ruckus with Dr Mason, who's not my favourite medico.'

Monclar was grinning now. 'So, you want to know why I had to leave the Queens?'

'Not unless you want to tell me.'

Monclar appeared to seek his response in those hundreds of exploding bubbles, then he raised his head and looked at her. 'Don't let this go any further, but I had to speak out about a couple of consultants, a physician and a surgeon who were mixing up medical practice with money-making. You know the sort of thing, using scare tactics to keep their private practices busy, hinting that pimples were potential breast cancers, and people with a touch of prostatitis were heading for the grave unless they were treated surgically. They were running a profitable little racket and also doing abortions on the side to boost their takings.'

'What happened to them?'

'They were medical mandarins, consultants, and I was a lowly registrar. So I had to quit while they're still on the books and still in business.' He gulped the rest of his whisky. 'They were aided and abetted by a couple of plastic surgeons who had decided to make their fortune doing face-lifting, bobbing noses, paring away double chins and pumping silicone into flat-chested women, knowing it would ruin their health and shorten their lives.'

'And Mason knows them all?'

'It would seem so.'

Monclar glanced at his watch and rose. 'I'll go and ring the intensive care unit and see how our patient is,' he said, as though wishing to cut short her inquisition. When he returned, he had a smile on his face and two more whiskies in his hands. 'She's pulling round and her heart has begun to beat regularly,' he said. He handed her one of the glasses. 'Drink that up and I'll drop you at your home. Somebody may be wondering where you've got to.'

'You don't tune in to the practice gossip, do you?' she said and noted the genuine surprise in his face. 'I've been living apart from my husband for the past month.'

'I didn't know, and I'm not interested in gossip.'

'I gathered that,' she said, and they both grinned.

Monclar fixed her with that professional face he put on when dealing with patients.

'That's not to say I'm not interested if you want to talk about it.'

'No, not tonight.'

'Well, if you have to get back ...' Monclar gestured at the pub counter where they served meals then at the half-dozen tables at the rear of the saloon bar. 'I was thinking of eating here,' he said. 'I used to on quite a few nights when I was doing my hospital year at Charing Cross. It's short-order cooking and nothing fancy, but the steaks and salads are good and they have some drinkable French and Australian wines to wash them down. What do you say?'

'Yes, if you let me pay my corner.'

'Fine, but only if you let me buy the drink.'

They found a corner table at the back and Monclar fetched their food and wine. They had Scotch rump steak lightly grilled with chips and salad; he had also brought Boursault cheese and biscuits and a bottle of Beaujolais.

'It's a feast,' she said.

She tried to draw Monclar out, but it was hard going.

'I take it you're not married.'

'No.'

'Never tempted?'

'By women yes, marriage no.'

From his attitude, Nancy concluded that anybody marrying Monclar might have to take second place to medicine, though many women would settle for that with somebody like this man.

For herself, she found Monclar attractive, too attractive. He had a low, undulating voice, maybe a bit rough round the edges and with a tinge of East End vowels and missing consonants; she particularly liked the way he only used his voice when he had something positive to say. It echoed his laconic style in the notes he wrote for his patients.

She chanced another question. 'It's an unusual name, Monclar. Where does it come from?'

Monclar chewed on his steak and swallowed it before answering. 'From a Frenchman who survived the St Bartholomew massacre in the sixteenth century, walked to Holland and stowed away on a Dutch barge for London. He was an engraver, but unlike most Huguenots, he didn't make a fortune or set the Thames alight. His widow and four children didn't have enough to bury him decently.'

After that lengthy speech, Monclar fell silent and when Nancy realized it was no pause but a dead halt, she counted each of her four left-hand fingers in front of him. 'I'm dying to know what happened during the four centuries between the time he disembarked and now.'

Monclar refilled their wine glasses. 'Not much,' he murmured. 'I'm the first member of my lot to have gone to a decent school and university or belonged to one of the so-called liberal professions.'

'And none of you had ever done any sort of medicine before?'

'Maybe a cut finger or two, and an aspirin for toothache.'

'So, why did you choose medicine?' she persisted.

'Why? I don't know. Maybe it was because when I was ten I fell out of a tree and bust my tibia or fibula or both and a Bermondsey GP of the old school called Benson splinted me, gave me a lesson on how to use a crutch and how to learn to walk again. Something like that.' As though to deflect her next question, he raised his glass to her and waited until she had done the same. 'That's more than ample about me,' he said.

'Are you always so laid-back about yourself?'

'Ah, but I make up for it by being an excellent listener which comes from my psychiatric training.'

'Why psychiatry?' she asked. 'I don't somehow see you sitting listening to someone on a couch in a dimmed room parading their phobias or manias or spinning out their fantasies.'

'Let's say I got interested in how our lives are shaped and influenced by mental processes and attitudes that are formed before we're aware of them.' He shrugged. 'But in psychiatry you know so little you can often come out of the same door as the one you went in, in the words of Omar Khayyám.'

'What sort of medicine are you going to practise, then?'

'I don't know, maybe general practice.'

'Though not in Shepherd's Bush, I take it.'

'Oh, it's not as hairy as that – and it's light years from the West End and Harley Street.'

After that, the conversation petered out. Monclar settled the bill, refused her share of it and escorted her to his car. When he had dropped her at her flat, he turned the car round and drove towards Hammersmith.

Next day, she found he had returned to Charing Cross Hospital to enquire about the woman they had revived.

Nancy wondered why he never mentioned the fact that the woman had suffered another heart attack and died while they were finishing their meal. She thought perhaps he never liked to lose patients, even those he had not known.

chapter VIII

His short bench wig made Judge Theodore Grantland look like an old spinster in curlers. It framed and emphasized his sallow, pinched features, thin lips, greenish-yellow eyes and a sardonic, curling nostril that sent a frisson through junior counsel. There were days when Gascoyne had to restrain himself from ripping the jabot off his neck and leaping over the bench to strangle the bilious old bastard with it.

This was one of those days. At his most misanthropic, Grantland kept short-circuiting his cross-examination, interpellating witnesses and spinning out the case to indulge his prurient, sadistic mind. Gascoyne had to restrain himself from throwing his whole vocabulary of four-letter words at the old bastard.

Any other judge would have treated it as an open-and-shut case; the husband had admitted his adultery with the woman named by Gascoyne's client, the petitioner. If corroboration was needed, they had a private detective to attest that he had seen the adulterers enter a Bayswater hotel and had even photographed them undressing and having intercourse from a flat opposite the hotel.

But Grantland had to hear everybody – the detective, the hotel maid who took the couple breakfast and the cleaning woman had had overheard them love-making in the husband's flat.

So, Gascoyne had to put them all on the stand. He was so angry and annoyed with Grantland that he muffed a series of questions. Grantland nearly broke his gavel by banging it to stop him.

'For God's sake, man, get your lines right. Do you want an adjournment for a week to study your brief?'

'No, Your Honour.'

'Well, get on with it.'

A titter ran round the public gallery and Gascoyne found his client staring at him. His mouth had gone dry and he could have done with a drink. He shuffled his papers frantically, searching for the details about the private detective.

To his horror and consternation, he realized he was gazing at several pages from *Lifelines*, his version of Nancy's novel which he had been working on the previous evening. How the devil had he mixed them up? He remembered his mind had gone blank on the story and parts of the dialogue and he'd given up, fearing an even deeper word block. Somehow, he must have shoved it into the divorce brief he had studied later that evening.

As he shuffled the papers desperately, he felt Grantland's little toad eyes on him.

'Pull yourself together, man, and get on with the case,' Grantland called.

'Apologies, Your Honour.'

Gascoyne was seeking a divorce on the petitioner's behalf on the grounds of her husband's adultery with a woman, presumed to be his mistress, on several occasions. Most judges would have accepted the evidence and granted the wife a divorce with a generous settlement. But Judge Grantland would have none of this. For him, the husband and wife had staged the whole affair to pervert the course of justice. If they had duped their counsel, which he doubted strongly, they would not dupe him.

'I would like to hear the witnesses, all of them, before listening to the stories of the husband and wife,' he said.

Gascoyne complied, calling first the private detective who had watched the husband and his mistress for two months. In that period, they had booked the same room in the Bayswater hotel at least a dozen times in the name of Mr and Mrs Samuel Beckett.

'Is this couple in court?' Gascoyne asked.

'Yes.' And the detective indicated them both.

'You accosted both parties as they left the hotel on the last occasion you watched them. What happened?'

'The man struck me with his umbrella, injuring me quite badly.

The woman screamed abuse at me which I would not care to repeat ...'

'Repeat it,' Judge Grantland put in.

'She called me a sleazy, snooping fucking bastard.'

'Was that all?'

'She said to her companion, "Give him a fucking good hiding, Bob."'

'Counsel, let the man tell us what happened in that hotel room. What did you see, man?'

'They had intercourse, Your Honour.'

'Details, man. Details.'

'The gentleman calling himself Beckett undressed the lady posing as Mrs Beckett. He unbuttoned her blouse. She was wearing a black bra. He then took off her skirt to reveal black panties with a black lace fringe. He removed the panties.'

'What about the stockings?' Grantland asked.

'He left those in place.'

'Then what happened?'

Gascoyne could see the old satyr almost salivate as he prompted the private detective at every phrase and made him describe explicitly in word and sound and gesture how the couple made love.

After Gascoyne had been compelled to put the maid and the cleaning woman on the stand and Grantland had dissected their evidence, he called the husband to corroborate the detective's evidence. It was during his testimony that a bizarre almost surrealist row broke out between the husband and the wife, despite Gascoyne's injunctions to her. When her husband declared he had taken a mistress because his wife refused to make love with him, she stood up in the well of the court and burst out:

He never loved me, never. He only wanted to use my body as a sex object.

HE: She even refused to sleep in the altogether.

SHE: He wanted to do it with me all in black. He's just kinky.

HE: She never puts toothpaste tops back on tubes and she used my shaver to do her armpits and legs.

SHE: He stubs out his cigarettes in cups and saucers and

smokes in bed and throws his clothes over a chair at night.

HE: She leaves her lipstick on everything and dismembers my *Times* before I've looked at it.

SHE: He smothers my best cooking in mustard, Worcester sauces and soya sauce. I could feed him tins of Whiskas and Good Boy dog meat and he wouldn't know the difference.

HE: She needs the *Larousse Gastronomique* to do a three-minute egg.

Grantland was leaning back against his high chair, lapping up every minute of this marital slanging match. He should have stopped it, but he didn't even bother to admonish the crowd in the public gallery, who voiced their approval and disapproval of the various accusations.

SHE: He's so bloody vindictive he murdered my favourite hibiscus by putting it out when he knew it was ten degrees below zero.

HE: That was because she smashed my computer to stop me from working.

SHE: He broke my Rod Steward CD out of petty jealousy.

HE: I broke it because the man can't sing, he's got hair on his vocal cords and he was driving me up the wall.

SHE (tearfully): He forgot my birthday, our wedding anniversary, he even forgot I existed.

HE: Nobody could forget that, alas!

At that point, Grantland decided to intervene and banged his gavel to silence the couple and the hubbub in court.

'I have heard enough to convince me that as a couple you are ideally suited through your incompatibility to live unhappily ever after. My verdict is therefore that the divorce is refused. Next case.'

Gascoyne looked at the judge with absolute incredulity, but already the bench was empty, the court as well. He found himself looking at the two people who remained, both as shocked and bewildered as himself.

To his own astonishment he was staring at his client, the petitioner, his own wife, Nancy. And the husband? Gascoyne might have been looking in his shaving mirror. This was the moment when he woke and realized that it was a variation on the dream he had experienced half a dozen times since Nancy walked out. It puzzled him, this dream with its admixture of the real and unreal, the rational and irrational. It pointed to something more than just his attitude to Nancy and his interpretations of her attitude to him.

Why was he defending *her* in the dream and not himself? Why did the pages of his novel, *Lifelines*, turn up in the middle of his divorce brief? Did his tongue-tied confusion when he saw those pages symbolize his real mental block when faced with the continuation of the story? And that slanging match between the parties? It was only too true. And what did it mean that Grantland dismissed the case on the grounds of mental cruelty and compelled them to cohabit?

Gascoyne climbed out of bed feeling hungover and with fragments of that dream still sticking to his mind. Pity he hadn't strangled Grantland with his jabot; even in a dream it would have given him much satisfaction. He still wondered what it all meant, but his attempts to resolve the conundrum ended in a headache.

One thing did stand out: he'd been an idiot to pour petrol on their quarrel instead of dousing it, and letting Nancy go. He wanted her back. But how to win her back? He knew her temperament, and he remembered how she had seen off a Rabelaisian character like Congden. With her, it was all or nothing.

He opened a drawer to search for a couple of aspirins and spotted the debit card Nancy had left behind. It brought a flush to his face, for when he had discovered it and wondered why she had not taken it, he had rung their bank to enquire whether she had drawn money after her departure. Not a penny, they told him, to his shame. Yet since she had contributed as much as himself to that account, she had a right to use it.

Now he picked the card up and turned it over in his hand. Was it a sign that she meant to return – or the gesture of someone who had no intention of returning?

Where, in all his divorce-court wrangles, had he met one

instance of a woman, or a man, who'd left debit cards when they stalked out? Gascoyne never expected such action from women especially. In divorce wrangles he had always made allowances for the woman's acquisitive instinct, her hunger for possession. He often pondered if it was acquired, genetic or just socially conditioned, this urge to attach things to themselves. This card in his hand, and the fact that Nancy had gone without taking many of the things she had bought with her own money, proved that she did not conform to the impression he had of women generally. He could imagine Anne Howells in Nancy's place – he might have saved a bed, table and a chair if he was lucky!

Gascoyne swallowed two aspirins and went into the shower room to sluice himself all over with hot and cold water. He was due in court at ten o'clock and had done little to prepare his brief on a divorce case, which he looked like losing. He had bungled two cases in the past fortnight by doing too little work on them and Tyndall, his QC, had taken him to task about the second case. If he did not watch it, he would be looking for another chambers.

By the time he stepped out of the shower he had made up his mind to find out where Nancy lived, go and apologize to her and ask her to come back on her terms.

chapter IX

When she came on duty half an hour late, Nancy realized Pat had some small crisis on her mind; she was wearing that face Nancy remembered from the day Marcia Clarke had been attacked and nearly raped by a male patient she had committed for psychiatric treatment and had been released by mistake. Pat gestured her into the corner behind the computer and by the filing cabinets. She had already hung up her white coat and was preparing to go.

'We've a new patient,' she whispered. 'Watch your step with him.'

'Why? Is he dangerous?'

'He's an oddball. I don't like the look or the sound of him.'

Pat pointed to the form she had completed with the man's name and address.

'Congden? John Congden?' Nancy murmured the name, trying it on her mind, wondering about the bell it rang. Was it really the man she had set on fire when he propositioned her? 'What's he like, this Congden?'

Pat reflected for a moment. 'He's thirtyish, a bit of a smoothie with a pale face and la-di-da accent. You know the type.' Pat dropped her voice. 'I think he's had a few and he's really cagey. I asked who sent him and he said nobody – I asked who his previous doctor was and he said he didn't have one. He wouldn't say why he was here or give me any idea what was wrong with him.'

'Who've you put him down for?'

'Monclar – he'll sort him out if anybody does.'

They stopped talking when Marcia's door opened and one of her regulars, the arthritic Mr Simmonds, shuffled out. Pat grabbed Nancy by her blouse sleeve. 'He's sitting over there in the corner by the window,' she whispered. 'I'll go and call Marcia's next patient and you can have a quick look.'

She went to the waiting-room door, opened it wide and called Mrs Agnew. Under Pat's arms as she held the door open, Nancy glimpsed the man who had booked in as Congden.

It was Robert.

Her first panic thought was to hand over to Pat and plead a sudden migraine or vertigo or anything that would prevent her from facing him. 'Congden.' So he had deliberately chosen that cocky little lawyer's name, the one who had stomach-butted and crotch-frictioned her the night they had met at the ad agency party. When Pat returned, Nancy had her story ready.

'Sorry, Pat, I forgot I have to do a five-minute errand. Do you mind keeping the shop for a few more minutes?'

'No bother. Did you see him?'

'Yes. I think you should switch him from Monclar to Mason, who hasn't got anybody waiting after the woman who's there now. And you can fill Mason's ear with the fact that Mr Congden might have a problem he fords difficult to discuss.'

'You know what he'll think that is.'

'Mm-hm! What he thinks everything is. But let them both sort each other out.'

Nancy left. She walked to the nearest café where she sat and drank a coffee slowly until she was sure that Robert alias Congden had been called. When she returned, Pat thumbed at Mason's door and jerked her head to signify that Congden had gone in.

'Keep your ears open about him,' she said. 'I'd like to hear what happened.'

'Don't worry, I shall,' Nancy said, tongue in cheek. She wondered whether to tell Pat it was her husband, Robert, who was evidently trying to contact her, but she decided to wait. 'How long has he been in there?' she asked.

'Five, six minutes.' Pat hung up her blouse and drew on her coat. 'What I wouldn't give to be a fly on Mason's wall.'

From the moment he stepped into the practice, Gascoyne had asked himself whether he had not made a desperate error trying to corner Nancy at her workplace. He had expected to find her behind the office desk; instead a pixy-faced chit of a girl started an inquisition about his medical background and from his stuttered, halting responses all but implied he had some form of venereal disease before pushing him into the waiting room. He had complied and sat down, thinking Nancy would eventually turn up and he could talk to her.

Now he was sitting across a desk from a quack with greasy hair, bloated pink cheeks and piggy eyes the colour of pond scum.

'Private or health service?' Mason asked.

'Er, private.'

That merited a handshake across the desk. Mason's hand matched his pink cheeks and slicked hair; it felt like wet foam rubber, boneless.

'Sit down, Mr Congden. Now what's the problem?'

'Well, that is ... it's difficult to explain. You see ...'

'I know exactly what you mean, so let me help you. At a guess what I call condomitis or what I call the Pre-empted Condom Syndrome.'

Gascoyne stared at Mason, wondering what sort of nut he was tangling with. 'The what?' he got out.

'Oh, it's nothing to worry about.' Mason smiled. 'It's my trade term for any form of sexual frustration. You've seen boys go into chemist's shops to buy a condom and come out with a packet of throat pastilles or razor blades ...'

Gascoyne could only gaze, dumbfounded, at that pink face which now had a smile on it.

'It's sex, isn't it, Mr Congden? That's your problem and you're a trifle embarrassed to talk about it. Right, am I?'

'Well ...'

'Priapism or impotence?' Mason asked, gold pencil poised over a notepad.

'What?'

'Priapism are those who can't get it down and impotence those who can't get it up. Which is it?'

'Neither.'

'Ah!' His Ah! sounded deep disappointment, yet he came back strongly. 'But it's trouble with the enemy, the opposite sex, eh?'

'I suppose so.'

'Then tell me, is it the breed generally – or do you have any particular woman in mind?'

Gascoyne took his time before replying and Mason did not rush him. He put down his gold pencil and picked up the stethoscope on his desk, polished the bright metal end-piece with a red, polka-dot silk handkerchief then studied his own reflection in it while he waited. Gascoyne was thinking that perhaps this narcissistic satyr might have some answers to his problem.

'You see, I have this ... er, difficulty with my wife.'

'Who doesn't, o' boy? I've had three and I know the score, God knows I know the score. Let me see, you can't get it up with her, is that it?'

'In a way,' Gascoyne mumbled. 'But I have a mistress as well ...'

'Ah, now that's more serious. With the wife it's natural, but the mistress. Extra-conjugal impotence can be serious. Can't change her for another one, can you?'

'But I'm in love with her.'

At that, Mason's eyebrows nearly collided with his hairline and Gascoyne thought he heard him mutter, 'That old chestnut,' before he caught himself up and said: 'Isn't it a question of what turns you on? I suppose you've had a go at the usual remedies – flagellation, fellatio, cunnilingus, that sort of thing.' Gascoyne shook his head and Mason again raised those eyebrows. 'Well, it's worth a shot. Then there's the black bra and knickers, or even simulated rape in evening dress. Tried that, have you?'

Again, Gascoyne shook his head. From Mason's attitude, he sensed the doctor was dismayed about his lack of sexual initiative.

'What about pot? Had a go at that?'

'Once or twice,' Gascoyne said, truthfully, although he added that it had done nothing for his sexual appetite.

Mason plunged a hand into a drawer and produced a card which he passed over the desk. 'Have a look at this ... it's a new porn cinema called the Hole-in-One, somewhere in Soho. Haven't been there myself, but they tell me it's white-hot.' He had another card in his hand. 'What about psychoanalysis? This chap's good on sexual problems.'

'I don't believe in Freud.'

Mason nodded. 'Don't blame you. For me he was a sort of sexual potholer who went down deeper, stayed down longer and came up dirtier than all the others of the Vienna écurie, but he didn't really take us anywhere much.'

Mason was shuffling several cards in his hands as though about to deal them. 'Ah! Here's a non-Freudian quack who's good on sexual aberrations....'

'I don't suffer from sexual aberration.'

Mason looked both disbelieving and disappointed, then his scummy eyes glinted and he nodded as though agreeing with himself about something. A pin finger reached out and punched a button on the intercom.

'Mrs Gascoyne? Can you come in and bring a packet of patient cards with you?' He looked at Gascoyne under his eyebrows. 'Just wait till you get an eyeful of this....'

As Nancy entered the consulting room, Gascoyne gazed at her; but she kept her eyes on the cards she held in her hand and made her way to the desk and placed them there in front of Mason. When she turned to go, Mason held up a hand to detain her then quizzed her about two of his patients before handing her cards for the patients he had treated that afternoon. Still acting as though Gascoyne did not exist, Nancy made her exit.

'Well, what did you think of her?' Mason said in a whisper that had gone suddenly hoarse. His face had also turned a deeper shade of pink.

'She's very pretty,' Gascoyne murmured.

'Ah yes, her face.' Mason fixed puzzled eyes on Gascoyne. 'That's not all you looked at, is it? Didn't you look where any normal man would look? At that glorious rump, the swell of those beautiful thighs and the wonderful parabolic curves of those breasts. Every time I see her, I think that nature has done a wonderful job putting all that flesh in just the right places.' Shaking his head in sorrow, Mason murmured several times, 'Her face! Her face!' Then in a louder voice, addressing himself to Gascoyne, he said, 'Now that's the sort of woman I could never chat up face to face and I didn't think anybody else could – if you get what I mean.'

Mason caught Gascoyne staring at him with a grim look in his eyes; his slick head shook from side to side and his face wore a resigned smile.

'I know what you're thinking, Mr Congden. Have I?'

'Well, have you?' Gascoyne had to throttle back his anger and keep the snap out of his voice.

'I have, ol' boy, thousands of times. But never in the flesh, dammit. Never in the flesh.' He shrugged. 'Anyway, she already has a bad case of iatrophilia.'

'What's that in plain English?'

'Doctor love – she's gone on the young locum we have here.'

'But you called her Mrs Gascoyne ... so she's married, isn't she?'

'Hmm, to some jerk of a lawyer who didn't appreciate her, so she walked out on him.'

Mason had his pen hovering over a prescription pad. 'Now what do you want me to prescribe for you – an aphrodisiac, pep pills, testosterone, that sort of thing?'

'Nothing,' Gascoyne said. He paid Mason the twenty pounds he charged for the consultation. As he went to leave, Mason pulled another card out of his pocket and handed it to him.

'I have another small practice there, in the West End,' he murmured. 'If things don't work out, come and see me there.'

Gascoyne took the card and thrust it into a pocket. As he left the practice, he looked round for Nancy, but she had disappeared.

Gascoyne glanced round the saloon bar of the dingy pub in Holland Park Road that he had blundered into after his unnerving session with that nut of a doctor. How many of these men and women around the bar were also looking for liquor to solve or dissolve their problems?

He ordered double whiskies which he threw down neat, but he stopped himself at three, knowing he had to drive back through thickening afternoon traffic to the flat and might tangle with another drunk driver or the law.

As he slalomed through the traffic in the back streets of Hammersmith and Kensington, he played back that surrealistic interview with Mason. One word stuck in a groove of his mind: Iatrophilia. It hadn't taken Nancy long to hook somebody else. Well, she was good-looking, that lecher was right. And could he blame her when he had betrayed her first with Anne Howells?

Without realizing it, he shot through the lights at Hammersmith as they changed to red and a concerto of horns dinned in his ears. A car jolted to a halt within inches and the driver cursed him for an imbecile. He felt thankful to slot the car into his parking space outside the flat.

Once inside, he realized he had forgotten there was nothing in the fridge and he should go to Tesco and fill up his trolley from the shelves. He couldn't face it. He'd have a liquid dinner – he still had several bottles of gin, whisky and brandy in the drinks cabinet.

He poured himself a half tumbler of Scotch, took a gulp and sat down with the bottle in his hand. What did that sex-obsessed doctor, Mason, this new locum and so many others see in Nancy that he didn't?

Mason and Congden could only have had gut reactions, or even epidermic reactions to Nancy. But could he reproach them when he had not looked much deeper? He had dismissed her three novels as so much schmaltzy, romantic rubbish without giving them much more than a glance. Maybe he should have studied them more closely.

Gascoyne put down his whisky and the bottle and walked through to Nancy's writing room to fetch the third of her novels, *Dreamland*, which he had not read. Why hadn't he seen in Nancy half of what Mason and others seemed to see? Perhaps he hadn't looked hard enough. Perhaps this book might give him a clue.

Dreamland, her last book, was set in a publisher's office, and here Nancy had got the background and atmosphere right. Gascoyne had almost forgotten she had once worked for a publisher. To his surprise, he found her writing better than in the two previous books – clear and concise with well structured, well knit sentences and paragraphs. And as he read the book, he realized she had given something of an original twist to the love triangle. *Dreamland* was the story of sexual rivalry which centred round a young poet who had echoes of Byron in his looks and his romantic poetry. In his publishers, the young woman editor who put his poems into book form had fallen in love with him while the head of the publishing house was in love with her.

Lisa Blake was so smitten with the poet, Michael Rigdoon, that she imagined and then became convinced that his book of love poems had been written for her. She wanted to give herself to him, totally, to let him do whatever he desired with her.

He did not even spurn her advances. He ignored her completely.

It took her long weeks to discover that he loved himself and his own poems and nothing else.

Nancy had put these words into Lisa's mind: 'She had yearned for a word, a sign, a caress, a gesture that would mean that Michael had some affection for her. But she met indifference. She might have been invisible for all the interest he paid her. Indeed, he seemed to care more for the words he had written or even the paper that supported them than for her or anything else. She felt more of an inanimate object than the paper. His coldness, his disinterest hurt her more than she could describe; it left her heartsick and with a black hole in her mind.'

Reading this, Gascoyne wondered when Nancy had written these chapters. What was their own relationship then and did it have any bearing on a paragraph like this?

Anyway, he told himself, the book could not have been a metaphor of any kind for their relationship. For the publisher, who wanted to marry Lisa, revealed that her Byronic poet was living with a middle-aged man and had been in love with him for at least five years. Lisa walked out on the publisher. Had she stayed she might have murdered him for ruining any hope she had of winning the poet's love.

Gascoyne put the book down and refilled his whisky glass. Those phrases Nancy had written about her poet were still vorticing in his head. Where had they come from? What had inspired them? Did they have some oblique connection with himself? Or did they refer to someone Nancy had really loved?

Rising, he walked through to the study, still gulping his whisky.

Among Nancy's books he found a collection of poems by Malcolm
Royston – same initials as Michael Rigdoon – brought out by
Nancy's old publishing house. Riffling through the pages, he saw
they were love poems though they did not go very deep in expression or style. Yet the book looked well thumbed, as though Nancy
had read it time and again. It was also where she kept her own
books and the reference books she used for her writing. Had she
been in love with Royston? Gascoyne felt a pang of jealousy and
resentment that this man had moved her more than he ever
seemed to have done.

What had happened to Royston? He must find out. Suddenly it
became the most urgent thing in his life to discover what had
happened to this unknown poetaster. He swallowed the rest of the
whisky as he walked back to the living room and searched for the
Telegraph number. They put him through to the library where he
introduced himself and said he wanted to know about a poet called
Royston. Could they help?

Within minutes the library had rung back. They read him the
few cuttings they had in their 'morgue' about him, ending with the
one describing how he had died of a drug overdose which was probably suicide, although the coroner brought in an open verdict.
Gascoyne put the phone down. He felt confused, his fuddled mind
trying to wrap itself round the facts they had given him. Dead! But
Nancy could still be in love with him. The dead often meant more
to people than the living, for their frozen imago was idealized,
sublimated.

He threw the book of poems on to the coffee table, scattering an
ashtray and knocking over his empty glass. Now he was too drunk
to analyze what it all meant.

He kicked off his shoes and stared at the uncut toenail peering
through his sock. Another one! He had discovered a hole in his
socks the other day, and a rent in his cardigan sleeve. What were
they feeding the sheep on these days? He hadn't seen a hole since
his bachelor days.

His toenail wouldn't stay in one place. It and the hole were
wobbling around. When he looked up, the walls and the ceiling of
the living room were doing the same. His eyes wouldn't focus, nor

would his mind. He was drunk. And maybe because he was drunk he first blamed Nancy for his plight; she had blown up a tiff and his small indiscretion into a great storm, then deserted him. Hadn't she betrayed him with that dead poet, Royston? He cursed the quack at her practice who had turned Nancy's head. Drunk or not, he could see clearly what he had to do ... He'd ambush her in a dark alley and stick a knife in her. Nooh, that was too quick and therefore merciful. He'd garrotte her, bare-handed, filling her ear as he slowly strangled her with his justification for his act. He must watch that he didn't break her hyoid bone and kill her too quickly before she had heard and meditated the full prosecution case.

Nooh, nooh. Destroying her was too simple, too good for her. Dead she would feel nothing and she must suffer. Who said never kill your enemy, for you're left with nobody to hate? Whoever it was spoke truly. Make her suffer. Don't kill her. Destroy what she loves, destroy the quack who has stolen her. That was it – eliminate him for a start.

Those thoughts and that plan were worth what was left in his whisky bottle. It amounted to more than half a tumbler, but he tossed it back neat in his elation at evolving such a neat strategy. Tomorrow he would work out a detailed plan.

He was really drunk now. Too drunk to do anything but spray his clothes all over the bedroom and collapse into bed.

Yet before he went to sleep, in that strange area where the mind is half awake, half asleep, he began to perceive things more sharply through his alcohol haze than in his most sober moments, as if the drink had somehow edged open a secret panel into his subconscious mind.

He had decided not to kill Nancy because he couldn't. His jealousy was just another face of love. He was in love with Nancy. It had taken his own infidelity, his professional cynicism and his stupidity to bring him to the point of admitting his love.

Somehow he had to win her back.

chapter X

Nancy parked her bicycle outside the small café where she usually relaxed with a coffee after work. When Robert had gone, she had phoned Pat at home to confess that the curious Mr Congden was none other than her husband, and Mason had summoned her to illustrate the point he was making to his patient, obviously something to do with sex. Pat hadn't stopped laughing when Nancy put down the phone.

Now, as she clipped the anti-theft cable into place, she noticed a woman in the corner seat and wondered where she had seen her face before. She was vainly trying to remember as she walked into the café and found herself suddenly confronted by the woman.

'Nancy Gascoyne, isn't it?' she said, and when Nancy nodded, she continued, 'I've been wanting to meet you. May I buy you a coffee?'

Without waiting for Nancy's assent, she indicated two seats and called for two coffees as they sat down.

'You're wondering where you saw me, aren't you?' she said. Nancy nodded. 'It was on TV ... Court Number One at Wimbledon.'

'Of course, you were the one who wasn't watching the tennis,' Nancy said, and rose to leave before Anne Howells grabbed her arm and stopped her.

'Please,' she pleaded. 'I came to have a reasonable discussion with you.'

'If you've come to ask me if you can have him for good, the answer is yes. That's reasonable, isn't it? And there's no need for discussions.' Nancy realized she was talking so loudly the other four people in the café were staring at them.

'Nancy, sit down for a start and have some coffee.' Anne held tightly to Nancy's arm until the waitress appeared with the coffees. 'I've come to ask you to help me do something about Robert,' she said.

'Isn't that your role now?'

'I wish it were, but he doesn't love me. He loves you.'

'Oh, is that why he sleeps with you and shows you off at Covent Garden and Wimbledon?'

'Those things didn't mean anything at all.'

'Who to? Him, you, me – all three of us?'

Anne pushed the cream jug towards Nancy, who pushed it back. She left the coffee untouched but took out and lit the one cigarette she allowed herself after work. What, she was wondering, did Robert see in this powdered, painted face which had its black eyes fixed on hers? What attracted people like him to women who dressed and acted like this Welsh whore?

She stifled her prejudices. By now, Nancy knew quite a bit about Anne Howells, having subdued her shame and reluctance to go and make inquiries about the woman who had seduced Gascoyne and broken up her marriage. At the Howells agency, she had inquired about finding a secretary's job and made friends with one of the office girls who was only too glad to talk about her boss.

Anne Howells came from Abergavenny in South Wales; her father had deserted her and her mother when Anne was five, then her mother died when she had just turned eleven, leaving her with grandparents who brought her up. At nineteen, she arrived in London and did jobs as a sales girl and a tourist guide before one of the madames who ran a house in the West End noticed her and enrolled her as a call girl.

Before long, she had set herself up with three other girls from the house on their own, specializing in rich clients only. They said she had a diary filled with the names and numbers of titled heads, leading businessmen, wealthy Arabs, politicians and even a couple of judges who had all bought her services.

Several of these rich clients had financed her agency in return for the pick of the girls she still employed in her call girl net. Nancy did not doubt any of this information, but she did wonder what someone who had slept with hundreds of men endowed with wealth, intelligence and sexuality saw in Robert Gascoyne, no Casanova or Don Juan in or out of bed.

Anne Howells cut across her thoughts. 'Robert wants you back. He needs you.'

'What for? To make his meals, wash his dirty linen and be available on the nights when you're not or you don't fancy a bit of slap and tickle?' She shrugged. 'He needs me! When did he notice I'd gone? When he grew hungry or when his liquor cabinet ran dry?'

'That's unfair,' Anne said. 'But you have a right to be bitter.'

'Thank you,' Nancy said, sarcastically. 'But what about you? What's your part in this script? Don't tell me you've had an access of altruism and are sacrificing everything for your lover's happiness including your chance of grabbing him for good. I won't buy that.'

'I believe I'm acting in both your interests.'

Nancy laughed, shaking her head to show her amusement was ironic. 'My interests!' she said. 'Know what I think? You both want me back to lend spice to your sex on the side. What's up? Can't you both get your act together?' She saw from Anne's face that she had landed on the truth and pressed home her attack. 'Sad, isn't it?' she murmured. 'It's the approach of the climacteric, intervertebral disc erosion, the cracking of bones, the arthritic crunch of joints, the cold sweats. All very sad.'

'How would you know, never having got there?' Anne retorted and noticed Nancy's eyes sparking with anger.

'For somebody with as much bedtime as you've had I wonder you have enough hormones left to get there.' To reinforce the jibe, Nancy reached into her bag and pulled out her make-up case and pushed it across the table. 'You've lost some of yours,' she whispered, 'and a couple of square inches of your real age are showing through. Use as much as you like.'

Anne knocked the case back across the table, but seeing Nancy reach for it and rise, Anne grabbed the compact back and said, 'Thank you, I'll borrow some of your powder.' And to the other woman's surprise she began to make up her face. 'Why don't you sit down and discuss things without raising our voices and scoring

points,' she whispered as she applied the powder. Her small stratagem worked; Nancy hesitated for a moment then sat down.

'I'm listening,' she said.

'Do you want Robert back?'

'I don't know. If I did, would he come back whole, or with some
of his parts missing?' Nancy stubbed out her cigarette butt in the
saucer, and looked straight at Anne. 'That's not intended to be
funny. It may not be your way of looking at it, but I would always
wonder which bit of him was with me and which bit was with
somebody like you.'

'I only had a small bit of him.'

'But you wanted the lot, didn't you?'

Anne nodded then shrugged her shoulders. 'My trouble was you.
He's still in love with you, if you didn't realize it.' She stirred her
coffee, eyes on the eddies the spoon made. 'If you want to know, I
loved Robert and still do.'

'Along with all the others.'

'The others didn't count – that was business.' Anne looked at
Nancy, who noticed that she had curious dark grey eyes with flecks
orbiting the pupils. 'If I didn't love him I wouldn't be worried
about him and I wouldn't be here trying to persuade you to patch
things up with him.'

'You'd give him up, then?'

'If I knew he was happy.'

'Well, you needn't make that sacrifice,' Nancy said.

She was watching Anne produce a sheaf of typescript from her
handbag and spread this on the table. 'Pity, he could have lived
high off the hog's back with you. With me it was fishfingers and
deep-freeze chips, the odd Chinese takeaway and a slice of cold
ham. With you he'd have been on a steady diet of good red meat
with caviar and foie gras thrown in for good measure, all washed
down with the best wines. You'd have to wean him off his favourite
vodka, of course.'

Studying her, Anne perceived someone who was trying to
conceal her jealousy under that flippant manner, someone who
might still be in love with her husband but who could lose him and
part of herself through her pride and obstinacy.

Maybe she was making a mistake by endeavouring to save this wrecked marriage, but if she left things as they were, Gascoyne would become a drop-out, a drunk who was slowly committing suicide. She put a painted fingernail on the typescript while Nancy watched.

'Did you know that Robert was writing a book?' she asked. Nancy shook her head. Anne pushed the typescript across the café table. 'This is a part of it, but do you know what I think? He's been writing romantic potboilers under the pseudonym of Dorothy Armour.' She gazed at Nancy. 'You didn't know?'

'No.'

'You didn't see the three books on his study shelf?' Anne insisted.

'What he does in his study is his business, and we had several hundred books in the house.' Nancy had a question of her own. 'Where did you get these if he didn't give them to you?' she said, pointing to the pages.

'Afraid I picked them up when he wasn't looking and photo-copied them. Wouldn't you like to read them?'

Nancy hesitated for a moment then gathered the dozen or so pages and began running an eye over them. In a minute she was engrossed. Gascoyne was no longer rewriting her book but was creating a completely new narrative. And she had to admit that he wrote well.

As she read, she realized Robert was writing a love story and had built into it incidents from their courtship and marriage. There was that drive through Scotland which was a massive snowscape of brittle hills and frozen lakes, a drive they thought they would never survive. Their VW had slithered on one of the hairpin bends coming over the Devil's Elbow and buried itself in a snowdrift; from five o'clock in the afternoon until just before midday the next day they had huddled together with nothing but their own warmth and some heat from the car engine to keep them from freezing to death. A Land Rover found and rescued them.

There was that other incident after their marriage when they had been caught in the tide race at Mont Saint Michel and Robert had to sling her over his shoulder and run for dry land. He had to take off his trousers and wring them out and do the same with his socks.

They were staying in the best hotel in the resort and Robert arrived with his trousers rolled up to his knees and his bare feet squelching in sodden sandals. 'But I am wearing a tie,' he said to the high-handed receptionist who supervised their luggage, who saw neither the point or the quip.

Although these scenes had been transposed, Nancy recognized the details as belonging to both of them. He had elaborated on incidents like the day they accepted information from the Greek porter in their Athens hotel and took a boat to one of the nearby islands only to find it did not return for forty-eight hours; they did not even have a toothbrush between them and had to seek lodgings with the local mayor.

Nancy read the typescript quickly, reluctant to show too much interest in it, but even that quick glance told her that Gascoyne had written some brilliant pages. A pang of envy went through her when she thought of her own efforts. Handing the pages back to Anne, she murmured, 'You must be his muse. You've obviously inspired him in a way I never could.'

'So you've read his other books, *The Heart's Reason*, *Blue Horizon* and in my opinion, the best of them, *Dreamland*?'

'No,' Nancy said, thinking that Anne's wrong assumption did something to take the sting out of her lie.

'You should, and you'd wonder where he got all the schmaltz and the sort of dreamy romantic notions that some of my secretaries have about life.' Anne paused and looked at the dregs of coffee in her cup. 'I suppose he picks some of that stuff up in the law courts.'

'That would be the last place.'

'You're right. He specialized in divorce, didn't he?'

'What do you mean "specialized"? He still does.'

Anne shook her head. 'No, I think he has given it up – or it has given him up. He wouldn't say, but I think he or his boss has had a change of heart.'

'You mean he's doing criminal law or something else?'

'No, I mean he's not doing anything in the law courts.'

Nancy concealed her surprise and pointed to the typescript pages in Anne's hand.

'At least he did these,' she said. 'Why don't you persuade him to go on and finish it and perhaps it'll make him rich.'

Without waiting for Anne's reaction she got up, nodded then strode out of the café to collect her bike and ride off.

chapter XI

ascoyne was under no illusions when Geoffrey Tyndall, the QC for whom he worked, appeared late in the afternoon at his chambers following a long day in court and tapped him on the shoulder. 'Care to dip your nose in the wine bowl, ol' boy?' he murmured.

Gascoyne could only nod. Tyndall rarely returned to his chambers when he had finished pleading, leaving the routine to his chief clerk and heading for a rendezvous with his current mistress or some rich client. This appointment indicated that the wine bowl was going to be transmuted into a poison chalice.

Gordon Bowie, who had worked in Tyndall's chambers for two years and hated his guts, warned Gascoyne once: 'Watch out for Tyndall's back-clapping – he always has a knife up his sleeve or in his hand.' Bowie knew what he was talking about, for he had taken what he called the six o'clock walk through the Inns of Court to El Vino's. He compared it to the eight o'clock walk murderers took from the death cell at Pentonville or Wandsworth Prisons to the scaffold.

'He'll sit you on his repentance stool and loose off with some double-talk about the art of advocacy, then it'll be stake or chop, meaning he'll fry you alive or decapitate you.' In his years, Gascoyne had seen three juniors get the stake or chop treatment. He did not dislike Tyndall personally, but detested his cynicism. He believed in one thing only: winning cases and earning big money. He would resort to any legal skullduggery to convince a judge or jury to find for him.

Like all gifted lawyers, he could have earned a living on the stage, but unlike some actors he never dried or muffed a line. They said he prepared two briefs, one his own and the other his adversary's, and he argued both before a non-existent bench and jury before going into court. Unworried by questions of guilt or innocence, Tyndall would willingly have defended Hitler, Himmler, Pol Pot, Bluebeard or Jack the Ripper – and prosecuted them with equal eloquence.

Now, as they walked through Middle Temple Gardens towards Fleet Street and El Vino's wine bar, Gascoyne purposely fell out of step with Tyndall and a stride behind him. They were traversing alleys with names like Temple Lane and Mitre Court, which broke into squares of smog-grimed Georgian buildings bulging with lawyers and their retinues.

It would be odd, Gascoyne reflected, not to belong to this professional corps with its age-old customs and traditions; yet he could not help feeling an exhilarating flush of liberation come over him.

For his colleagues, El Vino's might be the last-chance saloon; for him it might spell freedom.

In its invariable twilight, El Vino's reeked of its vintage burgundies and clarets, sherries and port; their odours hung thick in the atmosphere, trapped by osmosis in the panels, wooden tables and chairs of the back lounge where Tyndall headed for the seat he always chose in the duskiest corner, in keeping with his maxim that foul deeds belonged to the darkness.

Instead of accompanying him, Gascoyne halted at the bar and beckoned Chris, the nephew of the man who had founded the wine bar. 'What's the most expensive vintage you sell by the glass?' he asked.

Chris scratched his earlobe. 'Château Lafite 85, I'd say.'

Gascoyne knew that Tyndall normally drank one of the expensive burgundies, Vosne-Romanée, and his juniors who valued their careers normally shared his preference. When Gascoyne joined him, the head of his chambers beckoned Chris. 'Two large glasses of Vosne-Romanée,' he called.

Gascoyne stopped Chris as he turned. 'Not for me, Chris.' He looked at Tyndall. 'If I may, I feel like a large glass of Château Lafite 85. Chris, can the house provide?'

Chris nodded, po-faced, and Tyndall looked surprised then glared annoyance at Gascoyne.

A chain-smoker, he lit one of the king-size cigarettes he had specially made in Bond Street off the smoking butt of his last, which he gouged into the ashtray. Having observed him over four years breathe nothing but smoke, Gascoyne wondered when he was going to get cancer of the fingers of his smoking hand. He was so addicted, he had to suck boiled sweets in court. Tyndall was also tight-fisted with everyone but himself, and was so superstitious that he stepped over pavement cracks and wore the same jabot that he had won cases with as a junior.

He was talking over the cigarette in his mouth and through smoke. 'Split a bottle with Grantland the other day at the club. Good judge, Grantland. One of the best. Might've made the appeal court or even Lord Chief Justice.' He was peering through his spiky eyebrows at Gascoyne then indulging in that old law-court trick of falling silent until the witness felt forced to speak. Gascoyne stared him out, compelling him to repeat himself.

'Yes, even LCJ, if he'd had a mind.'

'If he'd had a mind,' Gascoyne murmured and chalked up a hit with that innuendo.

'What do you think stopped him?'

'Oh, Theo likes the divorce court. Suits his temperament.'

'If you mean that his prurient and squalid mind gets a kick out of wallowing in sex and smut and he revels in beach-combing among wrecked marriages, I agree.' Gascoyne had unmasked his batteries, and saw from the flush over Tyndall's prominent cheek-bones that he had struck home.

Tyndall checked himself and said, quietly, 'Maybe it's because you think that way about him that you've lost the last five divorce cases.'

Gascoyne took a pull of his Château Lafite, and swilled it round his mouth as he waved his glass back and forth to negate Tyndall's suggestion. 'I forgot his nit-picking prejudicial mind,' he said. 'As a judge he's not supposed to like or dislike barristers or their clients, but the old bastard can't help it. He's also a sadist, and possibly a pervert....'

At that, Tyndall banged his glass on the table. 'A pervert,' he said loudly. 'You're holding in contempt one of Her Majesty's judges.'

'Well, that's how he strikes me.'

'So, it won't surprise you that it got to his ears that you accused him of being prejudicial in his judgments, a grave accusation against any judge.'

'It's not only me. Ask any half-dozen Silks or juniors around the divorce court and they'll give you the same opinion.'

'They don't shout it from the public gallery,' Tyndall said, then added, 'I do realize Grantland's not the most sanguine character, but that's no reason for you to go joshing and needling a senior judge who has a yea or nay over our cases.'

'I suppose he mentioned the spat we had over Bryanson v Bryanson.'

'Among others.'

'He was sore about it because he was looking forward to hearing two days of marital mayhem with all the attendant filth and tabloid headlines.'

'Utter balderdash,' Tyndall said, shaking his head slowly from side to side in what looked like sorrow and bewilderment. 'What about you? Didn't you tell Joan Bryanson to give love another chance – when Bryanson was going to bed with everybody but her, when he's never declared a close season on his rutting, and when she's not so choosy either?'

'I told them both their futures were on the line if they decided to commit mutual hara-kiri.'

'Well, that piece of wisdom cost us a few thousand in fees and a lot of laughter in the robing room.'

Tyndall had called for another couple of half-pints of wine. He touch-lit another cigarette that looked all of six inches to Gascoyne and pulled half an inch of smoke into his mouth, grimacing as he expelled it. 'What about Mrs Fowler who had a cast-iron case for divorce? I've looked at the petition and she had the lot on her side – Fowler's a wino and a weirdo, he beats her up just this side of intensive care, he's spent most of her substantial fortune on slow horses and high-priced whores. So what do you do? Talk her into patching things up.'

Tyndall wagged the cigarette between his yellow fingers at Gascoyne. 'If he finally does her in you should be up as an accessory to murder.'

'Joan Fowler happened to be in love with him.'

Tyndall snorted smoke through his teeth and down his nostrils into his glass where even the Vosne-Romanée trembled with his indignation. 'That bloody word,' he muttered. 'Why did you handle Mrs Brewer the way you did? She had money to burn and a cast-iron case against her millionaire husband. And you go and talk them into making it up! Why?'

'Because she had a cyanide tongue and vinegar in her veins and she was determined to make him pay for spending one night with another woman. She was after money.'

'So nobody got any. You cost the firm several thousand pounds on that case alone. It's little wonder Grantland reckons you're in the wrong business. You should've gone in for marriage counselling or perhaps forensic psychiatry.'

'Grantland looks at every divorce case as another encounter in the battle of the sexes.'

'Who says he's wrong?' Tyndall came back. 'That battle has been going on since Adam and Eve dropped their fig leaves and took a bite of the forbidden apple.' Tyndall was warming to his topic, aided by more Vosne-Romanée 'Look, it's none of our function to pour a few words of wisdom into couples' heads and send them back into the conjugal front line. If what God hath joined together isn't strong enough to withstand marital tension then we have to use our spare key.'

'Spare key?' Gascoyne queried.

'To unlock the handcuffs,' Tyndall replied with a chuckle. 'The priests may handcuff them in the name of God, but fortunately for them the law gives us a spare key.' Again Tyndall chuckled. 'I've used my own three times.'

Yes, Gascoyne said to himself, and it has cost you a packet. Everybody knew Tyndall was on his fourth marriage and even that was heading for broken water and the rocks; he was paying a good half of what he earned in alimony to his three former wives and half of what was left to put his four children through college and university. It tinged his whole outlook on legal divorce work, and he rationalized his cynical views by arguing that he was entitled to earn enough from the divorce court to cover his alimony and other costs.

'Well, maybe it's because I think the whole divorce business has got out of hand and is now as sordid as Grantland's mind.'

'Spell that one out for my dim mind, would you?'

'You know what I mean. Lawyers create divorce situations because it pays them. They set parties against each other and feed judges like Grantland with their daily fix of sadism and soft porn. There'll come a time when they take divorce and all the smut attached to it away from the courts and hand it over to independent arbiters who'll help couples to sort out their problems or arrange their divorces amicably.'

Tyndall looked at him with great sorrow on his round, jowly face. 'You know, Gascoyne, I made a serious error of judgment about you.' He paused to take in more smoke. 'Know why I took you into my chambers?' Gascoyne shook his head. 'Your name – Gascoyne. I thought – irrationally as it turned out – he's a Gascon. A swashbuckling type with the boldness and the tongue of Cyrano de Bergerac. He has the gift of the gab and he'll have a go at anything and anyone. That's what I thought.'

'Sorry I didn't live up to my name,' Gascoyne said.

'So am I.' Tyndall jabbed a yellow finger at him. 'People have got to live up to their ancestry,' he said.

Like everybody in his chambers, Gascoyne knew that Tyndall boasted of his descent from William Tyndale, the translator of the English Bible, who was martyred by being burned at the stake for heresy. Like everything about Tyndall, it was slightly larger than the truth.

'Don't get me wrong, Gascoyne. As an advocate you're very good, but very good isn't good enough. The brilliant advocates have to be passionate, ruthless, prejudiced for their clients and have the killer instinct of a tiger shark.' Chris came with more wine, and Tyndall stubbed out his cigarette, seized his glass before it hit the table and downed half its contents. His dewlap quivered with what Gascoyne took for passion, prejudice and killer instinct as he said,

'The law's no trade for a man who wears his heart on his sleeve.'

'All right, I'm fired,' Gascoyne said. 'You were going to fire me whatever I said in my defence. Which is why you suggested the six o'clock walk.'

'Six o'clock walk?'

'It's what your juniors call these little sessions, which are renowned throughout the Middle Temple and as far away as Lincoln's Inn. I suppose my cards are stamped up and I can collect them tonight.'

Tyndall seemed confused, wrong-footed. He drained his glass, called for and paid the bill without a glance at it, then said, 'Sorry it didn't work out, ol' boy. If you've any idea where to find another chambers I'll put in a word.'

'Thanks, but I'm going to have a break before I take on anything else.' Gascoyne had decided not to reveal that he was giving up the law, or what he intended to do.

'Well, wherever you land, best of luck.' Tyndall levered himself out of the armchair and looked down at Gascoyne, then held out his hand.

Gascoyne waited until his huge, bulky figure had stepped into Fleet Street before he moved himself, making his way through the back alleys to the chambers.

It was only when he had cleared his desk, picked up his cheque and cards and gathered together his belongings that he had a blinding thought. Those arguments about divorce and love that he had deployed against Tyndall might easily have been used by Nancy.

chapter XII

Her local supermarket was the last place Nancy expected to find Gascoyne. Yet she should have been alerted when Pat announced that she'd seen him in her local supermarket, Waitrose, a couple of weeks before. 'Know what he had in his trolley?' Pat said, then reeled off the inventory. 'Six tins of sardines, two packets of frozen chips, ditto crisps, two packets of spaghetti, one of ravioli, half a dozen apples in plastic and a family-sized tub of Häagen-Dazs.'

'No liquor?'

Pat shook her head.

'Then he couldn't have reached the drink shelves.'

'But he was going out. He was at the cash desk, and he paid with a card.' Pat hesitated.

'All right, what else?'

'Well, either he's starting to grow a beard or he's run out of razor blades. He was ... Well, a bit dithery, and he looked as if he'd been on hunger strike.'

'It's probably withdrawal symptoms from forgetting to fill his drinks cupboard,' Nancy retorted, only half-believing Pat, who was given to fanciful language.

However, when she came face to face with Gascoyne, she realized that, for once, Pat had not stretched the truth. He looked washed out, unshaven, his jacket and trousers might have been slept in and his shoes had not been polished for weeks. From his appearance, she wondered if he was putting on an act to win her sympathy. She dismissed that notion when he cornered her by the bottled-water shelves, swinging his trolley in front of hers and blocking her passage.

'Could you get out of my way and let me pass?' she called, but he made no move.

'Look, Nancy,' he said, 'give me just five minutes.'

'To do what? Pick up the row where we left off? Let me pass.'

Gascoyne was still standing firm, blocking the passage, but a moment later someone said, 'Excuse me, can I get over there?' An elderly man pushing a trolley in which a pert little Yorkshire Terrier was sitting, unwittingly breaking the law about dogs in food stores, pointed to the Malvern water on the shelf behind Gascoyne, who still did not budge.

'What do you want?' he asked the man.

'He wants to do his shopping,' Nancy snapped, bulldozing her trolley against Gascoyne's.

Through the space she had cleared, Nancy shot off racing her trolley along the biscuits and breakfast-foods aisle towards the cash desk.

But too quick for her, Gascoyne took the short cut round the detergent and kitchen equipment shelves, headed her off and cornered her again in the angle of the fruit and vegetable counters.

'Nancy, you've got to talk to me – just for five minutes.' He was pleading, not in his legal style but sincerely and sounding slightly desperate, she felt.

Since she was boxed in, Nancy decided she had no alternative but to hear him out. However, she was going to play things cool. 'Very well, you have five minutes to make your point – but only in your capacity as a divorce lawyer.'

'Didn't you know? I'm no longer a divorce lawyer.'

'I don't keep in touch with the comings and goings of the family division of the High Court,' Nancy said, coldly. 'You're still a lawyer.'

'Only in name,' Gascoyne came back.

'No matter,' Nancy murmured with a shrug. 'I'll let you handle our divorce since you have all the inside knowledge and a head start.'

'I don't want a divorce.' Gascoyne had raised his voice to a shout that stopped several trolleys in their tracks. 'I want you to come home.'

'I want to get home, too, lady,' a voice said behind her and a man steered his trolley past hers and Gascoyne let him go by but blocked the way again.

'Come home, Nancy,' he said.

'Home is where I live now and your home is where you live. Let's leave it like that.'

She pointed to the back of the supermarket. 'The vodka shelf's that way. I'm going to the cash desk if you please.'

'I don't drink vodka any more.'

'Well, well! You don't sunder other married couples any more, you don't practise your trade, you don't drink vodka and you do your own shopping. What's happening? Oh, I know – the future Mrs Robert Gascoyne is obviously much tougher than I ever was. Good luck to her.'

She could observe that Gascoyne was growing more and more exasperated and was only just holding his temper in check.

'There's no future Mrs Gascoyne,' he said, banging a fist on the trolley handle. 'It was just a flirtation, I tell you. I've never loved anybody but you. I swear Anne Howells never meant anything to me, and I haven't seen her since you walked out.'

'Liar.' Nancy uttered the word loudly enough to stop another couple of trolleys. 'I've seen your new beloved and read some of the pages of the novel you're collaborating on.'

She read genuine puzzlement in Gascoyne's face before he said, 'Ah yes, she came round twice to see how I was and must have picked up pages of the novel that I'd left lying around.'

'From what I read she seems to have inspired your literary talents as well.'

'Nancy, darling, I swear she means nothing to me. How can I prove it to you?'

'Not by darlinging me. It's too late.'

'What do you mean it's too late?' He was pleading again. 'Does it mean you've found somebody else?' When Nancy did not reply, he went on, 'I know who it is – that new quack in the practice where you work. It's him, isn't it?'

'He's not a quack.'

'So it is him.' Gascoyne accompanied his shout with an upward flick of his hand to dismiss her response. 'You're mad. You'll be toiling twenty-four hours a day as his secretary and nurse and cooking and washing for him. He'll exploit you as I've never done. Then you'll wonder where your women's lib and your sexual equality have gone.'

'At least he's in love with me,' Nancy said to needle him further.

'There it is – that four-letter word again.'

'That four-letter word means I'm treated like a human being and not a chattel. Anyway, we have more in common.'

'Oh yes. What, for instance?'

'Music, literature, drama ...'

Gascoyne's laughter echoed along the lines of biscuits and cornflakes and bounced off the tins of cat and dog food. 'Does that mean you give each other readings of *The Constant Nymph* and Barbara Cartland on the hearth rug before the romantic log fire?' He guffawed again. 'And then what – bed, book and canoodle.'

'If you're thinking of citing him or anybody else, you've no evidence,' Nancy said to stop his laughter. 'All the divorce evidence is on my side.'

'Who mentioned divorce? Anyway, on what grounds and what evidence?'

'Your adultery for a start. Then sexual, social, domestic, artistic, physical and aesthetic incompatibility. You're the divorce expert, so I would imagine you can write the script in your sleep. I would think that Miss Howells would only be too pleased to spare my lawyer the trouble of cross-examining her about your long-standing adultery.'

'But Nancy, I don't want a divorce.'

She looked at him. His voice had risen half an octave and had something of a wail in it. She almost felt compassion for him, but said stonily: 'I thought that was what you and the Howells woman wanted more than anything.'

Gascoyne moved round his trolley to approach her, but Nancy side-stepped, backed off and placed her trolley between them.

'Look, darling,' he said, 'I wanted to suggest something. Why don't we have a trial period, a making-up period, say a month or two months? If you still feel you don't love me then I'll give you a divorce.'

He sounded so earnest, so anguished, that Nancy might have given in had someone not come between them. A woman pushing through to reach the avocado pears and grapefruit and shouting 'Excuse me' in a loud, irritated voice.

Nancy seized her chance; she left her trolley with what she had chosen in it and ran through the gap the strident woman had opened up. At the cash desk she wormed her way past the queue and out of the store.

She retrieved her bicycle and pedalled off before Gascoyne could pursue her. But as she navigated carefully through the thick traffic between Shepherd's Bush and Hammersmith, she wondered about Gascoyne. He looked like someone in the throes of a midlife crisis. He had certainly changed. It was perhaps not a complete transformation, but his temper and sarcastic tongue had softened; she had never thought of Gascoyne and humility as having anything in common.

But something had humbled him.

chapter XIII

Monclar realized something was amiss when he released the handbrake of his car and tried to back out of his space in the car park beneath the practice. He felt a slight resistance as the car moved, then a ripping noise came from the wheels. When he had cleared the parking space he could not believe what he saw; he had, in fact, left half the tread of his front tyres behind. Switching on his headlights, he got out of the car and looked at the tyre treads. They were stuck fast to the concrete floor.

Monclar kept staring incredulously at the tyre treads and the mined front tyres of his car. He recalled that when he had tried the car lock, he found the door open and had assumed he had forgotten to lock it. He had also noticed that he seemed to have left the car about a yard further from the wall than he normally did.

Evidently someone had opened the door, smeared the tyres with one of the epoxy resin glues and pushed it back until the glued section of the tyres was in contact with the floor.

Who had it in for him? A patient or a relative? One of his oddball cases, or someone he had given psychiatric treatment?

This was not the first time his car had been tampered with; ten days before, he had tried to open both front doors only to discover that someone had filled the keyholes with instant glue. He had to break into the vehicle and drive it to a garage to have the glue dissolved.

Then there were the calls and the parcels. Three times in the past week he had been wakened in the middle of the night by a

caller; on the first occasion it sounded like a man with a handkerchief over his mouth putting on a lisping castrato voice. He said it
was an emergency, that someone was vomiting blood at an address
in Shepherd's Bush and a patient of Dr Monclar had suggested
calling him. When Monclar reached the address and woke the
family, they denied that anyone was ill.

Two nights later, the voice came on again; this time it had
changed down an octave though Monclar reckoned it was the same
person by his rapid delivery, as if the man feared he might give the
police time to trace the call. 'Dr Monclar,' the voice said, 'if you've
been screwing that bitch of a secretary in your practice and
weren't fully covered, have yourself tested for HIV before you start
infecting other people. She's a whore.'

Monclar had no time to question the caller or even open his
mouth before the line went dead. He was more than ever certain
he was dealing with one of his patients who blamed him for a
wrong diagnosis and treatment, or for refusing to supply him with
drugs. He ignored the third call, which he later discovered to have
been another hoax. Worse was to come. His postbox began to fill up
with every form of junk mail –information and offers on everything
from Savile Row suits, hiking boots, mountaineering equipment,
sailing boats, marine radios and compasses, double glazing, the
latest in hi-fi systems and personal computers, a £500 cruise to the
Caribbean and a martingale for winning the national lottery. It
seemed he had written to half a hundred firms demanding the
information with a strong hint that he was in the market for such
merchandize.

These hoaxes began to lose their funny side when parcels began
to arrive. Undoing one of them, Monclar found himself almost
engulfed by the full-sized plastic doll which materialized out of the
box, hissing as she pumped herself up with air. On her alpine
breasts was painted: TRY ME FOR SIZE.

He received a food parcel from Harrods paid with what the store
claimed was his credit card, though when he checked it was
someone else's number; from the same store he had a fur-lined,
ankle-length coat delivered on approval, again backed by a credit
card. Monclar thought of contacting the police but decided against

this on the grounds that if the caller was a patient, he needed psychiatric treatment rather than conviction by a court and a possible jail sentence.

Something else stopped him: he had an idea it might have something to do with Nancy's husband.

After the phony night calls, he began to be more vigilant on his rounds. A few days after the first call he noticed a Rover 75 dropping into his wake on certain house calls; once or twice he saw what he took for the same car parked near the practice.

But now, as he took stock of his ruined tyres, he considered the man had gone too far and there was therefore no alternative to contacting the police. First, he had to get the car to the late-night garage on Goldhawk Road and have the tyres replaced and, at the risk of ruining the wheels, he decided to limp there.

Getting into the car, he felt something hard under his right buttock. When he located it and pulled it free he was looking at a small cigarette lighter. He put it in his pocket, thinking it might help to catch the hoaxer.

Before he had time to contact the police, news of the ruined tyres had spread round the practice. When Nancy taxed him about it, he disclosed the facts about the mysterious calls, the junk mail, the parcels and the Rover which was tailing him.

Nancy listened then asked, 'Have you cancelled what you have of this voice on your answerphone?'

'No, I think the last call's still on it.'

'Can I listen?'

He nodded. After they had finished that evening, he drove them to his flat in Holborn. When she entered, he must have caught the surprise on her face. 'I know, it's a trifle cramped but it's all I need.' It was no overstatement. His flat was smaller than her own. One room with a tiny kitchen walled off, a bathroom with a sitz bath, shower and WC.

'Where do you sleep?' she asked.

He pointed to the sofa. 'It opens out and it's quite comfortable – even big enough for two.'

She let that hint pass. Gazing round the place set her wondering why someone like Monclar, who earned more than four times her wages, stuck himself in a cell like this on a main road polluted with traffic fumes and with few amenities.

Nancy's attention went to the walls, two of which were covered with drawings and paintings. Grotesque subjects, some of them erotic or even obscene, they seemed to have been done by children.

'No, no,' Monclar amended when she asked. 'They were all grown-ups, from twenty to eighty. They were patients in the mental hospital where I trained. I gave them drawing and painting sets to see whether what they did with them might yield some insight into their mental state and suggest treatment.'

Monclar apologized for the disorder in his flat, saying he did everything for himself, including the dusting and Hoovering.

'It's no worse than mine,' Nancy remarked.

Monclar showed her the junk mail and parcels piled up on the large knee-hole desk in his one room, which obviously did duty as a study, living room, bedroom and dining room. As she flipped through the material, he located the call still on his answering machine and played it back.

Nancy listened intently, shaking her head as he repeated it several times. 'Could be anybody,' she said.

Monclar put a finger to his temple then went to a drawer, opened it and produced the small gold lighter he had discovered in his car when the tyres had been vandalized.

'But that's Robert's lighter,' Nancy exclaimed. 'I gave it to him a couple of years ago for his birthday.'

'So I'm tangling with a jealous husband, am I?'

Nancy shook her head in bewilderment, then pointed to the pile of mail and parcels.

'I didn't think he had either the imagination or the spunk to do anything like that,' she murmured.

'You know what it means, though?' When she shrugged he went on, 'It means he's as jealous as a tiger cat – and it means he's in love with you.'

'You mean he believes he is.'

'Isn't it the same thing?'

She looked at the pile of mail and the answerphone. 'I didn't think he could be that jealous,' she said.

Monclar grinned at her. 'You underestimate your ... your appeal. He's jealous all right, and jealousy is often in direct proportion to the desire felt for the loved one.' He widened his grin. 'But it can also be the sign of a wounded ego causing heartache and even some form of mental derangement.'

He opened the cupboard door to show her the rubber doll lying deflated on a shelf.

'That's a sign of mental wobbling,' he said. He cast an arm round the scene. 'And this could only be a start.'

'Are you implying he could become dangerous?' Nancy asked, then laughed. 'I can't see Robert doing anything violent. After all, he's a lawyer and he knows what it might cost him.'

'Jealous husbands don't begin to consider the legal or other consequences. In fact they're a bit like psychopaths.'

Nancy picked up the rubber doll and the latest thing Monclar had on approval from one of the London stores, a boxed edition of the Kama Sutra, an illustrated *Decameron* and two more volumes of erotica in deluxe editions.

'I'll send them back when I've read them,' Monclar commented.

'What are you going to do about whoever it is? Tell the police?'

'No – he's more in need of a doctor than a copper. Give him time and he'll break surface or simmer down and sink without trace.'

'I'm still worried.'

'You think he might do me in?' Monclar said, drawing his hand across his throat then wrapping both hands round his neck. 'If you do, you'd better start by telling me about this husband of yours ... what he's like, what he does, whether he might work with a gun or cyanide, why you fell out ... in short, everything.'

'That's going to take time.'

'We've got that.' Monclar opened a cupboard in which was concealed a TV and hi-fi system with several bottles and glasses on the shelf above them. 'What would you like? Gin, whisky, sherry ...'

She opted for sherry and he half filled two tumblers with Manzanilla and gestured towards the tiny kitchen. 'You wrestle with the salad and I'll make us a cheese omelette if that's OK.'

Nancy nodded and followed him into the kitchen where he handed her an apron and explained where to find lettuce, chicory, mushrooms and radishes in the small fridge.

While she prepared the salad she watched out of the corner of her eye as he mixed a couple of spoonfuls of milk with a little flour then broke three eggs, separated the yolks and added these to his mixture with grated cheese. He poured a spoonful of olive oil into a small iron frying pan and as it warmed over the gas he whipped the three egg whites into a solid mass and added these to his previous mix.

Nancy had to stop and watch. 'But this is cordon bleu stuff,' she said, marvelling. 'Wherever did you learn to break eggs one-handed, juggle the yolks and whites apart and concoct an omelette like that?'

'On my own and like everything else I've ever learned,' he said. 'The hard way.' He let the mixture simmer for more than five minutes, slipped it on to a plate then threw a little oil into the hot pan. 'Hurry up with that salad,' he said, taking the omelette and reversing it on to the pan. 'Ready in three minutes,' he said.

They ate off the small coffee table in the living room, sitting opposite each other. Monclar opened a bottle of supermarket Beaujolais Villages and was filling the tumblers they had emptied in the kitchen when she stopped him halfway up the glass. 'I haven't got the head for this,' she said.

'Leave what you don't want.'

Monclar studied her as he helped himself to salad then chewed on his omelette. Did this woman know how pretty she was? Or the effect she had on primitives like Mason, and this jealous husband of hers? She breathed and exuded sex, was highly intelligent, and sensitive. What more could anybody want?

He wondered idly how it would be to make love to her. That would probably be much easier than trying not to fall in love with her. Lechers like Mason saw no further than the sex act. But he, Monclar, might allow his real feelings to run away with him. It would be too easy with this girl opposite. No, he would hold his hand. Not only until he was sure of her, but more vital, until he was sure of himself.

'Where do you want me to start telling you about Robert Gascoyne?' she said, cutting across his thoughts.

'I don't know.' He raised his glass and clinked it with hers, lightly. 'I even wonder if I'm interested in your irate husband ... Anyway, not as interested as I am in you.' He sipped his wine and eyed her over the glass. 'If we were to play this scene properly, I should try to seduce you. I should begin by saying that you're not only the prettiest girl I've ever met but the most unusual combination of beauty, intelligence, wit and ...'

'Stop it, Dr Monclar.'

'The name's Ted.'

'Whatever it is, stop it.'

'Why? It's only a script I'm talking. So why shouldn't I pour compliments into your head and liquor into your glass then establish epidermic contact, first by hand and then ...'

'And then what part do I play in this script that you've written for us?'

'Ah! You listen, half amused, but half convinced by what I'm saying. You want to believe the flattery and you're intrigued by my approach. So, you sip your wine and act a bit more tipsy than your alcoholic content would suggest, you respond to my hand squeeze by trundling your pointed fingernails along my lifeline, maybe even influencing it, you allow yourself to be kissed and perhaps even fondled around your breasts and thighs, but when you're pulled into a tight clinch you call "break" and set yourself up for the next meeting and the next sequence of heavy petting and mutual heart-pounding.'

Despite herself, Nancy had to smile at the scene he painted. 'Is that how it usually happens in your experience?'

'Not in my experience. In most scenarios – so they tell me.'

'Well, you may be right. But life isn't a script.'

'That's where you're wrong. It *is* a script. And it's a script that most people write and act themselves with dialogue they haven't thought out properly and sentences they utter or throw out, if you like, without the slightest reflection about them. Our future may be decided to a great extent by our genes, but we have to write in the missing lines.'

'I'll think about that,' Nancy said.

'While you're thinking about it, you still haven't told me why you walked off stage and left your husband with a monologue, no audience and a sore ego.'

Monclar stopped when he realized Nancy was smiling at what he had said. He asked her to tell him why.

'Because you don't know how near the truth you are,' she said, explaining they had quarrelled over a script, something she had written and he had taken the liberty of correcting. That led her on, prompted by Monclar, to confess she was a spare-time writer of romantic novels, had published three and was working on a fourth when she had the row with Gascoyne and left him.

'Forget Gascoyne,' he said. 'Just go back to the beginning and tell me about yourself – everything.'

'What does that mean, everything? You're not going to analyze me, are you?'

'No, just interested.'

He caught her looking at him dubiously so to give her time to decide without embarrassing her, Monclar picked up the plates, knives and forks and carried them through to the kitchen where she heard him slot them into his small dishwasher. A few minutes later, he reappeared carrying a plate of different cheeses – Roquefort, Bel Paese and Parmesan plus two side plates. Another trip to the kitchen and he returned with a slab of Marks and Spencer's fruit cake. 'I've put the coffee on to percolate,' he said.

'Where do you really want me to start?' she said.

'The beginning's quite a good place.'

'It's very boring.'

'Not to me,' he said, then added, 'Oh, not because I'm a head shrinker but it's simply that I'm interested in people and their origins, and I'm doubly interested in you.' So she began, hesitantly, telling about her bank-clerk father who never opened the gold pocket watch his NatWest colleagues inscribed and gave him for forty years of faithful service because he might soil its face or wear out its spring or jewels or the lining of his waistcoat pocket.

He was like that with everything in life, leaving so much of himself unused and finishing with a wardrobe full of unworn suits and shoes; she was sure most of his brain cells, his sex cells and most of his other cells were intact when he died at sixty-seven, two years, three months, four days and fifteen hours after his retirement by the gold watch he never wore.

Even the Hillman he bought twenty years before still had its original tyres and only 22,000 miles on the clock. Nancy had never known him show any emotion, but he did take small pleasures in certain things – for instance, his ability to add up three columns of pounds, shillings and pence at a glance and carry this facility into the bank's decimal era. She said her mother was still alive, in her mid sixties and living on Merseyside where her father had worked. They rarely saw each other, though her mother rang her every other week. Had she listened to her mother, she would have been a member of some typing pool in Liverpool, or a shop assistant.

Her mother always took the safe line, which was why her father had never moved from his Liverpool branch of the bank, or gained promotion. Still living in Victorian times, her mother believed people should remain in the social stratum where God had placed them. To move down was humiliation, to move up was risking another form of humiliation from one's betters.

Hers was the caste system and she took her time in religion from the local Methodist minister. She watched *Coronation Street* and displayed all the petty foibles of her class. Everything worried her and she worried about everything; she even worried sometimes that she had nothing to worry about. She worried about the tear in the ozone layer and the greenhouse effect which might provoke planetary genocide; she worried about endangered species such as the oryx, the Himalayan black bear, the Chinese tiger, the rhino and Prince Charles. Would the monarchy survive and if so, was Charles fit to be a king having confessed to adultery? Diana worried her for years before her fatal accident; she was too highly strung, should stop eating herself sick and wearing mini-skirts that would give her cystitis. A Tower of London raven fell sick and Mrs Elliott worried that the Empire might collapse (unaware that it had gone long ago).

'So you escaped and fled south,' Monclar interjected.

Nancy nodded, describing how she had worked for an advertising firm and how an incident at one of their parties had brought her and Gascoyne together, how he had wooed her for six months or more and finally she had agreed to marry him.

'Were you in love with him?'

'I thought so. He was something I'd never met before. What my mother would call class, he had it stamped all over him. Public school, Oxford, the Inner Temple, the wig and gown and a pure white jabot round his neck and his name in the papers and his face on TV when one of his divorce cases made the news.'

'Do you still think you're in love with him?'

'I don't know. I wish I did.'

'But you walked out.'

Nancy explained that she had discovered he was seeing another woman, a former client he had defended.

'So that was the real reason for leaving him.'

'No ... well, maybe it had something to do with it. But I got mad at him for daring to rewrite the book I had started and that triggered the quarrel. Anyway, it was a quarrel waiting to happen.' She held both hands up palms outwards. 'But I write under a pseudonym and nobody knows and I don't want anybody to know, so you must keep my secret.'

'On the heart and soul of Hippocrates himself,' Monclar said, clapping a hand over his heart to confirm the pledge. 'But there's a quid pro quo,' he said. 'I'd like to read your books.'

'Why? They're hardly your sort of literature.'

'Wait a minute.' Monclar tilted his nose in the air. 'I smell the coffee doing something stupid.' He rose, took the cheese plate and hurried into the kitchen. A minute later he returned with a coffee pot and two cups and saucers on a tray. As he poured the coffee, he said, 'Your three published books – did your husband read them and if he did, what did he think of them?'

Nancy reflected for a moment. 'It's a few years back but I think he read the first one and I can't remember that he made any comment about it. Why?'

Monclar did not reply directly. He dropped two sugar lumps into her cup at her request, but sipped his own without either milk or sugar. Hers felt black and thick enough to stand a spoon in and so bitter that she added a third lump.

'Why do I want to read your books?' he asked, then answered the question.

'Because I'm interested in what makes someone like you what you are and they may give me an insight.'

'You won't find that insight in my books,' Nancy said. 'I didn't put it into them.'

Monclar nodded his head slowly to contradict her. 'You know, while I was doing my Diploma of Psychological Medicine I worked in a mental hospital handling schizophrenics for the most part. Did you realize they shy away from mirrors because they often don't recognize the face they see there and thinking they see another face frightens them? Some of them believe there's another side to the mirror. Normal people don't have that problem, but they're fooled, too, for they think the mirror reflects their real self when they are really seeing only a projection of themselves – and most often the person they'd really like to be.'

'What has that got to do with my books?'

'Books are a sort of mirror of the person who writes them, whether they're fact or fiction. If you think about it, pretty well all writing is self-portrait in some form or another if you can put the right part of the jigsaw together.'

'If you're going to dissect me line by line I won't even tell you what my pseudonym is or what I've written. Anyway, you've had me telling you all about myself and you've told me nothing about yourself.'

Monclar could see that she was serious. 'Don't worry,' he said, 'I won't try to psychoanalyze you, I promise. I'll even make a pact with you. Let me read your three books and the bit of the script you quarrelled about and I'll take you and introduce you to the Huguenot Monclars of Bermondsey, and you'll see what a quantum jump I've made to get this far west and into this small pad.' He held out his hand. 'Is it a pact?' he asked.

'It's a pact,' Nancy said.

He drove her home and picked up the three books and a typed copy of what she had written of her fourth novel.

Nancy had not expected him to try to kiss her – yet she was disappointed that he didn't.

Perhaps it wasn't in his or her script.

chapter XIV

Monclar fascinated her. Although she saw him for several hours a day five days a week, she found her eye irresistibly drawn to the way his reddish-fair hair sprouted on his high cheekbones and stood out on his temples and formed a circumflex over his deep blue eyes; his mouth had a slight sardonic twist which reflected the sort of barbed observations he threw out. If Nancy was truthful with herself, she was already half in love with the man even if he had given no hint of sharing her feelings.

She realized that in the love game there were invariably the hunter and the prey.

Until now, she had been the prey, fending off hunters and predators because that seemed a woman's traditional role. Now she had turned hunter and was finding Monclar a difficult stalk; if she took a false step or made a clumsy approach upwind, he acted like some cunning old stag and went to ground in thick cover.

His attitude puzzled her so much that she broke one of her rules and confided in Pat, telling her what had happened when Robert played the jealous, enraged husband and how Monclar had revealed this to her and invited her to his flat.

'You could hardly swing a mouse in it,' she said.

'Never mind the surface area, have you tried the sofa-bed for size yet?' When Nancy shook her head, Pat looked at her with surprise and perplexity. 'Nancy, you must be slipping,' she said.

'I can't fathom him. I'm sure he's got a block about women somewhere.'

'Maybe he has one hidden away somewhere, too mad or bad to put on show.'

'No, he's too honest. But why does he live in such a poky flat in a grim old building when he could afford one with two or three rooms around Holland Park or Kensington?'

'Ask him, and when you're about it you can find out why he works in a dump like this with two quacks like the Clarkes and a kinky, sex-crazy charlatan like Mason when he has youth, good looks and talent.'

'I've asked myself why. Pat, I tell you, he's brilliant. If he opened a consulting room in Harley Street he'd make a fortune.'

'Maybe he doesn't want to make a fortune. Maybe he's one of the half-dozen doctors in Britain not dedicated to increasing their bank balance or lowering their golf handicap at St Andrews or Wentworth,' Pat said with only half her tongue in her cheek.

A week later, Monclar invited her again to share his evening meal in his flat. On the way there, he stopped at a butcher's to buy a pound of fillet steak then shopped in the supermarket at Notting Hill for several tubes of sauce, potato crisps, salad and spices.

'What is it this time?' Nancy queried.

'Wait and see.'

Again she prepared the salad while Monclar cut the meat into chunks about three-quarters of an inch thick. To her astonishment, he produced a copper fondue pan and spirit burner and set it on the coffee table; he poured a bottle of olive oil into the pan, lit the burner under it and left it to heat. On two of his largest plates, he disposed a dozen sauces, various types of mustard, then chopped capers and gherkins.

'Do you like it hot enough to call out the fire brigade?' he said, holding up bottles of chilli and tabasco sauces and pointing to a dish of paprika sauce.

'I've never tried them all, but I'm game,' Nancy said.

'Hey, I forgot to ask if you like fondue.'

'I love it – specially the ritual.'

They sat opposite each other chatting until the oil began to sizzle in the fondue pan. Monclar speared a piece of meat with his fork, dunked it in the boiling liquid for a moment then passed it to her. 'Blow on it,' he said and she did then gathered some béarnaise sauce on it and took a bite.

'Well?'

'It's out of time and place,' she said.

Monclar twirled a cube of meat in the oil and tried the garlic sauce and smacked his lips. 'You've got to try them all,' he said.

'If I survive the first hot one,' she said, harpooning a piece of meat and frying it.

'Why did you choose fondue?' she asked.

Monclar shrugged. 'I like it, and I thought you'd like it. And it's not the sort of dish you can eat alone, is it?'

Nancy wondered about that remark. Was it some sort of hint, or did it have overtones that her antennae were meant to catch. She had to make some response.

'I'm wondering why you invited me,' she said.

'Why? I like you, I like your company, you're intelligent, you're very attractive, you don't talk if you've nothing to say and you don't mind if I do the same.'

'And that's as far as it goes?'

Monclar gazed at her with that sardonic twist to his mouth. 'If you mean would I like to sleep with you, the answer's yes – but I don't steal another man's property.'

'That sounds like hypocrisy.'

'Nooh.' Monclar was holding his fondue fork as she had seen him hold a hypo, between his thumb and index finger; he impaled a piece of meat, dunked it and watched it sizzle in the simmering oil until it changed colour. 'It's no hypocrisy. I play honestly. I don't say to a woman, "I love you, I love you, I love you" because I know that phrase is like a bad tune or a big lie – if you play or say it often enough it becomes the truth for those who listen to it.'

'That means when you say it, it will be true?'

He nodded and looked into her eyes. 'Another thing ... if we went further I might get too fond of you.'

'And so ...'

'And so nothing.' He blew on his meat then picked up some chilli sauce with it before replying. 'Let me say this sincerely – if I were the marrying kind you'd be my type of girl.' He gave her that sardonic grin. 'I like women who are themselves, who don't go in for disguise, who won't wear false eyelashes, who don't wear eyeliner, who don't hide behind a face mask.'

'There are a lot of negatives in that.'

'To me it means you're what you look – honest, straightforward.'

'The sort of girl who comes home with the Sunday school prize?'

Monclar reached over the table with the wine bottle in his hand to replenish her glass, but she placed her hand over it to stop him. As he filled his own glass, he said, 'No, but maybe the sort of girl who might win the Golden Heart award for her romantic novels.'

'So you've read them.'

'Mm-hm. All three and the typescript of the fourth as far as it goes.'

'And you didn't like them.'

'On the contrary, I thought they were good of their genre. If I can paraphrase Abe Lincoln, "Those who like this sort of book will find these the sort of book they like."'

Nancy laughed. 'I don't know what to make of that.'

Monclar was turning the salad she had made in its bowl and passed it to her to help herself. 'Look, Nancy, I wasn't reading your books as a literary critic or a romantic novel buff. I was reading them to discover something about you. For instance, I see you wrote the first one just over three years ago.'

'Does that mean anything?' Nancy asked, perplexed by the comment.

'Well, in my psychiatric book, it's difficult to be in love and write about it. Love is something most people write about before or after the event, not when you're in the throes. At least, that's the way I see it.'

'So you think I had stopped loving Robert when I began writing *The Heart's Reason*.'

'It's a working hypothesis.'

Nancy stared at him, wondering if he was joking, but from his expression she realized he was dead serious. He might have something. Indeed, she had often reflected herself that she might be channelling her frustration and lack of affection into writing the sort of stories she might have liked to live.

It could be, as Monclar suggested, her way of compensating for her failed marriage, or she may have been sublimating her anger at Gascoyne for his behaviour at that moment in time. He was running into trouble with Grantland, the divorce court judge, losing cases as a result and seeking his solace at the bottom of the vodka bottle.

'I'm wondering if it's a good thing for me – I mean being a working hypothesis,' she said.

'Well, you don't fit into any psychiatric slot.'

'Meaning?'

'Look at romantic novelists as a class. They're mostly blue-stockings with triple firsts in English lit, social history and church music, they have oil-barrel bodies, faces like a petrol refinery, skin like the Dead Sea scrolls and a bad case of sexual anorexia. Now, nobody could say that about you and that's what makes your case so interesting.'

'I'm not sure I want to be a case.'

'Oh, we all are, in some way or another. Think about it, the man-in-the-street and woman-in-the-street are just a handy abstraction. There's no such thing as the normal person or the average person outside maths. If we all conformed to type it would be a dull world.'

'Where does Dr Monclar come in?'

He grinned. 'Ted Monclar's a case as well, but of a totally different kind.'

'That's curious. I thought psychiatrists all went through a sort of twelve-month debriefing to iron out all their neuroses and personality kinks and leave them permanently in neutral gear.'

'Freudians maybe. I managed to hang on to all my manias and phobias, thank God.'

'I haven't seen any.'

Monclar went to say something then stopped himself; she saw his blue eyes inching over her face, reflection in them. 'I admit psychiatrists are always asking people to bare their soul and spill their secrets to them without much two-way traffic.'

'We have souls then.'

Monclar shrugged. 'It's a figure of speech. In fact, we're all programmed from birth by the two cells that come together to create us and set up the controls for the millions of genes that decide our lives.'

'Don't tell me we're like computer software – that would be dull.'

'Ah, but we have a dash of free will to make things a bit more interesting. Though in my book there's not much room for choice.'

'It all sounds like Calvinism or John Knox Presbyterianism.'

'Who's to say they were wrong?'

'I hope they were. I don't fancy having everything worked out for me in advance.'

Her voice had dropped a tone or two and sounded sad; he reached across the low table to touch her hand. 'Don't take it too much to heart. It's another working hypothesis.' He drank the wine in his glass and poured what remained of the bottle and drank it. 'You have Saturday off, haven't you?' Nancy nodded, and he went on, 'In that case, I'll fix it so that I'm free and take you on that tour of London docks that I promised you.'

'I'm looking forward to it.'

She realized this amounted to an important concession on his part, and although she wondered what was so important for him around Thames-side docks, she bit back the questions in her mind.

When they had together cleared the table and tidied the flat, Monclar offered her a lift home. She asked if he had finished with her books and the script she was working on, and he handed her the script, though said he would like to read the books again.

He had parked his car in the street. Before opening the door for her, he peered underneath the body. Inside the car, he released the bonnet lock and examined the engine to satisfy himself no one had tampered with it.

'Are you programmed to do this every time?' she said.

He grinned at the comment on his philosophy, but said quite seriously, 'I do, for you never know what's in the program of a jealous husband.'

chapter XV

A few evenings later, Monclar received a call from a practice
patient who said his daughter was sick and had five degrees
of fever. She normally saw Dr Mason at the practice, but he
could not be contacted. Would Dr Monclar please come? Although
it was nine o'clock and he might have passed the call to the depu-
tizing service they often used, Monclar was doing nothing and
decided therefore to answer the call himself. When he had located
the street in his London guide, he checked his car and set out for
the network of back streets between Goldhawk Road and Uxbridge
Road. So far as he could make out at that hour in the thick traffic,
nothing was following him. He found the address and spotted the
father waiting for him. He introduced himself as Vikram Mehta,
one of Mason's patients. Monclar had seen him twice in the waiting
room and was reassured.

'I am not able to make contact with Dr Mason,' Mehta said.

'How did you get my home number?'

'In the telephone book.'

'That's odd,' Monclar said. 'It happens to be an unlisted
number.'

'Then someone else maybe gave it to me.'

Monclar cut the man's explanation short and followed him
through the front door of the old building and along a narrow, ill-
lit corridor to a door opening into a flat at the rear of the ground
floor. Mehta had two rooms which included a tiny kitchen and a
cubicle containing a WC and a shower.

As they passed through the larger room to the bedroom where
the girl lay, Monclar noticed the small shrine to Siva, the god repre-

senting the ruthless, destructive force in the Hindu creed; beside Siva was Kali, his blood-lusting partner, her breasts covered with a necklace of human skulls signifying her power to slay. This many-headed version of Siva was painted white and his heads and four arms were draped in flower garlands. Monclar could smell the incense burning by the shrine and a thicker, more cloying tang of ghee, the clarified butter Mehta had used to anoint the effigies of his gods who bestowed life, sexuality and death. Monclar wondered whom Mehta was hedging his bets with – his Hindu gods or himself representing modern medicine.

'Shanta, my only daughter, is growing very tired, very, very tired,' Mehta murmured as he led the way. 'Too tired to be wanting to eat anything very often. I am worried about her.'

He halted before the bedroom door, put his two hands together and pressed both index fingers to his mouth in prayer. 'Doctor, this one is my only daughter. Her mother died when she was born. Nothing can happen to this one. Nothing.'

'Let's see what's wrong,' Monclar said, gesturing to the man to open the door. 'Anyway, when did this fever start?'

'Suddenly, very suddenly, only last night. But Shanta doesn't want to trouble doctors, that is what she says.'

Monclar had noticed Shanta Mehta several times in the surgery, probably because she was as beautiful as a tropical flower, with tawny skin, a lovely oval face and large, dark doe eyes. As he took her pulse, listened to her heart and breathing and palpated her chest and stomach, he quizzed her about where she worked and her previous illnesses. She was a sales girl in Marks and Spencer's in King Street, Hammersmith, and she had no previous illnesses.

Monclar noted her throat seemed inflamed, her pulse was faster than normal and she had four degrees of temperature. Something bothered him. It was nearly autumn and they had no flu, no aden-oviruses making the rounds, no epidemic of coryza or anything else. He prescribed one of the broad-spectrum penicillins and something to make the girl sleep, but gave Mehta pills for that night out of his bag. He should really refer the girl to Mason, her usual doctor, but to save time he wrote a note to the lab at Hammersmith Hospital and handed this to the father.

'Can you get time off to go with your daughter to the hospital, Mr Mehta?'

Mehta nodded. 'I work as a mechanic at a garage near this hospital. I can go.'

'They will do tests. When you get the results of the tests take them and show them to Dr Mason. Have you got that?'

Monclar had left his car fifty yards away under a streetlamp in a district where car theft and mugging were common. He was walking towards it when someone leapt at him from the shadows of a terrace house on the corner. A heavy blow struck Monclar on the head, glancing off the cap he was wearing and landing on his neck.

Stunned by the blow, he fell to the ground, and in a second the man who had attacked him was striking again at his head. Holding his medical bag over his head and face, Monclar tried to shield himself from the heavy cudgel that was raining blow after blow on him. Beneath the bag, he could see the man's legs straddling him, and he lashed out at one of them with his foot, his shoe striking bone and bringing a cry of pain.

Monclar scissored his legs round his assailant's ankle then pulled and twisted, throwing him off balance. Monclar thrust himself up on to his feet and as the man closed on him to use his baton, he stepped inside his swinging arm and buried his fist in the man's stomach, putting everything he had into the punch.

He saw the man stagger though he kept on his feet, getting in a last blow before he turned to bolt. Monclar sprinted after him, hurling himself at his legs and bringing him down with a rugby tackle. As he went down, the man hit a fire hydrant on the kerb and went absolutely still.

Monclar, who had heard the crack as the man's head struck the metal hydrant, turned him over and saw through the stocking mask he wore that he was unconscious. He went back to retrieve his bag, which he had let drop to pursue the man. When he returned, half a dozen people had gathered round the fallen figure still flat out on the pavement.

'Do you want me to call an ambulance – or the police?' one of the men said.

'No, just help me get him to my car, over there by the street-lamp.'

'But he tried to mug you and rob you, didn't he?' the man persisted.

'And look, he's wearing a stocking mask. I'll go and phone the police.'

Monclar grabbed the second man by the coat as he turned. 'Look, I'm a doctor and this man needs medical help or he may die. Now help me get him into my car and I'll take him to Charing Cross Hospital.'

He persuaded the man and two others to lift the unconscious figure and carry him to the car. Dumping him on the passenger seat, Monclar put half a mile between him and the crowd then halted in a quiet street and turned to the man. First, he cut through the stocking mask with scissors to allow the man to breathe more easily, then fished in his pockets for his wallet. In this, he discovered a card with the name Robert J. Gascoyne and a Kensington address which he found in his street guide.

Monclar was hardly surprised at the identity of his attacker; he had expected Nancy's husband to catch up with him sooner or later.

Gascoyne was still unconscious when they arrived at the flat, and Monclar had to carry him bodily to the street door. He had Gascoyne's bunch of keys and tried each of them until one opened the door to the block of flats. In the foyer he searched for the flat number and took the lift to the second floor, hoping no one would see the inert figure of Gascoyne in the lift, or if they did they would assume he was drunk.

When he had carried him into the flat and laid him out on the sofa, Monclar wondered if he should have taken him to Charing Cross intensive care unit. But his pulse was fairly steady, his blood pressure only slightly down and the bruise he had received by hitting the hydrant was on top of his head. Monclar noted that his pupils responded to his pen-torch light, his colour was good and he had neither urinated, defecated nor vomited. He injected a sedative and an anticoagulant to keep Gascoyne immobile and aid the resorption of any blood clot that might compress the brain.

He carried Gascoyne through to the bedroom, took off his clothing down to his underwear and covered him with a blanket then put out all but the bedside light. He decided that, as a doctor, he would have to wait until Gascoyne regained his faculties then re-examine him to ensure he had no serious injury.

Nice flat, he thought, glancing around. Large living room with a small balcony overlooking one of Kensington's walled gardens with well kept lawn and beds full of red and yellow roses, pansies under a couple of flowering cherry trees whose leaves were yellowing and tumbling.

He looked in at the kitchen, expecting unwashed dishes in the sink or on the table; but everything seemed as tidy as in his own flat. A half-bottle of supermarket Chablis stood on the working surface by the sink. A notebook lay on the table and Monclar saw its pages were covered with a fine, regular script which he did not read, not wishing to pirate someone's thoughts.

Along the corridor he came across a study with half a dozen rows of books above a desk on which sat a portable typewriter, but also a printer. He wondered if the computer had perhaps broken down and gone for repair. A sheet of typescript protruded from the machine and he noticed it contained half a page of dialogue. His eye also took in Nancy's three books among those on the shelves.

Was the script part of the book Nancy had mentioned her ex-husband was writing? Back in the living room, he picked up the copy of *The Times* from the coffee table and leafed through it. Curious, he had the impression of déjà vu reading the news and the commentaries on it; his eye went to the date, which told him why. It was three days old, the paper. A *TV Times* was also a week out of date. When he noticed unopened mail on the hall table, he began to wonder about Gascoyne.

Nancy and a couple of other people who knew him, insisted Gascoyne was a drunk; but the man who had attacked him was dead sober. And looking round this flat, where were the bottles, why was the drinks cabinet empty of everything but three bottles of tonic water, a couple of cans of lager and a half-bottle of gin that had not been touched? Monclar helped himself to one of the beers, snapping it open and drinking it out of the can. He wandered through to the bedroom to check that his patient was still alive and his breathing, pulse and blood pressure were within limits.

As he passed the open study door, his eye alighted on the thick folder by the typewriter which had at first escaped his notice. He slipped it open to find a bulky wad of typescript with a title on the first page, hand-drawn in letters two inches square: LIFELINES. 'Not bad at that for a title,' Monclar mused. 'Better than Nancy's three romantic titles.'

He realized he was stretching his personal ethic, but this title and the script tempted him, the more so since it might turn out to be a long night waiting for Gascoyne to break surface again. Still, he hesitated. After all, these papers should be considered private, like another person's mail, until they were published. He should choose something in the public domain from the bookshelves and read that.

But somehow, that pile of typed pages pulled him towards them like a dung heap to a fly; he picked it up and bore it through to the living room, opened another can of beer, sat down and began to read.

Anyone would have recognized Nancy's story after a few pages, though even then he could detect the changes, the injection of small but potent scenes and the heightened tone of the language; but after the first thirty or so pages, Gascoyne had completely taken over the book so that, even if he had preserved most of the plot, no one could ever have accused him of plagiarism.

Whereas Nancy's version had petered out like a flash flood in a wadi, Gascoyne had lifted the romance out of it and replaced this with hard, bitter reality. Love had figured in word and action very heavily in Nancy's story; here, the word was hardly used, and yet the sex scenes were drawn with such tenderness that the author must have believed in something much more than chemistry and kinetic energy and body language.

It gripped Monclar, pulling him into Gascoyne's mental landscape and the small world he had portrayed. It was a tour de force. When he had read to where the script ended, Monclar was compelled to backtrack through the book to the first pages and then read it again, this time with an analytical eye and also to discern how the author had transformed the original story.

This time round, he might have guessed that Gascoyne had spent most of his working life in a lawyer's toga, for some of the scenes read like courtroom dramas with the same sort of life-and-death dialectic worked out in cut-and-thrust dialogue pared to the bone. You could hear the divorce lawyer and the legal antinomy in those pages just as you could catch Nancy's character in the more mellow and muted prose she used.

Several times, Monclar found himself rereading paragraphs for the pleasure of the language. Gascoyne had cut out flabby adjectives and superfluous adverbs; he employed short, direct sentences, though often with an epigrammatic turn of phrase. Curiously, it reminded Monclar of Pope, of Swift, of Bunyan and even Hemingway.

A pity the story was unfinished. He wanted to read on beyond the point where the script ended to see how Gascoyne would resolve the accusation of murder against the call girl turned farmer's wife. At a guess, probably with a short, sharp sentence (handed down by the bench) and the slam of a prison door.

Monclar was finishing his second reading of the book when he became conscious of someone else in the room. Gascoyne was standing by the door, his hand on the right jamb to support himself, his face white but his grey-green eyes sparking with anger.

'What the hell do you mean by breaking into my apartment, ransacking my belongings, going through my private papers to say nothing of the technical assault you have carried out on me with your syringe!' He pointed a finger at Monclar. 'I could have you jailed and struck off for that,' he shouted.

'Then we'll probably share a cell in Pentonville since you tried to kill me tonight and I have half a dozen witnesses to back that statement. I also have evidence that you have destroyed my property, viz my tyres, that you have been making phone calls with menace and have been molesting me with the delivery of articles such as a rubber doll through Her Majesty's mails.'

'You haven't the slightest proof.'

'I can confront you with the witnesses of tonight's attack and even your wife will bear witness that it was your voice making the calls and your gold cigarette lighter found in my car the night you glued my tyres.' Monclar put down the typescript and rose to face Gascoyne. 'But I have no intention of pressing charges. As a doctor I'd say you need psychiatric treatment.'

'What I need is the wife you've stolen from me.'

'Your wife walked out on you and now that I've met you I don't blame her.'

'You know bugger all about me, you little quack.'

'Oh, I know quite a bit. I know, for instance, that you treated her as nothing more than a sexual implement to be used and discarded at your whim, you treated her as a cheap hand in the kitchen and around the house, and you betrayed her trust in you by working off your sexual excesses on some whore or other. I know Nancy stayed because she thought she loved you and believed you might have some love for her. She was wrong – I would say on both counts.'

'And now it's you who's fucking her, or using her for what you call a sexual implement.'

'You're several light years away from the truth there,' Monclar said, quietly. 'Although I must admit it has crossed both my mind and hers. However, we'll wait until she has been granted a divorce on her terms.'

'So she definitely wants a divorce.' Gascoyne's voice had dropped to a whisper. He walked, unsteadily, to the coffee table to pick up the silver cigarette box, find and light a cigarette. He drew deeply on it several times while Monclar observed him. 'I didn't realize she felt as bitter as that,' he muttered.

'Nancy's a romantic, didn't you know?' Monclar said. 'You didn't have to read her books to appreciate that, I hope. And romantics are all-or-nothing people.'

'Balls,' Gascoyne said loudly through a cloud of cigarette smoke.

'All right,' Monclar said. 'You've read her book, *The Heart's Reason* haven't you?'

'What the hell's that got to do with it?'

'Go back and look at the description of the hero then look at yourself in your shaving mirror and think about your character. You're all there, in her script.' He could see this had set Gascoyne thinking and rammed home the point by picking up the typescript of *Lifelines* and flipping through the pages until he came upon the scene he was seeking. When he found it, he handed the script to Gascoyne. 'You've written a wonderful portrait of the girl, Jane, your heroine. Do you know where you got it?'

Gascoyne put a finger on his right temple. 'It came out of there, every syllable of it.'

'A bit of it,' Monclar conceded. 'But more of it from here.' He placed a hand on his heart, then continued, 'She's nothing like Nancy, is she? Brown eyes where Nancy's are blue, dark hair where Nancy is blonde, promiscuous where Nancy is virtuous and loyal, instinctive and impulsive where Nancy is thoughtful and steadfast, primitive where Nancy is highly cultured. I could carry the antithesis a lot further.'

'It proves nothing,' Gascoyne retorted, though now with less conviction.

'Well, I'd say this woman—' He pointed to the script in Gascoyne's hands '—means something to you from the way you write about her. Tell me, am I right in thinking she's the sum of the parts of those women you betrayed Nancy with ...'

'Oh, for God's sake, it's only a book, it's only a book. And books aren't life or even about life.'

'You've got that round your neck, too, Gascoyne. Books are as much a reflection of the author's life as his dreams and fantasies. Admit it, Gascoyne, your book's about life. Your own life and much of Nancy's.'

'What has she told you about me, anyway?'

'You don't come much into our conversation. In fact, she has told me nothing about you, either to your credit or discredit.' Monclar paused. 'Your estranged wife's a very discreet and loyal person.' He indicated the script in Gascoyne's hands. 'If you'd been able to read between the lines of her books you'd have a better idea of what she really was, for she put into them what she couldn't confide in you.'

'And, of course, a trick cyclist like you can do this sort of decoding....'

'It's not all that difficult when you've met both the authors and find they're both writing different versions of the same script. You can see which is the true and honest one and which is the one who feeds his jealousy with the thought that the other is as adulterous as himself.'

From the way that Gascoyne glared at him and the clench of those hands around his script, Monclar knew his charge had struck home; he also realized that had this man felt strong enough he might have had trouble getting out of the flat alive. But he kept up his offensive. 'I wondered,' he said, 'reading the portrait of your heroine, if you could describe your wife in the same minute detail. For instance, what sort of eyes does Nancy have?'

'Blue, of course.'

'They're blue-grey. What else?'

'What do you mean, what else?'

'Haven't you noticed the flecks, the dozens of little grey, wedge-shaped flecks in the irises? You missed a whole constellation of them.'

Gascoyne shrugged. 'I haven't got a doctor's eye for that sort of thing.'

'All right, then tell me what she was wearing the last time you saw her, what sort of lipstick, perfume, face cream, deodorant she uses.'

'Not a clue, quizmaster.'

'When did you last tell her you loved her or took her in your arms?'

'For Christ's sake, stop it.' Gascoyne glowered at him. 'What are you trying to do? Grind me down more than I am now?'

Monclar shook his head. 'No, I know what you're feeling. You're feeling that five thousand million people out there on the planet don't begin to understand the pain and suffering that you're feeling. Isn't that how you feel?'

'If you want me to feel a helluva lot better just pick up your coat and cap and medical bag and piss off.'

Monclar picked up his coat from the sofa and put it on, saying, 'I was just trying to find out whether you really love Nancy or whether you're merely jealous because she ran off and might have found someone else.'

'So, what's your headshrink verdict?'

'Let's say the judge and jury are still out.'

Monclar fetched his medical bag and put his cap on his head, took a step towards the door then halted and turned to Gascoyne. 'When you feel better go and have your eyes checked at Moorfields or by a good specialist. You had a nasty crack on the head when you fell and it might affect your sight.'

Gascoyne did not reply or comment, only stepping aside when Monclar passed him on his way to the living-room door and the hall. There, he turned and pointed to the typescript still in Gascoyne's hands.

'Your book's good,' he said. 'In fact, it's better than good, it's superb. I'd love to know how you finish it and what happens to the two characters.' He grinned at Gascoyne, standing stony-faced. 'I seem to have met a couple of people like them.'

Driving home, Monclar had a touch of conscience about Gascoyne. He had purposely teased and angered him with that interpretation of his script. Even reading the book as quickly as he had, he could see behind the heroine a concealed, camouflaged portrait of Nancy through the refracted vision of Gascoyne.

There was tenderness in that portrait. Maybe even love.

chapter XVI

When Monclar picked Nancy up on Saturday morning, he kept quiet about his brush with Gascoyne and the fact that he had read *Lifelines*, his version of the script. Thick traffic and a river mist hanging over Hyde Park and the Embankment claimed all his concentration and not until they were driving through Southwark and into Bermondsey did the sun start to burn off the mist over the Thames.

Nancy had never visited that part of London and gazed at the web of old buildings and slums broken here and there by high-rise flats and office blocks. Monclar parked the car in a side street and they walked through to the Thames. Upriver, she saw the Tower Bridge and downriver the complex of modern buildings on Canary Wharf.

'It's black and tan as well as white, this place,' Monclar said as they walked along the streets near the river. She understood what he meant from the number of people of Indian or Jamaican origin they met and the kind of shops that served this community. Peeling paintwork, smog-grimed masonry and the smell of Thames mud – those were the impressions her senses retained as Monclar pointed out his haunts as a boy in this district. He showed her the comprehensive school that he had attended before going on to study medicine. 'Hardly anybody there ever got anywhere near university or technical college let alone studying medicine,' he said. 'In Bermondsey you were supposed to stay on station.'

'But you didn't – I mean stay put. Why?'

'Oh, I suppose because I had two brothers who left that school at fourteen and were earning enough when I left to pay for my books, bed and board.'

'And they're still here?'

Monclar nodded. 'You'll meet one of them today. The other's somewhere up north. He has a large van and he and his wife have a stall at dozens of markets selling pots, pans, kitchen gear, that sort of thing. They love that sort of life.'

'And your brothers suggested you should become a doctor?'

'No, I decided on my own, but they had to stake me while I studied.'

Something in his attitude and voice as he uttered the words checked the next question on her tongue.

'Sorry, Ted,' she said. 'I'm far too inquisitive.'

He shook his head and gave that wry grin. 'I would wonder about me if you weren't.'

They walked back to the car and Monclar drove them past Southwark Park to a collection of old, red-brick buildings around a concrete and glass admin centre. A high wall with broken glass embedded in its concrete coping surrounded the complex. Nancy read on the metal panel by the iron gate: BOROUGH-HALL PSYCHIATRIC HOSPITAL.

'Ever seen the inside of a mental hospital?' Monclar asked. She shook her head, slightly perplexed. 'It's where I spent two years after getting my basic medical training. Would you like to have a look?'

'If it's not catching,' Nancy said, flippantly, though wondering why he was spending part of their Saturday morning among patients when they took up most of his week. Evidently he had given them advance warning, for they were welcomed in the staff room where several men and women doctors were drinking coffee. Monclar introduced her to Dr John Wingfield, the medical super-intendent, and Dr Paul Rhys-Evans, the chief psychiatrist, then reeled off the names, which she failed to catch, of the half-dozen other psychiatrists.

For ten minutes, Wingfield and Rhys-Evans chatted with Monclar about his spell of training at the hospital for his Diploma of Psychological Medicine, and the changes since his departure. They gave him carte blanche to visit his former patients.

Monclar lifted a bunch of keys from a wall cabinet and beckoned her to accompany him. A lift took them to the first floor where a locked door gave on to a catwalk with a high grille enclosing both sides. Nancy pointed to it.

'Does that mean patients might want to jump from these gangways?' she asked. He nodded.

Monclar could slide his key into the lock, open the door and slip into a ward without disturbing the inmates. Nancy had often remarked the fluid way he moved around the practice, his gentle approach and light-handed way of treating patients. It probably came, she thought, from his experience in this mental hospital.

'You have to remember all the time that most mental illness has its roots in fear of some kind, and patients feel under threat most of the time,' he whispered.

They were moving down a long corridor enfilading several wards. White lavatory brick on the walls, white tiles on the floor, white ceiling and an odour of carbolic acid and detergent mingling with the smell of people in an ill-ventilated environment.

A dozen people stood or sat in the condor watched by three male nurses dressed in white trousers and smocks. One man stood stock still, an arm raised in what might have passed for a fascist salute; another was playing tennis without racquet or ball; a couple of patients sat on the tiled floor, hand in hand, gazing into each other's eyes.

An elderly, white haired man stood in Monclar's tracks. Ramrod straight, his arms stiff by his sides, thumbs on the seams of his hospital trousers, his feet at the regulation ten minutes to two. Monclar eyed him up and down as though inspecting him.

'Very good, Danny.'

Danny shouted. 'Can I stand the men down?'

'Yes, stand down, Danny. Kit inspection over.'

As they walked on, Nancy said, 'Do you know him?'

'Everybody knows him. He's been here for more than thirty years.'

'He looks like an old soldier. What was it? Shell-shock?'

Monclar shook his head. 'No, he was a conscientious objector in the fifties and they gave him three months in Wandsworth Prison, and he swapped the prison for this one and brought his fantasies here, and he'll die here.'

'Can nobody do anything to rehabilitate him?'

'It wouldn't work. People like Danny get used to life in institutions like Borough-Hall. Send him out and he'd wither in months. Here, his little manias and the hospital routine keep him going, pull him along from day to day. It's as though he's wound up by the nurses every day.'

In the common room, patients were sitting mostly staring into a void or turning their gaze inwards on themselves; three of them, two women and a young man, were shuffling round the room as though picking their way along an invisible path or following secret instructions.

In a corner, an elderly woman sat at a table, head bent over a dozen rows of cards, playing patience; she had dead-white hair brushed close to her skull and coiled in a tight chignon at her nape. Monclar whispered that she was a schizophrenic like the others in this room. A former maths teacher, she had started by quarrelling with Copernicus, Galileo, Newton and everyone else who believed the earth moved round the sun. For her, the earth was as flat as a cowpat, moved up and down to create the seasons and lay in the path of a comet a hundred times the size of Halley's and was therefore doomed. Suspended from her teaching job for such scientific and mathematical heresy, she locked herself away and began to work out a completely new cosmology and at the same time tried to square the circle and solve the lost theorem of a Frenchman called Fermat, something that had defied the greatest mathematicians for three centuries. She arrived at Borough-Hall in a straitjacket.

'Like a lot of schizophrenics, she rejected the real world and invented her own version, a doomsday version. And this is the only place where she's free to live in her own creation.'

'Now what is she doing?'

'Oh, she plays patience from morning to midnight using three packs of cards and her own system. And in five years she has never once completed the sequence or paired all the cards.'

'Why does she do it? Why does she go on losing?'

'She doesn't want to play a perfect game. She doesn't want to solve her problem. That would mean leaving here, and she's scared of the world outside. So those cards and her insoluble patience system are her lifeline in a way.'

Outside, in the corridor leading to the ward where the depressives were treated, two women patients yelled at Monclar who stopped and waited until they approached in that tentative, almost furtive manner. They looked like two of Macbeth's three witches, both with a cloud of wispy grey hair enclosing scrawny faces crosshatched with age, and sunken eyes, their frail bodies swallowed by white hospital smocks.

'Ted, you've come back,' the smaller woman shouted. She came close, standing on tiptoes to peer at his face.

'Just for a wee while, Anna,' Monclar said, gently.

'And you've brought Liz, you've brought us back Liz.'

At that, the older woman came within inches of Nancy, who tried not to flinch as the faded eyes inches over her face, screwed up to focus better.

'That is never Liz, you foolish creature.'

'It is. It is Liz,' Anna insisted.

'Silence, Anna,' the other woman cried then turned to Monclar. 'Ted, where have you been, and where is Liz? I demand to know this truth.'

'Yes, we have looked everywhere, Maud and me. Where is she?'

'Shut your mouth, Anna.' Maud kicked her friend on the shin with her slippered foot, bringing a howl from her.

She was gripping Monclar's hands so fiercely that her own had gone whiter than her face, and he was wincing.

'You put Liz away, didn't you? You put her in a home.'

'Liz has gone to her own home,' Monclar said, quietly.

'She will not return here? Never?'

'No.'

Maud released Monclar's hands and turned away, desolate. Anna had begun keening and moaning, holding her face in her hands. At that moment, Monclar did something that moved Nancy almost to tears. He put both arms round Anna and pressed her to his chest until she stopped crying and whimpering.

'Liz is all right,' he whispered.

He beckoned one of the women nurses with a finger and she came down the corridor with a colleague to lead the two women away.

Anna turned and shouted: 'Ted, you'll come and see us. We miss you and Liz. Bring Liz with you.'

As they walked on, Monclar explained they were mild schizophrenics with no family. Maud had taught at one of the local schools and Anna was a shop assistant; they had both been in Borough-Hall for more than ten years.

'Who was the Liz that made such an impression on them?'

'She was a patient here.'

'She was discharged, then?'

'You could put it that way.'

Monclar's offhand attitude and curt replies meant that he wished to cut short this line of talk; he launched into a short history of the hospital then showed her the wards where they treated depressives and after that the cubicles where they did electro-convulsive therapy and insulin treatment, which he described as medieval torture that should have been outlawed fifty years ago.

Word had gone round that Monclar was visiting. When they returned to the staff room, a dozen doctors had gathered to shake his hand, ask what he was doing and reminisce about his stint at the hospital.

Nancy was relieved when they finally said goodbye and drove through the heavy iron gate and left the psychiatric hospital behind them. Monclar stopped at a pub between Jamaica Road and Grange Road. 'I feel like having a beer after all that,' he said. Nancy did not demur, and they found a seat in the saloon bar. She opted for a Cinzano and soda. 'Well, what did you think of it?' he said putting their drinks on the table.

'Interesting, but a bit depressing.'

He nodded. 'Mental illness is always depressing, especially for the medical staff who realize they can do so little for it. It's more often than not up to the patient to decide if he or she wants to be cured. So many choose unconsciously to stay patients in institutions where they feel safe. Some rebel against the system and a few decide there's no point in living and do themselves in.'

Nancy was gazing at the soda bubbles breaking on the surface of the amber liquor in her glass. 'What I wondered was why ... why you wanted a busman's holiday.' She paused to sip her drink. 'I've been taken dancing, horse-racing, boating, scrambling, motor-racing, swimming ... I've been escorted to garden parties, clubs, rock concerts, fashion shows ... but this is the first time anybody's thought of conducting me round a ...'

'Loony bin,' he prompted, then added, 'I wondered how you'd react to it.'

'I didn't scream or throw a fit.'

'No, you were fine.'

Nancy looked at him. 'But I did wonder how you stuck it for two years without going round the bend yourself.'

That question she could see bothered him from the way he gulped his lager. But he finally grinned and said, 'I don't know. All I do know is that I went in there one person and came out another.'

'But you left your mark on the place as well,' she said. 'So many patients remembered you.'

'No one can forget them,' he said.

She sensed a reticence in him, a reluctance to be drawn further. He had wanted to gauge her reaction. In her turn, she felt he had acted in that two-hour visit as though he were testing himself or trying to exorcise some demon from his mind.

chapter XVII

Nancy took to Monclar's brother and his wife straight away. Bill was as dark as his brother was fair, with dark hair and eyes and a dark shadow on his clean-shaven face. He was bald on top and touchy enough about it to wear a floppy cotton hat which his wife, Jill, declared he only removed in bed. He was strong and stocky though light-footed, and quick spoken in a rasping Cockney which would have grated on her mother's ear as lower class. Jilly was blonde and looked like Pat with an inch more flesh all round. However, it became her and she laughed about being a stone overweight, but affirmed there was no good flesh near the bone. She was much more intelligent than Bill, who acknowledged this freely.

They and their two teenage children, a boy Norman, and a girl, Meg, lived in a terrace house in one of Bermondsey's average streets of terraced houses. Bill had bought the house and had the men who worked for him rip out the inside to create a large L-shaped living room incorporating a dining room and kitchen. Upstairs there were three bedrooms.

Their living room gave on to a walled garden measuring forty yards by ten, which Jilly had filled with every conceivable kind of flower – roses, delphiniums, hollyhocks, asters, lupins, day lilies, fuschias. Three small patches of lawn broke up this undisciplined array of flowers and shrubs. The middle one had a small fountain with a bird-bath; at the end wall, on a cherry tree, Jilly had rigged several tiny wooden nesting houses for birds. If gardens represented their creators, Jilly was an eclectic with a live-and-let-live outlook and an easy-going temperament.

Against the southern wall, Bill had built a summerhouse with a small annex which he used as a design and drawing office for his building work.

Since it was fine, they ate in the garden, sitting around the buffet that Jilly had prepared: a dozen plates of cold chicken, cold salmon, ham, a range of salads, cheeses and an apple tart she had baked herself.

'Bill offered to grill us steaks, but the last time he lit the barbecue it blew up on him, we nearly had to send for the fire brigade and he couldn't use his right hand for weeks. So we're eating cold.'

Monclar was unusually silent during the meal as though tuned in to some inner conversation. Nancy observed Jilly shoot sideways glances at him from time to time and she and her husband made the smalltalk about Bermondsey an all-too-obvious way of directing Monclar's attention away from the family.

From the gist of their remarks and Monclar's questions, Nancy inferred that he did not visit his brother's family often. She was relieved when they finished eating and Bill took his brother upstairs to see the new terrace garden he was building on the roof. It seemed a pretext for leaving her alone with Jilly.

For a few minutes, they sat in the garden chatting, with Jilly asking most of the questions: how was the practice, how was Ted fitting into it, how were they getting on together?

When she dried up, Nancy looked at her, smiling. 'Haven't you overlooked the main question: Have we slept with each other? Everybody wants to know the answer to that question. And the answer is no.'

'I'm sorry about that.'

'Why?'

'Because he's in love with you.'

'He hasn't said so.'

'Maybe he never will – maybe he's scared you'll say no to him.' Jilly glanced up at the roof garden from where they could hear the murmur of voices. Bill and Ted seemed to be arguing about something. She brought her gaze back to Nancy.

'Maybe he's scared you'll say you share his feelings and he'll get too deeply involved with you.'

'I don't follow. Why scared?'

'Ted's not very sure of himself. He's mixed up.'

'That's not the impression he gives as a doctor.'

'I know … he's sure of everybody and everything but himself.'

'I still don't begin to follow you,' Nancy said. 'But they do seem a complex breed, the Monclars.'

'Not Bill, or Mike. Only Ted.'

Jilly poured herself another cup of the coffee she made with the colour and consistency of Thames mud. Just like Monclar's. Nancy refused and watched Jilly light her third cigarette since they had finished the apple tart.

'Who's Liz?' she asked, suddenly.

Jilly's coffee cup stopped halfway to her mouth. 'Did he mention Liz to you?' she asked, wide-eyed.

'No, but when we were going round the wards, a couple of patients wanted to know where she was.'

'Did he say?'

'No, he ducked the question with them, and with me – but it seemed to hit him there.' She pointed to her navel.

Jilly sipped her coffee and smoked silently for several minutes, and Nancy let her reflect. Finally, she rose and beckoned Nancy to follow her to the end of the garden, glancing at the roof as she went as though fearful the men might see them.

'Liz was his sister. She turned schizophrenic. Don't ask me how or why; it's a touchy subject.' Jilly spoke in a whisper.

'Where is she now?'

'She's dead.'

'Oh. I didn't think schizophrenia was fatal.'

Jilly shrugged. 'In Liz's case it was. She killed herself by jumping from a three-storey window in Borough-Hall.'

'She was in Borough-Hall at the same time as Ted, then?'

Jilly looked down the garden at the house then her gaze went to the roof where the two men were standing watching them. She waved, then said out of the corner of her mouth, 'Ted found her dying on the courtyard in front of the main door. That was three years ago and I think he still has nightmares about it and I don't think he'll ever get over it.'

'I wonder that he went in for looking after mental patients.'

'You don't know Ted. He went in for psychiatry because of Liz –
to help her and perhaps cure her – and her death made him all the
more determined to help people like her.'

'What age was Liz when she died?'

Jilly's brow puckered and she caught her lower lips between her
teeth. 'Now let me see. Ted's thirty-one now … that would make
her twenty-eight.'

'You mean, they were both born in the same year?'

'On the same day,' Jilly whispered. 'Liz was ten minutes or a
quarter of an hour older than Ted.'

Nancy stared at Jilly, the light dawning on her. 'Twins! So they
were twins … they were twins!'

'Yes, they were twins,' Jilly confirmed. 'And that's the problem
and what worries Ted even now, and it's not a topic he'll discuss
with us … with you … even with himself.' Jilly flicked a glance
again at the roof garden. 'I know what you're thinking, for we've
all wondered about it – since it runs in families and hits twins
harder, does it mean Ted might go the same way?'

'I wouldn't know,' Nancy said. She was wondering why Monclar
had kept from her the fact that he had a twin sister who suffered
from mental illness and had died as a result. Did he really think
that, as a twin, he might be afflicted? Did he blame himself in any
way for her death?

She remembered his concern for the woman who had collapsed
in the street, and those patients he followed into hospital and those
he worried about when the Masons, the Clarkes and even old
Fothergill saw them as so many cases to be treated, or as clients
seeking a form of service; their desks might have been any office
desk or shop counter and their minds turned off when they shut
the drawers or the door. Monclar's did not.

Jilly unlocked the door of the summerhouse, saying that Bill
really built it for Liz when she was staying with them. Nancy
followed her inside. Through the door into the small annex, she
noticed Bill's drawing board and large desk.

In the main part of the summerhouse there was a large desk on
which sat a portable TV set and hi-fi system; above this, shelves

containing rows of books, cassettes, CDs. Three easy chairs and a divan bed made up the furniture; she also saw a small electric cooker and a fridge against the inside wall. Her eye went to a guitar in its canvas case which hung on the back wall.

'Did Bill play?' she asked.

Jilly laughed. 'Bill's tone deaf in both ears and he's got hands like bunches of bananas. No, it was Ted who played when he was in his teens.' She looked through the window at the roof garden to where Ted was standing. 'He was good, really hip. Bill and I used to go and watch him play. Liz, too. They both wrote a couple of tunes that his rock band put out on a cassette and it did well.' She sighed. 'Ah! Ted in those days. Through him we knew Miles Davis and Charlie Parker and Thelonius Monk and Brubeck and Jimmy Hendrix, the lot. He might've made a career out of it.'

'If he hadn't chosen medicine ...'

'That was Liz. When she turned odd and began to go mental Ted decided to study medicine.'

'Would he have done something else?'

'Who knows? Maybe he'd have done architecture and gone in with Bill. But he's a good doctor, they tell me.' Jilly looked round the interior of the summerhouse, at the divan bed and the table and chairs. 'Funny thing,' she mused, 'when I'm cleaning this place or sitting here of a summer evening, I get the oddest feeling Liz is at my elbow. Silly ... but Liz looked on this bit of the house as home when she was staying with us.'

'So they let her out from time to time?'

'Oh, she wasn't all that mad, and for months on end she could get by on drugs.' Jilly pointed to the divan. 'She'd sleep there during the summer months, and she even cooked her breakfast and lunch on the little cooker and did her own housework.'

'What did she look like?'

'Just like Ted.' Jilly turned and smiled at her. 'And not unlike you.' Searching under the TV set, she produced a key and opened a wooden filing cabinet, extracted a photo album and flipped through its pages. 'That's her from five until the year she died.' Nancy gazed at the pictures. Jilly was right, Liz looked like her twin brother, though with a more serene face. She looked younger than twenty-eight when she died. Nancy thought that the years hadn't imprinted their trace on Liz's mind and face in the way they had on her twin brother's which, in those photos taken together, appeared more tense, more scarred by time.

No one who did not know Elizabeth Monclar would have guessed from these photos that she suffered from schizophrenia, that she had withdrawn from the real world into one of her own making with its own disturbed logic, its oblique view of other people and their 'normal' world, its traumas and irrational phobias and manias.

Through the window, Jilly was still keeping half an eye on the two brothers on the roof. She waited until Nancy had closed the album, then repossessed it and replaced it among the files in the cabinet. 'Ted doesn't know about the album, although he has one or two pictures of Liz,' she said.

Noticing Nancy's eyes go to the shutters on the doors and windows, Jilly hesitated then said, 'When Liz slept in the summerhouse we often had to lock her in. Sometimes she could become violent and we'd have to replace the window glass every other week.' She sniffed. 'We had bad times with her, even though we all loved her and understood what she was suffering.'

Nancy saw that Jilly had tears in her eyes as she thought and felt back to those days. She described how Liz's illness had altered their whole lives and even now left indelible traces on the whole family. Even if mental illnesses like Liz's was no longer stigmatized by society or considered some form of divine retribution, it had sewed doubts in the minds of everybody related to Liz.

Ted would never have gone into medicine, Bill would never have stayed in Bermondsey and Mike would have worked himself a job in some city financial institution, for he had the head for figures. Instead, they had taken turns to care for Liz, and Ted had sacrificed advancement in his profession to be near her in Borough-Hall. Jilly wiped away her tears. She unlocked the filing cabinet again and probed with her hand under one of its drawers to detach a fat envelope and pull it out.

'Nobody else knows about these,' she said. 'Not Bill, not Ted or Mike.' She handed Nancy the package. 'They're bits and pieces of writings and drawings Liz did here and in the summerhouse, and maybe in the hospital as well. They were her secret and I've kept it. She hid them under the carpet and I came across them when I was cleaning up after she died.

'When I saw what it was and read the poems I didn't have the heart to hand it over even to Ted. It would've upset him more than he was. I even thought of destroying the lot, but I didn't have the heart to do that either. They were Liz's, her sort of will, if you like. I'm glad now I didn't, for I'm sure Liz somehow wanted Ted to read all this.'

'What makes you think that?'

In response, Jilly again reached under the files, exploring the back with her hand and ripping away adhesive tape to emerge with a tiny cassette measuring just over two inches by one and a half. 'Liz had one of those miniature tape machines which Ted gave her so she'd talk into it and perhaps help him and herself to treat her illness. The machine wasn't here or in the hospital and I expect she threw it away. But I came on this cassette inside a file where she kept newspaper and magazine clippings. I listened to it once and put it away. It was too sad to hear her voice and her thoughts.'

Jilly handed the cassette in its small plastic container to Nancy.

'What do you want me to do with all this?' Nancy asked.

'Take it away and read it and listen to the tape recording. You'll see why I couldn't bear to let Ted have it. I was ... well, kind of scared what he'd think ... and do,' Jilly paused. 'When you've read it and heard the tape, if you think Ted should have them, give them to him.'

'But I'm not even a member of the family,' Nancy protested.

'Ted loves you. He may not know it, and maybe you don't. But I know it. It's a chance for you both to talk about Liz and for him to get it out of his system.'

Nancy folded the envelope and thrust it into her handbag. She felt dubious about the responsibility Jilly had placed upon her, but none the less intrigued by everything Jilly had revealed about Monclar and Liz. She was also curious about what Liz's written and spoken testament might contain.

Monclar drove back in silence and she left him to his thoughts. He did not invite her home but dropped her at her flat.

When she had settled in her one easy chair, Nancy opened the package first. It consisted of about a hundred pages, some of them typing paper but a third looked as though they had been torn from a school exercise book; most were smeared and fingerprinted and a few were even charred round the edges. Glancing through them, she noticed the writing varied from page to page, even from paragraph to paragraph; sometimes it was backward-sloping, at others upright, though it was mainly in italic hand. Almost every page had dozens of erasures and marginal additions or corrections. On the back of several score pages and on the margins, Liz had made curious drawings – gargoyles, of gruesome, grotesque faces, of scarecrows, of sphinx-like creatures, half-animal, half-human. Many of these drawings reminded Nancy of something before she realized what – they resembled the paintings in Monclar's living room. Had they been done by Liz?

For the most part they were pencil or ink drawings; some looked as though done by a child, but others proved that Liz had an artistic hand. Anyone with psychiatric insight studying and analyzing these drawings would have inferred a psychotic condition, most likely schizophrenia; if they had looked more closely they might have noted hints that Liz Monclar might take her life.

Nancy gazed at one drawing representing a face, its eyes closed, its mouth a thin line, the hair spiky and awry; this grotesque face was enclosed in a bottle with a label where the neck would have been. The sort of bottle that pharmacies and hospitals used for keeping pills. It was framed in the sort of symbolic and structural chemical formulae of scientific textbooks. What was the formula? Poison, or the pills she was swallowing for her illness?

Then there were buildings like those Nancy had seen at Borough-Hall, though with dozens of additional windows. High windows. Windows within windows like an infinity of mirrors reflecting each other. But windows with black borders like death announcements.

Liz Monclar had killed herself jumping from a high window!

Nancy regretted that Monclar had not seen these drawings

before his twin sister had killed herself, although he could perhaps have done nothing to prevent her from taking her life in one way or another.

Another of her themes was birds. Eagles, giant hawks, ravens, vultures – birds of prey and birds of death which she had depicted at windows or flying through the walls of her hospital room with its rows of beds.

From the sick drawings, Nancy turned to the poetry, which was scattered haphazardly through the bundle of papers. It was as morbid as the drawings, speaking of death and the words without rhyme or reason, curious neologisms and words spelled backwards or in twisted, senseless anagrams.

But some of this poetry set Nancy wondering about this woman that she had never known, who had decided to die rather than face the dread of living a constant nightmare. Bits of verse proved Liz was a poet and as she read them she was reminded of what Monclar had said once about schizophrenics – he called them the strangled and stifled poets of our time.

Liz had written:

time
time is as time was as time will be even when the world is not
   and we are naught
i was here when the world was young, when life's first whisper
kindled the cold ash
and the sun warmed it into me.
i will be here when the sun's glow dies and the light turns
   again to dust.
where will time be then?
can i bid it stand still for me?
will my inner voices be stilled?
will there be light
or eternal night?
will my love survive death?
if i could ask him who is flesh of my flesh ...
but i have this heart-wrenching dread,
what becomes of ted

when i am dead?
without him near i would not want to live;
without me would he survive?
if he said that dead I would be within him
i would sacrifice my death for him.

Now Nancy realized why Jilly had hidden those poems, deciding
not to show them to Bill, and especially not to Monclar. What
would he have made of that poem. Or this one:

look never in the looking-glass for your face;
there you will see the faces of others
with yourself mirrored in their eyes,
your mind possessed by them,
their lips whispering with hate,
their hands twitching with the desire to strangle.
such fiends are between you and your reflection,
between you and your being.
white-coats call them paranoia
and when you voice your fear of them,
they laugh their slow, sad laugh.
so you shut your mouth, your mind, your heart.
let them think you mad.

Liz's poetry reflected not only her thought but her state of mind,
her moods, her very being. A pity, Nancy felt, that someone like
Monclar or another psychiatrist with experience of schizophrenia
could not have access to this literary testament to give them a
deeper insight into the mind and emotions of an intelligent and
sensitive schizophrenic. Towards the end of the bundle of papers,
which had no order to them, Nancy came upon a poem entitled
'timothy', with the name worked in beautiful illuminated script in
oil pastels that must have taken Liz hours to accomplish.

timothy
i see an infinite universe in timothy's eyes;
they are deep-blue and star-flecked,

the hue of the night skies.
they reflect the wisdom of the world.
timothy, why did you seek patronage?
when it's you who are the sage,
knowing more than i or anyone
in that round head and whiskered face.
timothy knows that i, too, belong to the animal race;
and when i discourse with him about divine, godlike humanity,
he opens his mouth and yawns in my face.
his message to me is more eloquent than the wordless
    eloquence of melody,
more meaningful than mathematical constructs like relativity.
timothy, you are not only my ally,
you have taught me how to live and how to die.

When she put the poems and drawings back into their envelope, Nancy had to phone Jilly and tell her how much they had moved her. Then she asked one of the questions which had prompted her to ring.

'Who was Timothy?'

She heard a catch in the voice at the other end of the line, followed by a long sigh.

'Ah, Timothy! Timothy was an alley cat that strayed into Borough-Hall. Ted adopted him then passed him over to Liz. When she was really ill and hallucinating and even aggressive, Timothy was the only creature that could get through to her and even calm her down. He talked to her in his own way, rubbing himself against her, purring and mewing, sleeping beside her and going for walks with her in the grounds. He lived with her for months on end in the summerhouse, but he never adopted any of us, only Liz and Ted. He tolerated us as friends of theirs.'

'What happened to Timothy?'

'I wish we knew,' Jilly replied. 'When Liz killed herself, Timothy disappeared. We and everybody in the hospital hunted for him everywhere. We posted notices in the police station and the shops, put ads in the local paper and the local radio and searched the streets. But nobody has ever seen him from the day Liz died.'

'Now you know why I hid those poems,' Jilly said. 'I couldn't bear to read them again myself or think about poor Timothy or Liz. I couldn't let the others see them.'

Over the line, Nancy could hear her sniffing and sobbing before she excused herself and said, 'Do you think Ted should have the papers and the cassette?'

'I think he should,' Nancy said. 'But now's not the time. I think the moment has to be chosen very carefully.'

'Perhaps if and when he decided to talk to you about Liz.'

'Maybe.'

When she had rung off and was locking the envelope and cassette in a drawer, she wondered how that cassette with Liz's poignant voice and those poems would affect Ted. He looked tough and mentally robust, but still she wondered.

She might never know how they would affect him. Never once had he mentioned Liz and her illness, or the way she died; yet those were evidently the most traumatic events in his life. He might never bring up the subject with her.

Yet, he had gone halfway by taking her to Borough-Hall. Would he dare go all the way?

chapter XVIII

Monclar took the envelope from Vikram Mehta and looked at the Hammersmith Hospital stamp on it. He needed a few seconds to place where he had met this Indian and remember having examined his daughter late one night and sending her for blood tests. He did not open the envelope but pushed it across the desk to Mehta, who did not touch it.

'You and your daughter are Dr Mason's patients, so you should let him have this. Unfortunately it is his day off.'

Mehta eyed the envelope on the desk. 'I would like you to look. You ordered the tests for Shanta.'

Monclar hesitated. He did not wish to provoke Mason any more than he already had by treating one of his patients, but something about Mehta's attitude intrigued him. This man had deliberately chosen Mason's day off to bring these test results to him. Did he know more about his daughter's illness than he had admitted that night ten days ago? Or perhaps he had steamed open the envelope and was aware of what the hospital had found.

'Please, Dr Monclar,' Mehta pleaded.

'Why didn't you bring your daughter with you?'

'I wish to see you alone first.'

'But you realize I may have to pass these on to Dr. Mason.' When Mehta nodded, Monclar slit open the envelope and pulled out the two documents it contained.

'These are dated from last Thursday. You could have seen Dr Mason that day or on Friday.'

'My time is taken up on those days.'

Monclar felt the hard edge to the Indian's voice and those obsidian eyes fixed on him before he turned to the documents. They had run two tests on the girl and both had produced the same result: Shanta Mehta was sero-positive with significant and growing numbers of HIV virus in her bloodstream and lymph. No wonder she had looked drained of energy and colour when he saw her that night.

'You have read this, haven't you?'

'No, I have not.'

Monclar picked up the reports and placed them back in the envelope, handing this to Mehta.

'Take this to Dr Mason when he returns tomorrow. You're his patient and it's for him to read the report and decide on the treatment.' He rose and went to show the Indian out of his consulting room, when the man caught him by the arm.

'Doctor, forgive me, I have read this report and it has frightened me.' He was weeping, still holding Monclar by the arm. 'Please, please, Doctor, take Shanta and give her medicine.'

'Mr Mehta, I can't do that even if I wanted to. Dr Mason is quite competent to treat your daughter.'

'She does not wish to see him.'

'Why? Does she say why?' Mehta shook his head. 'Does Shanta know that she is running the risk of Aids, an illness that can kill her?'

'Yes, she knows.'

'Does she know who she got it from? Who she had sex with?'

'Shanta is always denying having sex with any man.'

'Then does she have boyfriends?'

Mehta looked injured and offended by that suggestion. He shook his head. Tears still ran down his sunken cheeks.

'But you realize she must have been infected by someone,' Monclar insisted.

'Doctor, she is afraid of saying, she is afraid of going to prison if she says anything.' Mehta shook his head slowly from side to side as though bewildered by everything. 'I do not understand. Shanta is a very pure girl. No boyfriends, not many girlfriends. It is a mystery. Shanta is very studious; she is taking night-school instruction in commercial studies.' Mehta wiped away his tears with a red silk handkerchief.

Suddenly, his voice hardened and he said, slowly, spacing out the threat: 'If I ever find this man who is poisoning my daughter, Shanta, then I will kill him.'

Monclar put a hand round Mehta's thin shoulders and motioned him to a seat and came to sit down opposite him.

'Mr Mehta, why don't you want Dr Mason to treat your daughter?'

'It is a personal thing, sir. I do not like this man at all.'

'All right, you don't like Dr Mason, but I have to work with him and I cannot take his patients. Now listen carefully. You must never mention that I sent your daughter for these tests. You can take them to another doctor.'

On his scrap paper, Monclar scribbled the name of a young GP who was starting a practice in Chiswick. He handed the chit to Mehta. 'Take the tests to this doctor and he will treat Shanta. I'll ring him and let him know you're coming with Shanta and why. He will know how to treat her as well as myself or anybody else. You needn't come back here and you must not tell any of our patients that you have found another doctor. Is that clear?'

Mehta nodded. He grasped one of Monclar's hands in both of his and bowed. As he took the note and test results and rose to leave, Monclar stopped him. He gave instructions about changing the routine of his household so that he and any friends they had would avoid infection from Shanta; he should also inform the manager at the girl's workplace.

When Mehta had gone and Monclar had rung the young GP, he buzzed Pat and ordered her to delay his next patients for several minutes, which gave him time to recall the circumstances in which he had seen Shanta Mehta, and her father's attitude then and now. Mehta was hiding something and even the sound of Mason's name seemed to arouse either fear or hate in him.

There was a mystery somewhere. But whatever it was, he felt it did not concern him. He had already run a professional risk by referring Mehta and his daughter to another doctor; if Mason or anybody else in the practice discovered this, it would cost him his job and perhaps trouble from the GMC.

Yet the whole affair niggled at him. When he had finished his consultations for that morning, he waited until the practice closed for lunch and the other doctors had gone, then lifted Mason's key off the hook in the office. He went into his consulting room and closed the door behind him. He switched on Mason's PC, then found and inserted the disk listing the patients by age, sex, illness and treatment.

Mason had the fewest patients in the group practice, but running his eye down the list, Monclar observed that he had more black patients than the rest of the group put together. He brought up on the screen the forty-odd young women of Asian and West Indian origin, and their treatment charts. Curiously, most of them had minor illnesses like the common cold, migraine, skin allergies, earache, sore throat – things they could easily have treated themselves.

But Monclar's cursor halted on four of these girls. Two Pakistanis aged seventeen and eighteen, a Hindu aged seventeen and a West Indian aged nineteen, were being treated with zidovudine, one of the drugs used in suppressing virus proliferation in patients who were HIV positive. Yet there was no mention of test results or HIV infection in these patients.

If these patients were HIV positive, with Shanta Mehta that made five potential Aids cases in Mason's books. A very high proportion for one small list!

Was it a coincidence? Or did it point to some skullduggery on Mason's part?

Monclar waited until Nancy appeared to take over the afternoon stint and called her in to explain what had happened with Shanta Mehta and her father; he disclosed how he had checked through Mason's list and found four more sero-positive or Aids cases. Had Mason reported them to her?

Nancy shook her head, and confirmed they had no record of such cases on her master computer; there, she found the same information as Monclar had on Mason's PC. So, if these four girls were suffering from HIV infection, Mason had broken the rule about informing the other doctors in the practice.

'Ted, how do you think these girls have been infected with HIV?'

Monclar shrugged to signify he did not know. 'And we can't bring them in and quiz them,' he said. 'Mason would blow his top. He'd consider it unethical interference and could lodge a professional complaint or even sue us for slander. In Hippocratic terms it's worse than the five As.'

'The five As?'

'Alcohol, Addiction, Abortion, Adultery, Advertising – and I suspected that Mason has one or two of those ethical afflictions.'

'But if he's running some sex racket, which would be more his style ...'

'We can't do a thing unless he's caught in the act.'

Monclar switched off Mason's PC, removed the disk, replaced it in its holder and locked the door. He handed the key to Nancy. 'If we both keep an eye on him and those girls, perhaps something will give him away,' he said.

Other things put Mason and his HIV positive patients out of their heads. Peter and Marcia Clarke returned from visiting Fothergill, who had left hospital for home and was undergoing treatment to enable him to regain some use of his paralyzed right arm and improve his slurred speech. He had told the Clarkes that he had decided to resign from the health service and the practice, leaving Peter Clarke as the senior partner.

Clarke called Monclar into his room and explained about Fothergill then asked, 'Would you be prepared to take over Dr Fothergill's list on a permanent basis?'

'Can I think about it for a week or two?' Monclar replied.

'Of course, but don't leave it too long.' Clarke was standing at the window and he turned to look at Monclar, who could not help noticing that Nancy was right: he had dropped into his Neanderthal crouch. In fact, Clarke looked like a small, hairless gorilla with his knees bent, his shoulders thrust forward, his arms dangling. 'I think you should know, Dr Monclar, that we're all delighted with your work here and would like you to stay and become a partner. But it's entirely up to you.'

Before he went on his afternoon rounds, Monclar buzzed for Nancy and told her about the offer.

'Think I should take it?'

'If you want my honest answer – no.'

'Why no?'

'Because you're quite simply too good for this lot here. You could have your own practice where you choose, you could become a hospital consultant or set up in Harley Street as a psychiatrist.'

'Harley Street! Palpating and auscultating well-heeled layabouts and fat-cat businessmen, stroking minor neuroses, bruised egos and bent psyches? Writing three and four-figure cheques for wealthy hypochondriacs?' He stabbed a thumb at his chest. 'Me, Ted Monclar, in Harley Street!'

'All right, if it offends your principles or your conscience you can open a clinic in the East End among the natives. Anyway, here you'd moulder away and finish like Fothergill or as a premature Alzheimer.'

'You sound as though you'd like to get rid of me,' he said with a wry smile.

'No, I'm just looking at the Clarkes and Mason and I don't see you retaining your sanity working with two mediocrities and a sex maniac.'

'What about you?'

'I'm only a filing clerk and general dogsbody, and anyway I do it for the money.' She saw disbelief in his face, also the hint of another question; but he obviously thought better of posing it, and instead ended their discussion by looking at his watch and saying he was running late.

Nancy returned to her cubicle, wondering why Monclar would go so far then confront some wall of plate glass. Why didn't he want to practise psychiatry, which he could do brilliantly, when he had invested so much time and effort in it? All right, she understood it had much to do with Liz's illness and suicide, but he ought to realize these were problems he had to resolve for himself before thinking about his role in medicine. It had started to pelt with rain and it drummed on her window and bounced off the building and the street outside and filled the waiting room with damp, malodorous humanity. She felt as bleak as the day as she worked mechanically through the three lists and stuffed their data into her computer.

As she was waiting for the last patients to emerge and leave, her phone rang and she heard Anne Howells' voice. She sounded fraught and began by apologizing for ringing; she wanted to know if Nancy had seen Gascoyne lately. When Nancy said no, Anne explained that she had called the flat several times in the past four days and no one had answered the phone or the calls she had fed into the answering machine.

'He's probably just gone off for a few days' break,' Nancy suggested.

'No, I went round to the flat and found that he has given it to an agent to rent. All his personal belongings have gone.' Anne sounded really worried. 'Do you have any idea where he might have headed?' she asked.

'I don't, but doesn't the caretaker or the agent know?'

'No, the only address he gave was his bank. Even his old friends in his chambers have no idea where he might be.'

'Sorry I can't help,' Nancy said. 'If he gets in touch or I hear where he is, I'll let you know.'

It was odd, Nancy thought when she had hung up, that Gascoyne had quit and rented the flat he liked so much. And not only vanished, but taken care to cover his tracks. Knowing him, he was up to something, she was sure.

chapter XIX

Viewed from the basement of a small hotel, life had a totally different feel, Gascoyne thought, when he had spent the first week in his new lodgings. As though the whole planet had gone tilt. But it was exactly what he wanted: a complete break from his past routine and a place where no one would ever think of looking for him. This part of London between Bayswater and Westbourne Grove, with its plethora of small hotels, boarding houses and bedsits was ideal camouflage. He was a crocodile in a log jam. When he had decided to hand his flat to an estate agent and lose himself, he remembered the owner of the Athenaeum House Hotel in Bayswater whom he had defended successfully against an accusation of having failed to provide adequate fire precautions following a fire which had killed one guest and injured two others. Eric Marston, the hotel owner, thought him mad to give up a career at the bar and seek a job as a night porter, but had taken him on at a reasonable salary and installed him in a basement studio.

For Gascoyne it could not have been better. Between eight at night and seven in the morning, he looked after the hotel; his basement room was cleaned, his laundry done by the hotel and his meals appeared when he gave the word.

It meant he could devote most of his day to writing, for he was now possessed, even obsessed with the idea of finishing the book Nancy had begun and he had thought to revise. He had changed the story, the shape, indeed the whole concept of the book, which had become more his than Nancy's; in fact, he had obliterated almost all the traces of her version. To finish the book, he needed to put distance between himself and their old environment, both his and hers.

To himself, he admitted he was fleeing. Fleeing from the routine in which he had imprisoned himself; fleeing from Anne Howells who wanted to appropriate him; fleeing from the remonstrances of his brother and parents about his failure; fleeing from the false sympathy of colleagues and friends from his Inner Temple days. Finally, fleeing from himself, or that part of his self which measured life in Bloody Marys, gimlets, blockbusters, those things that had already disconnected him from reality.

For the first time since adolescence, Gascoyne was beginning to take stock of himself. Why had he allowed himself to be forced into a race of school and college prizes when he had reached an age to decide for himself? Why hadn't he rebelled when his parents press-ganged him into studying law at Oxford when he had a talent for photography, drawing, writing? And those grisly dinners in the Inner Temple! At Oxford he had felt like an aborigine among the scions of noble houses and the minor aristos, even among the upper-middle crust crumbs moulded together by nothing but dough. He was merely middle class. But he recognized the descendants of the robber barons who'd come over with the Conqueror and the offspring of the carpetbaggers who'd hoisted themselves up the social ladder on the bent, sweating back of low paid proles.

Little wonder that some of his Oxford companions reneged and turned to socialism or communism. He might have, too, had he had the guts to buck the system. But he had conformed – as he always had. He had bowed to the established order there, in his Inn of Court, in his chambers, in the law courts, everywhere. He had absorbed establish-men thought and behaviour through his pores; from colourless characters like Tyndall and Congden, he had taken the beat, the rhythm, even the words. He should have thrown his wig, gown, jabot, blue bag, the lot in Grantland's face instead of making grovelling verbal obeisances to that sado-masochist.

Well, all that was behind him now. Even the script Nancy had begun and he had revised seemed to belong to that part of him he wanted to renounce. He had transformed it from the title,

Lifelines, through to the final chapters on which he was now working. When he reread his script it did have some of the lifelines of Nancy, Anne, himself, even Monclar and that sex-obsessed quack in their practice as well as Tyndall and Grantland.

Monclar was right; he had been trying at one time to structure his script around that of another person who was writing completely different lifelines.

If as a writer he had a word to communicate, it should be his own word, no one else's.

For ten footloose days after leaving his flat, Gascoyne wandered the streets between Bayswater Road and Westbourne Grove; the area had dozens of small hotels like his own, hundreds of flats and rooming houses carved out of Victorian and Edwardian houses. Although mid-autumn there was a hot dry Indian summer spell and Gascoyne strolled round in shirt sleeves just observing people, listening to their talk in the pubs where he sipped the two beers he allowed himself these days and enjoying his freedom and anonymity.

It was in the Windsor Crown that he met the night porter of the Hotel Cockaigne, a block from his own. This man, Frank Chubb, in turn introduced him to two other night porters, from the Serpentine Hotel and the London-Pullman – Alan Mains who was a Scot, and Brent Williams from South Wales.

Their hotels were no more than three terrace houses knocked into one then split into between thirty and forty rooms. All three had some hairy stories about the sort of client they dealt with – everything from street pros to junkies and delinquents. Many of their rooms were let by the hour to prostitutes; others were reserved for those well-heeled clients who had regular dates with call girls or perhaps mistresses.

'I could write a book about a week in the life of the Serpentine,' Mains said once when they were in the Windsor Crown. Gascoyne just listened and put their stories down on paper when he returned to his hotel; they were good raw material.

When he left the flat he had also sold his car, having little need for it in town. Walking round the district, he did not regret the move; hardly a free parking space existed and most of the kerbside had been appropriated for resident parking. Those vehicles which strayed into those spaces or yellow-line areas were either clamped or towed away. Frank Chubb became a victim when his Mondeo was towed away from a resident's bay belonging to a friend. It cost him nearly £100, and he came into the pub that night fuming about the racket between the police and the towaway firm. To rub it in, they had damaged the track rod and steering rendering the Mondeo too dangerous to drive before being repaired.

Gascoyne listened, then said, 'Frank can you collect a dozen people who've been towed away hereabouts and have suffered damage?'

'Half a hundred in our street,' Frank said.

Gascoyne told him to have his damage assessed, and ask the others to do likewise. He wrote a letter in his best Inner Temple jargon to the towaway firm threatening legal action unless they compensated Mr Chubb and others for the damage and inconvenience caused; he also hinted that, as the plaintiffs' advocate, he meant to look at the firm's records over the past four months and interview the policemen who patrolled that part of the town and signed the towaway certificates.

Within a week, Frank and his friends were reimbursed for the fine and repairs. To celebrate, he invited Gascoyne and his other two chums to the hotel for a champagne lunch in his room. He had a much better set-up than Gascoyne at Athenaeum House, but then the Cockaigne charged twice as much for a night, and the same tariff for even an hour or two during the day. Frank made as much out of a night's tips as Gascoyne earned in a week.

'That's cos we have the carriage trade.' Frank grinned and winked. 'I've seen plenty of our short-timer and one-night-stand girls on the telly. Yeah, and you should see some of the swank cars they get out of ... chauffeur-driven an' all.'

'What about the gals, Frankie? Where do they pick them up?'

Mains put the question, but Chubb shrugged, pulled on his champagne and said, 'None o' my affair. All I know is they're not street hookers or that kind o' pro. My job's to see and hear and say nowt and pick up my hush money.'

'What about drugs?' Gascoyne asked.

Chubb emptied the champagne bottle into their glasses then put two fingers in his ears and one to his lips. 'What they do up there's none o' my business. But I wouldn't bet there isn't a bit of main-lining or coke-sniffing or the like goes on.' He paused to glance at the door as though wondering about eavesdropping. 'I've had to help carry some of them out to their cars half-dead,' he whispered.

From what Gascoyne gathered, the Cockaigne had at least a dozen rooms set aside for its high-class sex trade in a part of the hotel which could be reached by the old service staircase giving on to a back courtyard. Even Chubb barely knew what went on there; and the three maids who looked after those rooms were paid to shut their mouths. And since they were old pros, they did not mind doing a stint at their former profession. Gascoyne returned to his hotel that afternoon relieved that he had nothing like the problems of Chubb, Mains and Williams; he could spend his night reading and half his day writing. He had only one worry – avoiding having his cover blown by Anne Howells or Nancy before he had finished his novel.

He and Anne Howells had quarrelled when he found she had photocopied half the novel and shown it to two publishers without his say-so; he only discovered her treachery when one of the publishers wrote to him making a generous offer. The other, a woman from the Aphrodite Press, rang him out of the blue with an even more munificent offer. It was still another reason for his flight.

A couple of weeks after the lunch, Gascoyne was sitting behind his reception desk in the small hours when his phone rang. It was Frank Chubb, whispering hoarse-voiced with agitation, asking him to come to the hotel and help him with a problem.

'What sort of problem?'

'Can't say on the blower, but I need a hand and quick.'

Gascoyne locked the hotel door and stepped quickly through the deserted streets to the Cockaigne. Chubb was standing waiting for him on the steps.

'I've got a stiff in one o' the second-floor bedrooms.'

'A suicide?'

'No, I think his ticker's packed in, but he might've put too much of the wrong stuff in his hypo or up his snout.'

'Have you alerted the proprietor?'

'Hmm!' Frank snorted. 'He don't want to know. Told me to get on with it and keep the coppers out of it.'

'What can I do to help?' Gascoyne said.

'Do you know a quack you can trust?'

Gascoyne shook his head. 'Surely the hotel has a doctor on call for its guests.'

Chubb shot him a look, signifying he was acting like an innocent. 'We have a quack on call, but he'd ask all the wrong questions and we'd have the law down on us before you can sneeze – and God knows what they wouldn't find. We'd all be in the clink.'

'I get the point. Can I have a look at the man while I'm thinking?'

Chubb led the way upstairs and opened a second-floor bedroom with a key, pulled Gascoyne inside and locked the door again.

Gascoyne looked at the figure on the bed, covered with a sheet, and then at the room. Drab wallpaper, faded curtains, scuffed carpets. Nothing remotely romantic or even inviting about this room. Sordid. His eye went to the TV set on top of the drinks cabinet. Beside the screen lay the sleeve of a video which he picked up. *Three-Night Stand.* Crude porn. Evidently to help turn on clients like the dead man on the bed. His clothes had been carefully draped over one of the two chairs in the room. Gascoyne flipped the jacket panel open to note the Savile Row label; under the chair he had shoes handmade by Lobb. Obviously not nobody in life, this corpse.

On one of the bedside tables stood an empty champagne bottle with two glasses, one containing an inch of amber liquor, the other empty. A small heap and a film of fine white powder lay on the table.

'What do you think that is, Frank?'

'Coke. Most of 'em sniff it or give themselves a shot in the arm to make themselves feel high and forty years younger.'

'This the first time somebody has dropped dead?'

'Yeah, thank God ... since I've been here anyway ... two years, that is.'

Gascoyne went to the bed and pulled back the sheet.

For more than ten seconds he stared, transfixed, at the face before his memory matched it and his mind put a name to it. Of course, he had seen it a thousand times in all its moods, but always in the context of the law courts, always framed in a short, bench wig above a judge's robes. It hadn't changed much now, that face; its sneer which he had observed a million times had merely congealed into a death rictus and those greenish yellow feline eyes had lost their angry glare and turned glaucous.

Judge Theodore Grantland was not naked; he wore black silk tights slit at the crotch to reveal his limp penis and testicles. His forearms were covered with women's black silk elbow-length gloves with the fingers and thumbs cut off. Rolling down the right glove, Gascoyne noticed a constellation of pinpricks round the elbow crook where Grantland had injected himself.

It was then that he spotted the slender gold thread held tightly in the dead man's hand. Under the hand was a curious charm, a four-armed god dancing within a ring of flames. It was a Hindu amulet which he recognized as a Siva Nataraja, a representation of the Hindu god, Siva the Destroyer, probably worn by the missing call girl as a charm. He had difficulty prising the dead hand open and removing the amulet. Its gold thread was broken, probably signifying that Grantland had torn it from the girl's neck at the height of his last orgasm.

Gascoyne looked at the face. Round the dead man's forehead he had a thin black silk band wound so tight that it had bitten into the flesh. On the legs of the black tights were splashes of a white, viscous substance that were drying; he supposed it was Grantland's sperm.

For several long moments, Gascoyne stood there, his mind in a whirl as it tried to come to terms with Grantland's sordid death in this shabby hotel room. It explained much about this sex-obsessed judge, his attitude to divorce and marriage, his sadism and his lewd conduct in court. What his fetishisms meant, Gascoyne did not begin to understand.

'Do you know anything about this man?' he asked Chubb.

'No, but I've seen him off and on a dozen times. Noticed him cos he doesn't leave even a tosser in my offertory box.'

'Did you get a look at the girl he was with?'

'Yeah, Asian girl, about the usual age ... fifteen, sixteen.' Chubb pointed to Grantland. 'Him and most o' them like 'im like 'em that young.'

'Who runs this sex racket?'

'Search me, I don't even take the money for the rooms. It's too high-class.' Chubb held both hands up, palms outwards to halt Gascoyne in his cross-examination. 'I don't want any aggro about the racket. Just tell me how we get out of this.'

'Let me think.'

Gascoyne's first thought was to avenge every insult and slight he had suffered at this man's hands. Alert the authorities and let them handle it. Set the media loose on this old satyr and paedophile who'd be buried with bigger and more sensational headlines than he had ever created as a divorce court judge.

They'd have a field day, the press and TV, crucifying Grantland, raking up the dirt about the judge who flayed other people for minor sins like adultery while he himself went in for tawny-skinned nymphettes who indulged his sexual fantasies. They would really hit the drug angle; his coke-sniffing and mainlining, his fetishism. And in a week or two they'd have several other bites at the cherry when Her Majesty's coroner held the inquest into his sudden death.

He hated Grantland and everything he represented, but some-thing – his damned conformism? – stayed his hand. Grantland had a wife and two sons, both juniors in chambers, both acquaintances. This would finish them.

'No scandal, Frank – is that what you want?'

'That's it, Bob ... a quiet life, that's me.'

Gascoyne produced his address book and found Tyndall's number. A voice thick with Vosne-Romanée and sleep answered him, but he had to repeat the facts about Grantland twice before the head of his former chambers grasped the import. If Gascoyne had the impression Tyndall was shocked by the news, he did not seem really surprised by the circumstances of the death. As though he was aware of Grantland's real character.

'What have you done?'

'Nothing, so far,' Gascoyne replied. 'But you realize we'll need a doctor to certify his death, and since it's a sudden death we'll have to inform the district coroner.'

'Hold on a second.' Gascoyne heard the thud of the handset on what he supposed was the bedside table. A minute later, Tyndall came on the line again, presumably from his study. 'Now listen, Robert. Do nothing until I get there. I'll contact a doctor and bring him along ... somebody who knows Grantland and his medical history and can certify his death.' He paused for a moment – to draw in smoke? then said, 'What about the girl? Where's she? Did you see her?'

'No, she saw what had happened and took to the hills.'

'All right. Lock the door and stay there and I'll be with you in half an hour at the most.' Tyndall hung up.

While they waited, Gascoyne went through Grantland's pockets to come up with a phial containing white powder. He tried some on his tongue: cocaine. Another bottle had scored pink tablets which looked like the latest in pep pills. But nothing in the judge's pockets to identify him.

When Tyndall arrived in his own car, he had someone with him who looked familiar to Gascoyne. It still took him several moments to place the man as the doctor he had seen in Nancy's practice, the man obsessed with sex – Manson or Mason? Hadn't he even suggested a consultation on the subject of sexual perversion in his West End practice?

Gascoyne looked at Grantland's corpse and thought: There but for the grace of God go I....

From his attitude, Gascoyne felt that the doctor had not recognized him in that dimly lit room. Before he even looked at the corpse he was busy wiping the champagne glasses and bottle then looking in the wardrobe. Tyndall was quizzing both Gascoyne and Chubb, mainly concerned that nobody else had seen the judge enter the hotel, or knew that he was dead.

Mason had a quick look at the body. 'It's a heart attack,' he said to Tyndall, loudly enough for the others to hear. 'This patient of mine had a history of heart trouble and I've been treating him for coronary insufficiency over the past eighteen months.' He looked at Tyndall, then added, 'I'd like to make one or two tests in private.'

Tyndall took the hint and ushered Gascoyne and Chubb downstairs to the lounge and ordered them to wait until Dr Mason had finished. He returned to the upstairs room himself, and Gascoyne could guess what was worrying him and Mason.

Ten minutes went by before Tyndall reappeared. On his face he wore his best courtroom beam, the one that reassured his witnesses and sewed panic in the opposition.

'Well, Robert. Pleasure to see you again even in the middle of this unfortunate affair.'

Knowing what was coming, Gascoyne put space between his back and Tyndall's sledgehammer hand about to descend on his shoulder-blades with a couple of thuds. It hung in the air as Gascoyne explained how he came to be in Grantland's room. Tyndall listened then pointed to a corner table and two easy chairs and led them there. To Chubb, who now sat behind his reception desk, he called, 'Find us a bottle of whisky, a couple of glasses and some ice, would you?'

'Correction, Frank. I'll have a bottle of soda water.'

'Oh, I thought you liked your Scotch neat, Robert.'

Gascoyne shook his head. 'I don't take it neat or otherwise these days.'

Tyndall's spiky eyebrows went up a notch. 'On the wagon, are you? Not the lurgy, or the dreaded C, is it?'

'No, nothing like that.' He could feel Tyndall's remote, troubled eyes on him as he poured himself half a tumbler of whisky, floated three ice cubes in it, lit himself a six-inch cigarette and filled his lungs with smoke, some of which he washed into his stomach with whisky. 'You might say I can't afford it now I'm on the dole,' Gascoyne continued, rubbing it home to his old boss.

Tyndall gulped half his whisky and grinned at Gascoyne. 'Let's talk about that in a minute or two when we've squared all this away.' He gestured at the ceiling. 'It's a mite tricky, don't you think?'

'A coroner's job, I'd say.'

Tyndall snorted down his nose. 'Bugger all to do with the coroner.

Mason, who's his doctor, says it's a heart attack ... natural causes, and that's good enough for me.' Tyndall was expelling smoke in short puffs which said something for his state of mind. 'Only thing is ... well, people might start wondering how he came to die in a crummy little hotel like this a couple of miles from his home. Y'know what lawyers are – they'll concoct all sorts of yarns. Oh, I know what you think of Grantland, but there's his family....'

'Yes, his family,' Gascoyne murmured. 'They wouldn't like to find out he died having it off with an Indian prostitute all of sixteen and him wearing black tights and women's gloves and coked up to the eyeballs. If some of that came out at the inquest ...'

'For Chrissakes, there isn't going to be an inquest,' Tyndall hissed, gripping Gascoyne's arms in his agitation. 'It's a fucking natural death.'

Gascoyne grinned at the unwitting quip. He produced the phials of cocaine powder and pep pills. 'These were on the bedside table. I picked them up in case they got lost somehow.'

He caught Tyndall staring at him as though wondering how to tease the implications out of that remark and what they really meant. 'I noticed too from his elbow that he had been using a hypo needle quite a lot which, I must admit, shocked me in a man of his eminence. I wondered whether his addiction had something to do with his penchant on the bench for punishing without remorse anyone who had committed the smallest misdemeanour.'

'Robert, you have a right to be bitter.'

'It's not a question of personal bitterness,' Gascoyne came back. 'But those who live by the sword like Grantland deserve to feel its edge when they transgress themselves.'

'Come off it, the man's dead, isn't he?'

'It means that sometimes justice is done down here as well.'

That earned him another curious look from Tyndall, who fell silent for more than a minute as though wondering what to say. Finally, he managed to clamp a hand on Gascoyne's shoulder. 'Look, Robert, we've had our ups and downs, but we're still friends. I've been thinking ... you know George Congden's taking silk, so I have to find somebody talented enough to replace him as the leading junior. If wondered if you—'

'Not interested, Geoffrey. I've a nice little part-time job as a night watchman which leaves me free to do what I want to do.'

'Which is?'

'Oh, a bit of scribbling.'

'Fiction or fact?'

'Fiction.'

That seemed to reassure Tyndall, who had already left the remains of three cigarettes in his ashtray since they had sat down. After reflection, he had another question.

'Did you happen to see this Indian girl who was with Grantland when he had his heart attack?'

'No, and neither did the night porter,' Gascoyne lied. 'She went out the back way and I suppose in something of a hurry.'

Tyndall thumbed towards Chubb. 'Did he get her name?'

'No, I asked him. But she was a pro, so he thinks.' Gascoyne wondered why Tyndall was so interested in finding out about the girl. Probably to bribe her to remain silent, or even to threaten her if she talked. His legal experience whispered that the head of his old chambers knew more about Grantland's secret life and the call-girl set-up than he would reveal. He asked the question he might have asked had he been cross-examining in the law courts.

'Did you ask this doctor if he knew of Grantland's penchant for drugs, fetishism and call girls?'

'Good God, why? And how the hell would he know?'

'Well, if he was Grantland's regular doctor as you say he was …' He let Tyndall complete his thought.

'I only know Grantland consulted him from time to time,' Tyndall said in a hard voice, aware that Gascoyne was interrogating him. 'I wouldn't have rung him otherwise.'

'Sorry Geoffrey,' Gascoyne said, softly. 'I wouldn't have asked but I consulted Dr Mason once. He was a GP in a pretty run-of-the-mill group practice in the Shepherd's Bush area. But I suppose this—' He pointed an index finger at the ceiling '—is part of his private practice.'

'I know little or nothing about Mason,' Tyndall said, testily. 'My only interest is protecting Grantland's name and sparing his whole family crucifixion at the hands of the media.'

Tyndall struck his best defence counsel pose. 'As a colleague, Robert, don't you think we owe it to our profession and a person who, despite his faults – and who among us doesn't have faults? – graced the bar and the bench and does not deserve to have his reputation and his calling besmirched by a sexual peccadillo and a minor lapse in an exemplary life.'

Gascoyne looked him in the eye. 'Tyndall, you know and I know that Grantland was a vile, vicious, mean-minded, black-hearted, bile-ridden, sex-obsessed, depraved, degenerate sadist and one of the most iniquitous and unrighteous bastards ever to wear a judge's wig, and I'm overjoyed that he's lying up there stiff and cold and dead for all eternity and I only wish to heaven there is a God who'll damn him as he damned others and that he'll burn in hell.'

For a moment, Gascoyne thought Tyndall was going to strike him. Do it and I'll clobber you with the whisky bottle, he thought. Tyndall, however, pulled himself out of his chair, drew himself up to his full six-foot two inches and towered over the seated Gascoyne.

'Now look, Gascoyne, if you breathe one word about this I shall contest it in Chancery where I have many friends and you know I will win and damn you.'

'Now look, Tyndall, you know I can pick up the phone on Frank Chubb's desk and ring the Press Association and Reuters which would alert every newspaper, radio and TV channel in this and other countries and you and your curious friend, Dr Mason, would have a lot of explaining to do.

'If I haven't done it so far it's because it's not in my nature, and my friend, Chubb, would be involved. But if there's an inquest, or anyone cares to ask me what I saw I will not lie to save Grantland, you, Dr Mason or anyone else.'

Tyndall went to say something, but at that moment they heard a siren winding down as an ambulance drew up at the hotel entrance. Tyndall met the two paramedics at the door and showed them upstairs.

Gascoyne waited to see the body of Judge Theodore Grantland stretchered out of the hotel in a body bag before sitting down with

Chubb to have a glass of beer. He did not even bother to bid either Tyndall or Dr Mason good night. Nor did they tarry in the lounge, but slipped quietly out of the hotel.

As Gascoyne walked home, he felt something cold and hard against his right thigh. He had forgotten the amulet. Now he pulled it out to look at it in the lamplight where the glitter seemed to set Siva the Destroyer dancing in his flaming circle.

He had seen life-sized effigies of Siva, the dancing god, the destroyer of the Hindu trinity, who could laugh and caper and dance amid cosmic flames as he was doing in this amulet.

Who was the girl from whose neck this amulet had been torn in that sinister room?

He would have given much to know.

chapter XX

Nancy was working in her office when Shanta Mehta and another girl patient, Moora Numar, came into the practice and asked if they could see her for a few minutes in private. Nancy showed them into Marcia Clarke's consulting room, empty on her day off. She suspected that perhaps it was the usual trouble – Shanta's friend was pregnant and would want to know how to arrange an abortion without her parents' knowledge. But the frightened faces of both girls suggested that something worse was worrying them. Shanta, who expressed herself better, told the story. Moora had been with a man in a hotel. He had gone into convulsions when they were making love and Moora had fled, thinking he was dying. But she had left behind in the hotel room something that might identify her. A gold amulet her mother had given her of the Hindu god Siva whom they worshipped.

Moora's parents were very devout Hindus and had three amulets blessed by the priests in the holiest temple of Benares, the Bisheshwar; they gave one to their two daughters and the third to their best friend, Shanta.

'But Moora is wearing an amulet,' Nancy said, pointing to the emblem of the dancing god on a thin gold chain round the girl's neck.

'Moora cannot say she has lost hers. That would be a curse on the family from Siva. So I am giving mine on loan.'

'Won't your father notice yours has gone, Shanta?'

Shanta shook her head. 'I'm saying that it is being mended at a jeweller's shop.'

Shanta explained that Moora was too scared to go back to the hotel herself and retrieve her amulet. Would Mrs Gascoyne be so kind as to get the amulet back from the hotel before someone found it and traced it to Moora? She was pleading.

Although Nancy wondered about the relationship between these two girls and Mason and the possible connection between them and the girls with HIV infections, she refrained from quizzing the girls about their sexual activities. She took the address of the Bayswater hotel and promised to call there when she shut the practice that evening.

'You will not tell anyone, Mrs Gascoyne,' Shanta said, her large anxious eyes on Nancy. 'Not Dr Mason or Dr Monclar.'

'No, I won't tell a soul.'

As soon as she had seen the doctors out and shut the practice, she took a cab to the Cockaigne Hotel, which impressed her as the sort of seedy maison de passe which abounded in this area. A homunculus behind the reception desk high-handed her and denied seeing an Indian girl two nights before or having any record of one in his register.

'Have a look, Ma'am,' he said, thrusting a thick book at her.

She pushed it back without a glance. 'You had a dead man here that night, didn't you?'

'A dead man? Nooh, never seen or heard of that, I haven't.'

Nancy realized she would get nowhere with this man unless she put him under pressure. 'All right,' she said. 'I'll contact the local police and write to the hotel proprietor. You see, the missing piece of jewellery is unique and therefore very valuable.' Chubb thought about that for a moment then, as she turned to go, he called out, 'You might try the Athenaeum House Hotel down the road. Night porter there might have a clue about your bracelet.'

Nancy walked the hundred yards to the Athenaeum House, which did little justice to its name. Smog-blackened brick, peeling stucco round the doors and windows and railings flaky with rust. Pushing open the door, she found herself in a small entrance with four easy chairs and a low table and a reception desk behind which she noticed a bowed head.

'Excuse me,' she said and the head came up.

For a moment, she stood bewildered, almost stunned at the sight of Gascoyne's face which bore much the same look of astonishment.

'You're here!' she got out. 'Whatever are you doing in a place like this?'

'What do you imagine?' he said. 'Working. Earning my daily crust.' He grinned at her, putting down the page of typescript he had been reading on his desk. 'May I enquire what you're doing in a sleazy joint like this?'

'A girl from my practice left an amulet in the Cockaigne Hotel down the road – it's a sort of Hindu charm.'

'Like this.' Gascoyne opened a desk drawer and pulled out the Siva Nataraja and held it up.'

Nancy looked at the gold emblem of the dancing god, realizing it fitted Shanta's description of the one Moora had lost.

'That's it,' she said. 'Where did you get it?'

'Tell me who it belongs to and I'll tell you where, why, how and when.'

Nancy hesitated for a moment, remembering Shanta's strictures about secrecy. 'This is between us, but it belongs to an Indian girl who's a patient of Dr Mason at the practice. I don't know exactly what she was doing, but I think she was lured into that crummy hotel by somebody who paid her for having sex then died on her. Now she's scared she might be blamed for the man's death so she sent me to recover her amulet before they trace it back to her.'

'That's about the story,' Gascoyne said. 'But tell your girl nobody died there, so she can stop worrying.' He handed Nancy the amulet.

'How did you get this, then?' Nancy asked.

'In the hotel room.' He saw the look of mystification on Nancy's face and then a question, which she put:

'So she just thought the man was dying?'

'No, he was dying. And he did die.'

Nancy glared at him. 'Will you please stop your usual doubletalk and explain what happened there two nights ago?'

Gascoyne did not reply directly. Instead, he pulled a copy of the late edition of the *Standard* out of a pigeon-hole behind his desk and handed this to her. 'Read that and then I'll tell you what I know,' he said.

Nancy looked at the half-column he had indicated on the front page under a headline stretching across three columns. It said:

Judge Theodore Grantland died last night at the home of his friend and legal colleague, Geoffrey Tyndall, QC, in Camden Crescent, Holland Park. The judge had dined with Mr Tyndall, a senior Queen's Counsel, and his wife and was preparing to leave around midnight when he complained of feeling unwell with severe chest pains.

A doctor was called but while waiting for him to arrive, Judge Grantland collapsed. Efforts by Mr Tyndall to revive him by chest massage and the kiss of life were in vain. The doctor could only certify that the judge had died of a massive heart attack.

Judge Grantland was eminent in his profession. He had a brilliant mind and came down from Oxford with a double first in law and entered the chambers of Adrian Curtis-Menzies to specialize in civil cases. However, he made his name by winning several libel cases that made headlines and by defending British servicemen against accusations of wilful murder during the shoot-to-kill controversy in Northern Ireland. Equally successful in handling divorce cases, he became an obvious choice as a divorce court judge.

Judge Grantland was rarely out of the headlines because of his many controversial judgments in divorce cases; although professing to shun publicity and succeeding in doing this for his private life, he was often accused of backing into the lime-light professionally by his trenchant legal asides. He undoubtedly had a sour, sarcastic wit which he often exercised gratuitously on the parties and their advocates in divorce cases.

We shall return to Judge Grantland's life and career in a full obituary in tomorrow's editions.

Nancy handed back the paper. 'So, it was your old friend Grantland who died in that sleazy little hotel down the road.' When Gascoyne nodded, she pointed to the paper in his hand and added, 'And this is the cover-up by Tyndall and his wife.'

'You've got there in one,' Gascoyne said. He came round the reception desk and pointed her to a chair in the foyer before disappearing into a back room and emerging with a tray containing a bottle of whisky, two cans of soda water and ice cubes. 'Since it's a long and funny story you'd better have a drink and hear it from the beginning.' Nancy sat down and accepted a whisky and soda; she noticed that he left the liquor alone and drank only soda water. At this time of the evening, the old Gascoyne would have shipped the best part of a bottle of vodka or the equivalent, and shown it.

'I'm on duty,' he said, thumbing towards the desk.

She listened while he explained in detail what had happened that night and his part in the story. When he had finished, he had a thought.

'By the way, the quack Tyndall fetched with him to certify Grantland's death works with you. A sleek-haired, smooth-cheeked type whose mind seems only to be in sharp focus around the male and female genitalia. I met him the day I came to see you and you shunned me.'

'You mean Mason.'

'That's the name. He's the man who's fixing everything and presumably making sure there's no coroner's inquest. He seemed to know both Grantland and Tyndall well.'

Nancy did not comment, although the pieces of their puzzle about Mason's activities were dropping into place. Shanta, the four other Aids cases and now Grantland and Moora. What would Monclar make of it?

Gascoyne was rummaging in an inside pocket and produced the phial of cocaine and the bottle of pills. 'What are these?' he asked.

'He'd need a script for those.'

'Which the good Dr Mason would supply along with other accoutrements like cocaine, heroine, hypos, tourniquets and everything else a junkie needs.'

'Robert, are you going to keep quiet about all this?'

'What do you think?'

'For my part, I'd like to keep the girls out of it. They'd never live it down, and some of them have Aids probably through this sort of prostitution.'

'What about your quack? Does he get away with it? Sounds as though he'd be struck off and perhaps do five years at Her Majesty's expense if this got out,'

Nancy hesitated then disclosed that she and Monclar had suspected for some time that Mason had been running a call-girl racket, though they could never gather enough evidence to nail him. Even now, they could not ask the girls involved to testify against him since it would ruin them. But from now on, they would keep an eye on him and when he made another mistake they'd pounce.

'Let's hope it's soon,' he said.

Nancy caught him gazing at her as though he was observing something new about her, or sizing her up in the same way that she had while he had been talking. She could see that he had changed a lot. She got in first.

'You still haven't told me what you're doing behind the night desk in this ...'

'Squalid little Bayswater hotel,' he cut in, and when she hesitated, he went on, 'I'm taking a leaf out of the writers' handbook.'

'What does the leaf say?'

'Well, I've noticed that the most successful writers and poets started in garrets or cellars, they lived like saints abjuring food, water, even sex, they wrote at night by candlelight and were totally dedicated to their art.'

With a gesture, Gascoyne embraced the foyer, the reception desk and the steps leading to the basement under it. 'This little pad and my sordid basement room are the nearest thing I could find to the poor poet's corner – even if they haven't produced the same divine afflatus that they might have done with a Chatterton, a Blake, a Heine ...'

'So, you've come here to finish your book.'

'It's your book, too.'

She shook her head emphatically. 'No, it isn't any longer. Your girlfriend, Anne Howells, let me read what you had written over a month ago and it's a completely different story. I could never have done anything like it.' She raised her glass of whisky and soda in a toast. 'It's very good. In fact, it's better than very good and it'll earn you a lot of money.'

'You may be right, though it's not the object of the exercise. I've already turned down two offers from publishers.'

'Oh, you don't need the money?'

'I do, but wouldn't I be taking it under false pretences since the book was your idea in the first place?'

Nancy shook her head. 'I waive my rights as it's another book.' She shrugged. 'You said yourself everything's in the writing and the way you look at the story.'

As they were talking, Nancy had sudden mental flashbacks about how their own stories had evolved; from that spat about his changes in her script, and the broken computer symbolizing their break-up, their books seemed to have developed as an allegory of their lives.

Were they, as Monclar suggested, a sort of fragmented self-portrait where bits of themselves were projected on to the characters they were drawing?

As if Gascoyne were reflecting along the same lines, he suddenly said: 'Know something? We didn't realize it, but we were both writing different life scripts long before we put them on paper. The odd thing is that it took us six years and more to put it on record.'

'Have you been talking to Ted? I mean, Dr Monclar?'

'Yes, we had a discussion of sorts one night.'

Gascoyne gazed at her. Why hadn't they been able to script their lives with less abrasive dialogue? With more kindness? With more understanding? With more insight into each other's minds and hearts? Maybe they could have rewritten the text together, revised things between them. But it was perhaps too late.

'Are you in love with him?'

'Love. I didn't think you believed in that.'

'You know what I mean.' Gascoyne reverted to his old flip self. 'Do your two hearts beat as one and the night is always young and the moon is always new and you see stars in each other's eyes? The old story that everybody gives his own twist to. Well, are you?'

'One of us feels that way.'

Gascoyne raised his glass of soda water. 'I'm glad for you. Sincerely. I only wish you'd felt that way about me – and for that matter, I'd felt that way about you. But there it is.'

'I'm sorry,' Nancy murmured.

'You haven't said if he's in love with you.'

'I don't know that he is.'

'Well, I do. He told me so. Oh, not in so many words. But as an old divorce court hand, I can read the runes.'

'What about you? Have you seen Anne Howells?'

'Not since I went on the lam.'

Nancy looked at him closely; she knew him well enough to realize something was worrying him. 'What's wrong, aren't you hitting it off?'

Gascoyne grinned ruefully, then shook his head. 'Remember what I said about writing and love and writing and sex – they don't mix. Our story has screwed up my libido.'

Nancy could not help laughing, and Gascoyne saw the funny side laughing with her. 'It'll come good if you don't think about it.'

For a moment or two, Gascoyne contemplated the small bubbles exploding on the surface of his soda water then raised his head. 'I've nearly finished the script,' he murmured. 'I'll see about our divorce then go and find Anne and ask her to marry me. How's that for a program?'

Great,' Nancy said. 'From meeting Anne, I think you're both lucky. And I know she won't want to change one word of your script.' She pointed to the typescript on his desk. 'Either that one or your life script.'

Gascoyne escorted her to the door. To her astonishment, he took her in his arms and hugged and kissed her, then whispered in her ear, 'You'll invite us both to the wedding, I hope.'

Before she could reply, he had darted back into the hotel.

chapter XXI

A week after her meeting with Gascoyne, Nancy had just
arrived and begun her afternoon shift when she spotted
Vikram Mehta in the waiting room. He must have been
watching for her and came to the office to whisper over the counter,
'Shanta was taken ill overnight and is going to hospital and they are
keeping her there. She is ill. My only daughter is very ill.'

'I'm terribly sorry,' Nancy said, realizing this was evidently an
Aids crisis and hoping they would cope at Hammersmith. She
looked at Mehta, noting the bloodshot eyes in his lean, quarried
face. 'Have you informed Dr Mason?' she asked.

'No. I would prefer you tell Dr Monclar about Shanta.'

'He's on afternoon visits but I'll tell him when he returns.'

Mehta was turning to go when he suddenly halted and she
noticed his red eyes fall on the gold amulet. She had brought it into
the surgery to give Shanta when she next saw the girl. She cursed
herself for leaving it in view beside her computer. Now she picked
it up and handed it to Mehta. 'It belongs to Shanta. Perhaps you
could give it to her.'

'She lost this jewel here, then?'

Nancy hesitated, trying to think quickly on her feet. What had
Shanta told her about a jeweller? 'No, no, she didn't lose it. She
asked me to fetch it from the jewellers where she had taken it for
repair. The chain had broken.'

She read doubt in those red-rimmed eyes, which were now fixed
on hers. 'It cost how much? Tell me and I will pay you.'

'It was two pounds fifty – but Shanta can pay me when she
comes out of hospital,' Nancy said.

'No, I will pay.' Mehta produced a small leather purse, zipped it open and produced five fifty-pence pieces and handed these over. 'What did they do to this necklace?' he asked, and for a moment Nancy was flummoxed.

'As I said, it was the chain or clasp that was broken and they mended it.'

She could feel his suspicion as he scrutinized the amulet carefully before thrusting it into an anorak pocket. He muttered a thank you and left. She realized he suspected she was lying.

Mehta went straight home. He had no conscience about searching Shanta's room, turning out the drawers, the pockets of her coats and costumes, looking under the chest of drawers and at the wardrobe top, lifting the carpet and the bed mattress.

Finally, he found the hiding place: two plastic sachets stuck to the bottom of the dressing-table drawer where there was a space an inch thick.

Mehta emptied the plastic bags then stared, bewildered, at their contents – a bundle of money, a diary, a small box full of pills, a diaphragm. Mehta was worldly enough to know what this rubber-covered metal ring and dome was, but he felt a rush of blood to his face at the idea of his daughter using this contraceptive device as well as the pills. He thanked his gods that his wife, who had died giving Shanta life, was no longer here and did not have to suffer like him at the sight and meaning of these things on the dressing table. Rage blotted out every other sentiment and emotion in him as he went outside and threw the pills and the diaphragm in his dustbin. Returning, he picked up the diary and the money which he counted. £342. He held them in his hand.

Was this worth a life?

He turned to the diary, a small plasticized book with three days to a page. Page by page he went through it, noting meetings with known friends, and her few appointments. One thing struck him: those two nights she was supposed to spend at her night-school were often marked with an 'M' and a time, and some with a 'C'. No other indication. But in the notes at the back of the diary he found half a dozen phone numbers, two of them underlined.

He already had an idea who 'M' was. And in the phone book he found Mason's professional number in the West End matched one of the underlined numbers; he tried the other from a phone box and Mason's voice came up on the answering machine. One of the other numbers he rang turned out to be a hotel called the Cockaigne, which he assumed was the 'C' in the diary.

Now he had solved the mystery of Shanta's sickness, he must act.

However, he had one thing to do first. He went to the small shrine he had constructed in an alcove of the living room to honour Siva the Destroyer and his red-eyed, blood-thirsty wife, Kali. He anointed both gods with oil and ghee and prayed to them, asking them what he should do. Both Siva and Kali, with her necklace of skulls and girdle of serpents, had one simple and unequivocal message for him:

Vengeance.

With the blessing of his gods, Vikram Mehta sat down and drew up a plan of action.

First, he went to the garage owner, a Hindu like himself, and asked if he could have the ten days the repair shop owed him since his daughter needed his help to overcome her illness. His boss told him to take as long as he needed.

He already knew Mason's professional address in the Harley Street area and he managed to persuade a BT operator to let him have the address attached to the other number; this was a residential flat in York Avenue off Regent's Park. Over a three-day period, Mehta observed Mason's comings and goings between his West End consulting room and Shepherd's Bush.

He discovered the doctor was a bachelor with three failed marriages behind him, though he did not lack for elegant and nubile woman. Mehta caught sight of three attractive women in Mason's Bentley. He also hung around the Cockaigne Hotel between eight o'clock and midnight and watched girls like his daughter entering and leaving and men doing the same, obviously keeping sex assignations.

To carry out his plan, Mehta realized he would need a key to Mason's York Avenue flat and another for his Bentley. In the car park below the practice, he had ample time to examine the car undisturbed. He finally found what he was looking for: a spare key stuck inside the jack mounting beneath the chassis and so encrusted with mud he wondered if Mason had acquired it unwittingly with the vintage car. He cleaned it and tried it on the lock and the ignition then hid it.

Mason's flat presented his biggest problem. It had a street-door code, a day and night guardian and video cameras sweeping the whole of the foyer. He had to obtain the flat key and devise a means of thwarting the security system.

He knew Mason worked mornings and sometimes part of an afternoon at Shepherd's Bush. During a morning surgery, he consulted the doctor, complaining of severe back pain radiating down his right leg. As he guessed, Mason sent him for X-rays to Charing Cross Hospital. When he returned with them next day, Mehta left his coat and jacket in Mason's office before going into the examination room.

As Mason fixed the X-rays to his screen and studied them, Mehta excused himself saying he had forgotten to produce the radiologist's notes from his jacket. When he fetched them, he searched Mason's pockets, found his keyring and put it in his own coat pocket.

By elimination he realized which was the flat key, although he also took the one for the West End consulting room. He had both copied in two different stores in Holland Park and Shepherd's Bush within half an hour.

But how to return them without arousing suspicion? He thought of going back to tell Mason he was allergic to the anti-inflammatory pills he had prescribed and slipping the keys into the doctor's jacket. Too risky. And the Gascoyne woman was now on duty. Instead, he kept watch in the car park until a teenage boy from the flats above appeared and parked his bike a few places from Mason's Bentley.

Mehta called him over. 'Look,' he said, 'I've just found these keys by this car. I think it belongs to one of the doctors.' He handed over the bunch of keys. 'Why don't you take the keys to the surgery and he'll give you a reward for finding them?'

'OK,' said the boy, pocketing the keys. 'Thanks.'

Mason's keys duly arrived on Nancy's desk and she gave the boy a pound. She slipped the keys into Mason's pocket while he was busy with a patient in his exam room, and thought no more about it.

Mehta still had to solve the problem of getting access to Mason's flat and making his reconnaissance. There was the garage connecting with the flats by the back stairs. This proved easier to enter than he envisaged, for cars came and went frequently; by waiting until six o'clock when it was growing dark and keeping his head down, he managed to slip into the garage behind a Daimler. When the driver and passengers had disappeared, he emerged from behind the pillar and climbed to the second floor where his key gave him entrance to Mason's flat.

He had time to look round knowing Mason would not be home for at least another hour. This man lived in impressive style. Mehta understood nothing of Chippendale or Sheraton or Chesterfield, but realized the furnishings had cost a fortune; even the Chinese rugs on this floor and the Persian and Indian rugs in the other rooms would have taken several years' wages to buy.

His eye went to the heavy chandelier hanging by a stout chain from the living-room ceiling. A year's money at least. Paintings and tapestries everywhere, thick brocade curtains at the windows, colour TV and hi-fi systems everywhere. He noticed the videos were labelled in grossly sexual terms and were obviously obscene.

When he had finished sizing up the flat and memorizing its layout, he descended by the back stairs to the garage leaving in the same way he had entered, by waiting for a departing or arriving car to open the heavy steel door and slipping under it.

He had two nights to wait, having chosen Friday night, the beginning of the weekend when Mason's cleaning woman took a break and the guardians were busier with so many people trafficking in and out of the block.

Mehta spent the afternoons and evenings in the hospital with Shanta, who was isolated and lonely; her eyes were unnaturally bright and her forehead burned with fever. It had, thanks to his prayers to the gods, come down a degree and the doctors hoped she would get over the crisis in a week or ten days and they could discharge her. Sitting with her, observing the pain in her eyes and her fear gave Mehta the courage to do what he had planned.

He knew Mason called at his West End consulting room on Fridays to pick up mail and appointments and got home around seven o'clock. After dusk, just before six, Mehta slipped into the underground park and upstairs to the flat. He settled himself behind the larger of the Chesterfields.

Squatting there in the darkness, broken only by the flashing of street signs and car headlights, he felt scared by what he intended to do. But when he shut his eyes he could see the wan, exhausted face of his daughter; he also confronted the grim face of Siva and the fiery eyes of Kali. Had the gods not ordained this and was not he nothing but their instrument?

Seven o'clock was chiming from one of the church clocks when he heard a key sliding in the lock and a moment later the chandelier flared into sequinned light. Mehta heard Mason's heavy tread on the Chinese carpet then the click of the drinks cabinet door, the clink of a bottle and glass, the gurgle of poured liquor; he felt the pressure of Mason's body on the back of the Chesterfield.

Waiting, waiting until he heard Mason put his glass on the coffee table before him, Mehta rose slowly, and held his breath.

An arm's length away, Mason's head was slightly bowed over the evening paper. How easy it would be to slip the silk noose in his hand round that bull neck, pull it tight, twist it and keep twisting until he choked every atom of life out of this vermin. But would that be the vengeance of Siva and Kali?

Such a black-hearted villain must surely know why he was paying with his life; his last thought must be for those girls like Shanta whom he had sacrificed for his personal pleasure, his gain, his greed.

Mehta clenched his fists and tensed his thumbs and he aimed for the hollows on both sides of that bull neck just where it met the shoulders, just at that nexus of arteries and veins that supplied and drained the blood from the brain. He grunted with the effort as he dug his thumbs almost to their roots into that flesh; he felt Mason's head snap backwards, the neck go rigid, the head fall forward, the body slump on the leather couch. Using the silk cord he had brought with him, Mehta bound Mason's feet together then brought his hands round behind his back and tied these as well. He thrust a handkerchief into the slack mouth then propped the man upright in the corner of the Chesterfield.

A few minutes later, when Mason opened his eyes, they widened when he saw Mehta sitting opposite him. His gaze went to the thin silk rope dangling from the chandelier hook and his eyes widened further with terror. His face suffused with blood as he vainly tried to utter through the gag.

Mehta put up a finger to stop him. 'I will remove the handkerchief, but if you try to scream or shout I will put it back. Understand? Make a sign.'

Mason nodded his head and Mehta removed the gag from his mouth.

'Mr Mehta, what's the meaning of all this? If you want to rob me, go ahead. I won't say anything. If it's money you want I'll give it to you.'

'I am not wishing to rob you or take your money, Dr Mason. I want to kill you.'

'Kill me! Why, for God's sake?' Mason's lips were trembling so much he could scarcely articulate. 'Don't you know the penalty for murder? They'll put you in prison for life.'

'What is this to me?' Mehta replied. 'You have killed my daughter and you are now paying for that murder.'

'But your daughter is not dead, Mehta, only sick. Look, I promise to do everything to save her.'

'You are an evil man, Dr Mason. You are contaminating Shanta's mind and her body, and the minds and bodies of others like her.'

'Your daughter wanted money and she sold her body to get it like the others. Is that my fault?'

'Yes. You were their doctor. They respected and trusted you and you are tricking them and corrupting them ...'

Mehta had to stop speaking to collect himself and put the image of his daughter's pained and drawn face out of his mind. 'Shanta was a pure girl before you poisoned her mind and now she is dying before she is living. And this is the reason you are having to die.'

Before Mason could answer, Mehta moved quickly round the

back of the Chesterfield and brought the heel of his hand down with all his force on the nape of Mason's neck, knocking him out. Putting the gag back into the slack mouth, he then dragged the inert body over to the chair he had placed under the noose, which he looped round Mason's neck.

As Mason recovered consciousness, Mehta began to hoist him upwards, inch by inch, until his feet were dangling just below the level of the chair seat.

Mason's face had turned dull red then livid, his eyes swelling as though to burst out of their sockets; he was trying to speak through the gag, but the thin silk rope was cutting into his neck, gradually breaking the skin then the windpipe. Mason was wriggling desperately on the end of the rope, uttering a hoarse croaking sound then a whimper and finally a sigh as the rope throttled him.

Mehta stood watching him, unmoved, as the convulsions and twitching grew weaker until Mason choked on his own blood and vomit and died.

Mehta placed the chair on its side to give the impression Mason had mounted on it then kicked it over to hang himself; he removed the gag from the open mouth and the bonds from the hands and feet and pocketed these. He spent half an hour examining the room and removing any traces he might have left. He took care to lock the door behind him. He met no one in the corridor or the stairs leading to the underground car park. There, he hid until a car approached and he could slip outside unseen.

At Baker Street tube station he thrust the flat key into one of the rubbish bins before boarding a train.

Back home, he prayed for half an hour before his shrine. As he prayed, it seemed to him that the faces of those two fearsome gods, Siva and Kali, looked on him with a more benign expression.

Since Mason did not work on Mondays, no one at the practice learned of his death until the *Standard* and the local radio stations broke the story late in the afternoon. Both the Clarkes were shocked and puzzled, for Mason seemed free from any concerns about his job, about money, about life in general.

Monclar had two house calls to make, but when he returned he had already heard the news on his car radio. He had also bought a paper and read the story of how Mason had been found by his cleaner that morning, hanged in his locked flat. Police were treating it as a suicide.

'Do you think they're right, it's a suicide?' Nancy asked Monclar when he had shown out his last patient and they were alone in the practice.

'What else can they think? No sign of infraction, the guardians saw nobody and nothing came up on the video system. And Mason's doors and windows are all locked.'

'Yes, but don't you think as a doctor he really did decide to exit the hard way?' Nancy insisted. 'Why not pills, or gas, or a plastic bag over his head, or even a header out of the window. But that thin rope ... it brings me out in a rash thinking about it'

'You were the last person to see him here on Friday. How was he?'

'Nothing wrong with that one. He was his usual nasty, infuriating self with another bawdy quip on his tongue. Know what his famous last words were to me: "You'd be a great lay tied up."'

'Did he come out with that? However much truth there may be in it, he was pretty crude.'

'Ah! But what he said he said when I came back at him was: "'You're a great lady for tidying up."'

Monclar laughed and went on laughing as she mentioned half a dozen others of Mason's lecherous sallies. 'Sometimes I even felt the urge to strangle him with my bare hands.'

'I wonder who else around here might have had the idea?' Monclar mused then banged his forehead with the heel of his hand. 'Mehta,' he said.

'Mehta,' she repeated. 'You mean he blamed him for what happened to Shanta and might've murdered him?'

Monclar nodded. 'Now that I recall it, he said as much the day he brought me the positive HIV results. He said ...' Monclar paused, searching his mind for the exact phrase. 'He said, "If I find this man who is poisoning my daughter, I will kill him."'

'But how did he trace things to Mason? How did he find out about Mason's sex racket?'

'Shanta went into hospital and he might have been going through her things. People are careless and he might have fallen upon a diary, a phone number and address ... something pointing to Mason.'

'The amulet!' Nancy exclaimed, then told him how Moora had left an amulet like Shanta's in the hotel the night Grantland died, how she had recovered it from Gascoyne and had to lie to Mehta about it. 'I don't think for a moment he believed me. He already had his suspicions about Mason.' A sudden thought brought her up. 'There was something else that day ... he saw Mason for a back problem.'

'Did he? Normally he treated Mason as though he had a bad case of bubonic plague.'

Nancy looked at Monclar. 'You know, the more I think of it, you're right. On the afternoon that Mehta saw Mason, his keyring was picked up in the garage and I slipped it back into Mason's pocket without telling him, not wanting more sexual harassment. Somebody could have copied his keys.'

'And that explains the locked door of his flat.'

They stood there staring at each other, aware that their intuition and the evidence each had adduced to buttress it were enough to make Mehta at least a prime suspect in Mason's death.

'What are we going to do about it?' Nancy asked.

In response, Monclar traced a large imaginary zero with his index finger. 'Justice has been done,' he said. 'Oh, I admit it's the law of talion, an eye for an eye, a tooth for a tooth, but what does anybody gain by having Mehta locked away for ten or twenty years for avenging his daughter? Anyway, who'd look after her, sick as she is?' He looked at Nancy and shrugged. 'Had it been my daughter, I might have had the courage to do what we assume Mehta did.'

'So we forget it.'

'Look, Nancy, it's only supposition. We have one of the best police forces in the world. Let's leave it to them.'

chapter XXII

After Mason's death, officially registered as a suicide, the partners decided to share out his small list among themselves. Monclar had still not made any decision about taking over Fothergill's patients permanently but was staying to help out the Clarkes. He and Nancy had a drink or dinner after work at least twice a week, but neither of them made a move. Nancy had resolved to let Monclar take the initiative; on several occasions, she felt he was going at last to speak about Liz, but something always seemed to block his thought. It was frustrating playing a waiting game, but she had to be sure he loved her.

In the weeks that followed, she learned from the press and TV that Gascoyne's cover had been blown. His book had been auctioned among publishers and had fetched an advance of more than £250,000 and had already sold film and TV rights. American publishers were bidding against each other for the book rights and the spin-off rights. And, irony of ironies, it had been shortlisted for the Golden Heart award even before publication.

When she arrived at the practice one afternoon, Pat handed her a parcel: it contained two advance copies of Gascoyne's book sent by his publisher and hers, Aphrodite Press. It had an impressive jacket. Two hands occupied the whole of the front cover, palms outward and superimposed on each other. The larger man's hand was done in sepia, the smaller woman's hand in ivory tints. The lines of the hand – the life lines, the heart lines, the fate lines – were etched in different colours, shades of blues, yellows, reds and black. They converged, diverged, collided and criss-crossed; they broke in places and fragmented in others. The title *Lifelines* was done in bold italic script.

Gascoyne had written a note with the books on the publisher's memo-pad paper. It said merely: 'Lifelines for both of you.'

One copy she handed to Monclar, the other she took home to read that evening. Although the book ran to more than 400 pages – twice the normal length of her novels – she devoured it at one sitting which kept her up till three in the morning. Reading it, Nancy could not help feeling green-eyed. Never in a thousand volumes could she have handled a story like that or recounted it in such powerful prose. It hit you in the head and heart at the same time; it could set you smiling or turn your stomach. Some pages were written with such punch that she could hardly believe that others, done in delicate, filigree prose, were of the same author.

She saw that he had purged her version of the book of all its flabby narrative and focused on the storyline. And the scenes! They were diamond-sharp, especially the scene where the younger brother died under the horse's hooves, and the final court drama with the verdict poised on a razor's edge.

How had she lived with this man for six years and never realized he could put dialogue together that would stand up unaltered on the stage, never known that he could feel the emotion he had injected into this story?

Many things she recognized as his: the acerbic wit and that sarcastic bite she had experienced herself. In fact, she could see a composite portrait of Robert in the elder brother and the lawyer who defended his young wife on a murder charge. Did he realize how much of himself he had written into his book?

For she had to admit it was *his* book.

She arrived next afternoon dying to know what Monclar had thought of the book, but he disappointed her by saying he would have to think about it. Like her, he had read it at one sitting and reckoned it would sell in millions, but he wanted to read it with a more analytical mind.

To her, that meant he wished to discuss the book seriously and she expected he would invite her to share the cooking in his flat.

Instead, a couple of days later, when they had finished work, he drove them to the pub near Charing Cross Hospital. When they had ordered, he surprised her by saying, 'You know, Gascoyne's still a lot in love with you.'

'Now what makes you say that?'

'It's all over his book if you've read it properly. He's drawn a marvellous portrait of you.'

'Of me! Where? I haven't seen it.'

Monclar laughed. 'That's because – as Burns said – God hasn't the giftie gi'ed us to see ourselves as others see us.'

Nancy shot him a hard look. 'So I'm the whore, the call girl on the murder charge, am I?'

'She's no whore or call girl, she's the heroine and a very good one.' Monclar poured some of the Crozes Hermitage he had ordered into their glasses and raised his to her. She left hers, pointedly, where it was. 'All right, I'm sorry, but that's the way I see it,' he went on. 'Oh, he's changed things around a bit with author's licence. You're dark instead of blonde, your eyes are dark instead of grey-blue and he's given you an inch more in height and round your anatomy. And you wouldn't have bolted when the young brother was killed – you'd have stayed and fought. But that's for the purpose of the story.' He grinned. 'It's you all right.'

'So with all those changes what does that leave? The sex scenes, the wrestling on the stable floor ...'

Monclar laughed in that way he had which often left her wondering if she should take him seriously. 'No,' he said, 'I wasn't thinking of the sex scene. They weren't written out of experience.'

'How would you know?'

There was a hard edge to her voice, something he had never heard before, and he realized he had gone too far. He pushed a hand across the table to search for hers, but it had vanished before he got there. She had her eyes, narrowed and steady, on his. 'Nancy, please forgive me. You know I didn't mean to suggest ...'

'You know very well what you meant to suggest and I know what you mean to suggest, so let's leave it as one of your hypotheses until it's proved otherwise.'

'I've said I'm sorry.'

'I heard that, and I accept your apology – but only because I'm hungry.'

At that they both laughed and, to drive the contretemps out of their minds, their rump steaks, beans and salad arrived and kept them silent for several minutes.

Monclar broke the silence. 'Reading Gascoyne set me wondering about your version of the story. You haven't mentioned it for a long time. How's it coming along?'

'It isn't. I put it through the shredder.'

'Why did you do that? The bits I read were really good.'

'Why? It didn't read like the real thing, that's why.' She paused to consider carefully what she had in mind before releasing it. 'Didn't you once have another hypothesis, that nobody can write about love if they're in love. They either do it before or after the fact, like accessories?'

'Oh, it was just a notion.' For a moment he chewed on a piece of steak, irrigating it with the Rhone wine, while he looked at her through those curious russet eyebrows of his. 'When did you start writing your romantic novels?' he asked.

'Just over three years ago. Why?'

'Would you say that perhaps it was then that you were beginning to question your love for Gascoyne and his love for you?'

She shrugged. 'I wouldn't know now. But as far as Robert was concerned, he didn't believe in love, he believed in sex, which is probably why he can write so well about both.'

'Well, he's only got half the answer in that case.'

'You believe in love, then?'

Monclar nodded. He had a faraway look in his eyes so she kept silent, leaving him to his thoughts. Finally he said:

'Let me tell you a real love story about a boy and a girl born around the same time and brought up next door to each other. They loved each other naturally; they didn't have to have love explained to them by their parents, by their school friends, by the newspaper and telly oracles. They lived their love every day and they lived for each other.

'Then the girl fell ill with some sort of curious fever, it might even have been a bad flu. She had always been delicate, highly strung, but after her illness she began to behave oddly, abnormally. She began talking off the subject, talking to herself and making up nonsensical stories and rhymes; she would lock herself away for days without eating, without changing her clothing, without washing even.

'She began to suspect that everyone around her, including the boy who loved her, was plotting to steal her soul, to murder her with a gun, a knife or poison.'

Monclar had left his food and wine untouched while talking, and now he went silent for several minutes, just looking at his plate and toying with his steak knife. Nancy felt she had to prompt him, gently.

'Was what she had a form of schizophrenia?'

'It was schizophrenia,' Monclar replied. 'You only had to look at her domineering, selfish, possessive and devious mother to realize why the daughter had become a schizophrenic. Nobody seemed able to help her. Her brothers and their families tried though in vain, for she spurned their help and turned away from them.

'The young man who loved her suffered more than anybody, for she even distrusted him and thrust him away as an enemy. When she became aggressive towards her family she had to be placed in a psychiatric hospital where they fed her drugs which kept her calm enough to be allowed home for short spells, but she was no longer anything like her old self. She was a zombie, a sleepwalker.'

Monclar raised his head to look at Nancy. 'If you remember those patients in the mental hospital. That's what she was like.'

It was as though Monclar was soliloquizing in low and very slow speech as he continued:

'It is difficult for so-called normal people to understand the mental processes of schizophrenics; their anguish, their emotions, their lopsided logic, their vocabulary, in fact their whole world – all this is hermetic to us. We and they don't even begin to understand what is happening to them.'

Nancy broke in when he looked like halting again. 'And the young man who loved her and had to watch all this – how did he take it?'

'His own anguish was in direct proportion to his love for her. It was worse for him because he loved her so much and saw that she no longer recognized him or his feelings for her. Finally, they ceased to be able to communicate with each other. The girl had a cat, a half-Persian, half-alley cat and in some way they understood each other and the young man felt himself excluded and even jealous of the cat.

'He also felt frightened, for he saw not only anguish but anger in her eyes and wondered when this would boil over. When she attacked her mother and one of her brothers, she was again placed in the mental hospital. And there she killed herself by turning her anger inwards against herself.'

'What a sad story,' Nancy said, wondering if she should try to draw Monclar out more or leave him to his thoughts. He was running his finger round the rim of his wine glass, first one way then the other, which must have symbolized some mental process though she did not know what. However, it was he who asked the question she should have put as the person who did not know that the story had a true basis.

He said, 'Do you want to know the end of the love story? What happened to the young man who loved her?'

'What did happen to him?'

'He died of a broken heart.'

Nancy tried to conceal her surprise at that statement and was at a loss on how to react or reply. Of course, Monclar was not aware that Jilly had related what she knew of the real story of Elizabeth Campbell Monclar. Or that she had seen Liz's paintings, drawings, had read her poems and other writings.

But here was a psychiatrist, twin brother of a schizophrenic girl, recounting their story in a dry, neutral, impersonal style like some case history from his notebook. He had turned it into an allegory that gave nothing away about his own connection with the family drama.

She longed to shout at him that she knew most of the truth about Liz and himself; that he as a psychiatrist must realize he was fooling himself, that he was harming himself by repressing the emotions connected with Liz's illness and death, that he was repressing the truth as well.

Why no hint that he was talking about Liz? Why no admission that her schizophrenia had decided him to practise medicine and specialize in psychiatry?

Nancy said nothing. A word out of turn might have damaged or destroyed their relationship and driven him further into the stockade he had built around that whole episode in his life.

However, that story had told her one thing: Jilly had missed some vital clue, something that had created a whole constellation of repressions and inhibitions in Monclar, something that had congealed his emotions. She realized that unless he exorcised Liz and her tragedy and his own guilt about it from his mind, he would become an emotional cripple and life would be a constant torment for him and whoever tried to share it.

chapter XXIII

Monclar had never once stated his age or seemed curious about how old she was. She looked up his date of birth in his career entry in the Medical Directory belonging to the practice and found he would be thirty-one on 16 October. What could she do to surprise him that day? She tossed up between giving him a CD set of jazz classics or a CD set of Beethoven or Debussy, his favourite classical composers; her coin landed for Beethoven and she decided to give him the CDs of the five last quartets. She'd inveigle him into his favourite pub and make the presentation there.

But she had a thought. What if Jilly, Bill and Mike, the other brother, had arranged something? Nancy decided to clear her lines before fixing anything. She rang Jilly and asked if they were doing anything for Ted's birthday.

'Ted's birthday?'

Nancy heard the catch in Jilly's breath as she repeated the two words, then something like a sigh came over the line.

'No, we're not doing anything special.'

Nancy was surprised at her attitude, but said, 'In that case, I was thinking of inviting him to dinner and giving him some of his favourite music.'

'Nancy ...' Again there was a long pause and that sigh. 'Maybe you'll think this is a bit odd, but Ted doesn't care much for birthdays.'

'I'm sorry, Jilly, I'm an idiot. I should have realized it was Liz's birthday as well. I'd better call it off.'

'It's not only Liz's birthday ...' Jilly went silent for a moment then said, 'Let me think. I have to come into town to one of the computer shops to get Bill another program for his drawing office. Maybe we could meet halfway and have coffee? There's Harrods tearoom or there's a patisserie opposite and one round the corner in Sloane Street. There's something I should have told you and didn't, and you should know about it.' They arranged to meet in the shop opposite Harrods the next day, which left Nancy twenty-four hours to speculate vainly about Jilly's secret.

When she walked into the coffee shop the next day, it took Nancy a long moment to recognize Jilly under the floral hat she wore; she was an inch taller in high-heeled shoes and had on a fashionable pale-blue, lightweight coat over a print dress. 'It's my West End uniform,' she said with a smile when Nancy apologized for her double take. They ordered coffee and Jilly picked a slice of chocolate cake, damning its hundreds of calories and saying it would settle her stomach. She drank her coffee sweet and pulled nervously at a cigarette when she had demolished the cake. To set her at ease, Nancy chit-chatted about what was happening in the practice.

'I'm so glad Ted's working with you,' Jilly said. 'You've changed him a lot.' She looked at Nancy, then said, 'I wish we had a practice like you near us. Meg, my daughter, went to our GP yesterday and came back with the news he's packing up. Now we've got to go on the books of some fund-holder who's only worried about his profit and loss and his cash flow and doesn't give a fig about hacking coughs or heart trouble.'

'Ted's a very good GP.'

'I'm sure he is,' Jilly said, then as though remembering what she had come for, she pushed her cup, saucer and plate aside, leaned over the table and whispered, 'I didn't think to tell you that day we met, but Liz killed herself on her birthday – that is, on Ted's birthday. That's why we don't want to remember it.'

Nancy took in this revelation without knowing how to digest it or what to say. 'On their birthday,' she breathed. 'What a dreadful shock that must have been to Ted.'

'Not only to Ted! To everybody. We were bringing her home for

her birthday. She felt better. Everybody was going to be there.'
Jilly's eyes moistened, she sniffed and stubbed out her half-smoked
cigarette as she relived the memory of that day just under three
years ago. 'It was as though she'd done it to spite us all, to pay us
out for something we'd done or hadn't done.'

'But Liz was ... well, not normal. She wouldn't have known
what she was doing, even what day it was.'

Jilly looked at her. 'I'd like to think that – and so would Ted. It
haunts him.'

'You mean, she knew.'

'Something like that.' Jilly nodded her head. 'At least that's
what Ted thinks. We've never discussed it openly with him, but
we've thought a lot about it since and asked one of the psychiatrists in Guy's about it. He said that schizophrenics like Liz may be
abnormal in our view of things, but they're often not mad, they
have their own logic and their own truths. And Liz might have had
her reasons for what she did.'

'And that's what Ted thinks, too?'

'I don't know for sure, but I do know it had a terrible effect on
him. It took him a year to get over it, and how he got through his
work we don't know.' She turned moist eyes on Nancy. 'Know
something? We thought he was going to commit suicide as well. He
didn't come to Liz's funeral and as far as we know, he's never been
to her grave.'

'A lot of people don't like graveyards.'

Jilly twitched her head from side to side. 'There's more to it
than that. Ted hasn't seen his mother in ten years, for he blames
her for what happened to Liz. Oh, she was and is a bitch who
hasn't a friend left in the world, but he could still have shown up
once or twice.'

'Funny, I haven't seen that side of Ted,' Nancy said. 'He couldn't
be more considerate with his patients.'

'You've got a lot to do with that,' Jilly said. 'Meeting you has
done wonders for him. You wouldn't know that he hadn't been in
Bermondsey for over two years before he brought you to meet us.
And he hadn't set foot in his old hospital until he showed you
round.' Jilly raised her head to look through the window at the

thick traffic that was crawling down both sides of Knightsbridge, but her blue eyes saw nothing of it, for she was thinking back to the events of three years before. She mused:

'I wish you'd known Ted before Liz had her breakdown. He was, well ... champagne.' She shook her head, dreamily. 'Ted could talk on anything ... classical music or Jimmy Hendrix, philosophers like Hegel, Buddhism, the latest films and plays. He could pull a whole library of facts out of his head and keep us in stitches with jokes and stories. But they say when a twin dies, he takes half the one who survives with him.'

'I'll never believe that,' Nancy said. 'I think if Ted faces up to what happened to Liz and to whatever took place the day she died, he'd rid his mind of it for good and get back to his old self.'

'I think he knows that himself.'

'So, what's stopping him?'

'I wish we knew. We've worried that question to death and we're none the wiser.'

Jilly called a taxi to take her to her computer shop while Nancy chose the top front seat of a 13 bus to take her somewhere near the practice. She went over in her mind what Jilly had disclosed about Ted and his twin sister. If ever there was a case deserving the aphorism Physician Heal Thyself this was it. But Monclar seemed to have caught himself in some sort of double bind from which only he himself could devise an escape.

She was musing on these thoughts when someone clumped along the passage between the seats and came to rest on the opposite front seat, spreading a leg imprisoned in plaster and latching his elbow crutch on to the handrail. Nancy wondered for a moment why her gaze was fixed on that leg before her mind was illuminated with several ideas at once.

Twenty years ago, this young man could have been young Ted Monclar in splints and with a wooden crutch. Who had set and splinted his leg when he fell out of the tree? She must find out.

Instead of going home, she had a sandwich in one of the cafés at Shepherd's Bush and surprised Pat by appearing during the lunch break a full hour early.

'You're in for a grisly afternoon,' Pat said. 'Your boyfriend's gone to see somebody who's coughing blood which means he'll be running late. Peter's had to go down the road to a building-site accident, and Marcia's having kittens trying to decode some of Mason's fancy drug treatments and his habit of prescribing sex stimulants.'

Nancy took the medical directories, recent copies of the medical journals and the Yellow Pages into Monclar's consulting room and spent half an hour searching through them and making calls. She found what she was seeking and had relayed Pat before Monclar returned from his emergency call.

Next morning, Nancy took her place in the waiting room of Dr Richard Benson's surgery at the end of Tooley Road in Bermondsey. She had a good hour and a half to wait, for Dr Benson spent about twenty minutes with each patient and obviously had never heard of computers, keeping the records in his own hand in an ordinary filing cabinet.

Eventually her turn came and she found herself confronting an elderly man, bald on top, greying at the sides with a moustache and horn-rimmed glasses behind which faded blue eyes looked at her.

As he went to put her name on a card, Nancy said, 'Excuse me, Dr Benson, I'm not a patient. I came to ask you a few questions.'

'Not travelling for a drug firm, are you?' Dr Benson had a warm, vibrant voice with a slight Cockney accent.

'No, nothing like that. I wondered if you looked after the Monclar family.'

'Yes, I still do – those that are left in the area.'

'Do you remember Edward Monclar, the twin who broke a leg? I think you set it.'

'The one that became a doctor. Went through Guy's or Thomas's medical school then went into mental health. He had a sister who killed herself. That the one?'

'That's him. He's looking for a practice and heard you were giving up and selling this one.'

'I am. But why doesn't he come himself?'

'Well, it's like this. He wondered if I'd like the area and the flat that goes with the practice.' She caught Dr Benson looking her up and down and smiling at the idea of sending a woman to judge a medical practice on whether she would like the flat above it.

'Are you his wife?'

'Well ... that is, not yet.'

'So, it depends on the flat. You go with the flat, and he takes your word on both, is that it?'

'In a way, yes.'

Dr Benson said if she cared to wait until he had finished his morning surgery, he would let her have a look at the flat.

When his last patient had gone, he came and escorted Nancy through the surgery and upstairs to the flat. He apologized for its state; his wife had died two years ago and he only had a daily cleaner and made his own meals.

Nancy looked at the large living room, the three bedrooms, kitchen and bathroom; it had a sense of spaciousness and a wonderful view looking out over the Thames to the Tower of London and upriver to London Bridge. It also sat on the edge of a small park running down to the river, and had a walled garden twenty yards by ten.

'I'm afraid I've let the garden run to seed a bit,' Dr Benson said, pointing to the unkempt lawn and the rose bushes which were reverting to briars.

He let her wander round the flat, the surgery, the garden and when she had finished, he asked, 'Well, do you like it?'

'Yes, very much.' She noticed his face crease into a smile and his eyes twinkle. 'I think it may be what Dr Monclar is looking for,' she said.

'I'm glad. It's an interesting practice, a bit of a mixed bag, but interesting. Anyway, it's nice to know somebody will take it on. I'd hate to think they'd pull it down and build offices, or turn it into a video porn shop.'

At Borough-Hall she handed in her name and they rang to confirm her appointment with the chief psychiatrist, Dr Rhys-Evans, before conducting her along the corridor of the admin wing to an office overlooking the grounds and gardens of the hospital and asking her to wait.

Outside, patients were weeding the rose beds, thinning out lilies and irises and planting pansies and polyanthuses under supervision; a handful of them in hospital blues were wandering over the lawns criss-crossing or going round in circles aimlessly and without appearing to notice each other.

'Ah yes, I remember you.' Rhys-Evans had joined her at the window before she became aware he was in the room. Do all the medical staff move like stalking tigers in this place? she wondered. He offered her a seat, then said, 'Now what's the problem about Ted Monclar that you were trying to explain over the phone?'

'You know Dr Monclar well, don't you?'

Rhys-Evans nodded. 'I was in charge of the schizophrenic wards when he did his DPM. One of the finest postgraduates we ever had here. Pity we couldn't keep him, but you know the reason why.'

While he talked, Rhys-Evans doodled with coloured pencils and she could almost follow the tortuous workings of his mind in those whorls and parabolas and squiggles which he wrought into something like a Jackson Pollock painting. But this mannerism did not distract her like his Welsh voice, which lilted along in what seemed to her like three-four time and covered a range from baritone to contralto. It was like operatic recitative. Into the bargain, he was pedantic.

'Did Dr Monclar spell out his reasons for leaving?'

'No, not in so many words. But they were the reasons that brought him here in the first place. His sister was admitted as a schizophrenic patient and he thought – perhaps erroneously – that he could do more for her by having himself attached to her ward. And she killed herself.'

'You know Dr Monclar is still very much affected by his sister's death.'

'Well, it was a traumatic event which might well have precipitated a personality crisis in someone less robust mentally than Ted Monclar.'

'But it has left a mark,' Nancy said. 'And I wondered if we might help him to come to terms with his sister's suicide and resolve his own problem.'

'Of course I would like to – but how?' He was filling in the whorls and squiggles in blue pencil as he put the question.

Nancy thought for a moment. She had to enlist this Welshman's complicity in a stratagem she had devised, but she must try to pander to his vanity by conveying the idea that it was he who was fording the key to Monclar's problem.

'I wondered why he suddenly brought me here a few weeks ago – as though he might be seeking some sort of help.'

Rhys-Evans put that question in the form of five blue convoluted lines into his doodle which now assumed the aspect of a gigantic reptilian tussle between adders, vipers, anacondas, boa constrictors, mambas and cobras.

'Yes, I agree. I thought it odd myself after three years' absence, and on reflection I adjudged it a positive sign.'

'I wanted to ask you about the date Liz Monclar committed suicide. It was her birthday – their birthday. What do you think was the significance of that date?'

He added a couple of rattlesnakes in greens and purples and stared at the result. 'It had profound significance,' he said.

'Even in a schizophrenic who doesn't think or behave in any way like a normal person?'

'What is normality?' Rhys-Evans's voice went curving upwards as he uttered the question and his hand halted over the doodle. 'Liz Monclar was making a statement by committing suicide. An unconscious statement but no less meaningful for that. What that statement was we may never know exactly.'

'But if Dr Monclar had some inkling of what it meant....'

'If he did, he kept it to himself and I have never discussed Liz's suicide with him.'

He struck his thickest black pencil through the doodle several times as though cancelling it, then said, 'He knew his sister better than anyone, so he might have an insight into what her gesture meant. After all, they were twins.'

Nancy pounced on that comment. 'You were there on the ward that morning, Dr Rhys-Evans, weren't you?'

'Yes, I was on the second-floor wards.' He was on a fresh sheet, doodling this time in geometrical patterns, cubes, pyramids, triangles, squares and – was this meaningful? – an ogival shape like a rocket or shell. He hesitated then sighed as if undecided about what to say. 'Ted and Liz Monclar were in one of the interview rooms off the corridor leading to the ward.'

'You could hear them, then?'

'Clearly.' He was drawing something like the Eiffel Tower. 'They sounded as though they were quarrelling.'

'Violently?'

Rhys-Evans shrugged. 'You know how mental patients are – they shout and scream and rant and it may mean much, or nothing.'

'But this time it did mean something.'

'Unfortunately.' He nodded. 'Liz struck Ted so hard that he could not prevent her from running along the corridor and upstairs to the third floor. By the time he had recovered and pursued her, she had levered the window open and jumped.'

'She struck him! What with?'

'A broom handle.'

'Was he badly hurt?'

'He had a bruise on his temple and was bleeding from another blow on his cheek.' Rhys-Evans tapped his pencil on the desk. 'Those bruises healed.'

'His mental scars didn't – is that what you mean?'

'I fear so. They were twins, you see, and twins are not only genetically linked but often feel their actual destinies are linked, which may or may not be the case. Yet, there is no doubt many twins feel the loss of their brother or sister is the loss of part of themselves, and they think it diminishes them.'

Nancy had reached the point with this hair-splitting man where she had to weigh her proposition very carefully in case he took fright and refused to collaborate. 'Liz Monclar had two very good friends here, who were also Ted's friends, didn't she?'

'You mean Maud and Anna, who are still on the schizophrenic ward?' When Nancy nodded, he went on, 'Maud's been here for twelve years and Anna for just over ten. What about them?'

'Well, you know Liz wrote poetry and painted and drew things. I wondered if she had left anything with Maud and Anna.'

'No.' Rhys-Evans shook his head and when he did, she noticed there was a slight fall of dandruff on his white coat. 'If she had, one of the nurses would have picked it up.'

'But she might have,' Nancy persisted. 'They shared a room on and off for five years.'

She saw she had sent him back to reptiles, writhing and twisting across his memo pad, as much an indication of his confused mind as the chaotic wanderings of the patients outside. 'I'm not quite with you there,' he said, finally.

Nancy took the plunge. 'Dr Rhys-Evans, would you be prepared to tell the whitest of white lies if it helped Ted Monclar to recover his peace of mind, to get rid of his guilt about his twin sister's death and the fear and anxiety which is preventing him from fulfilling himself?'

'A white lie! What sort of white lie?' Now Rhys-Evans was giving her his full attention, his eyes behind his rimless glasses riveted on the large envelope Nancy had conjured from her shoulder bag. She slid it across his desk.

'They're Liz's poems, drawings and a cassette with a message she recorded.' She explained how she had come by them and the fact that Monclar had never seen them or even knew they existed. 'Perhaps you could listen to what she says on the cassette, look at the drawings and read the main poems and you'll guess what I'm trying to suggest.' No psychiatrist could have resisted opening that envelope to unravel something of the mind of a mental patient. Rhys Evans pulled out the papers, ran an eye over the drawings and took time to read some of the poems. 'These are very revealing,' he murmured in that up-and-down voice. 'I wish Ted had known about them either before or after it happened.'

'But he can know now,' Nancy said. 'If he were told they'd just been discovered in Maud's or Anna's belongings, that they'd hidden them waiting for Liz's return, that they didn't know how important they were ...' Nancy paused to gauge his attitude and when she observed that he did not appear hostile to the suggestion, she pushed her point home.

'Now, if he were told about the discovery of these papers and cassette and invited to come and have a look at Liz's creations, even on 16 October ...'

'The anniversary of Liz's death?'

Nancy nodded, adding, 'And their birthday.'

'It's risky.' Rhys-Evans took off his glasses to breathe on them and polish the lenses with a red silk handkerchief. 'What if it had the opposite effect and instead of releasing his repressed emotions about his sister's death, it triggered off a mental crisis in him?'

'Shouldn't we let Ted Monclar make that decision for himself?' Nancy said. 'He has a right to see what Liz wanted him to see and hear. And where better than his old hospital where he'd be among friends and colleagues?'

'Can you leave all this with me and let me think about it for an hour or two?' Rhys-Evans asked.

Nancy nodded her agreement. She fixed an appointment with him for six o'clock, realizing he would probably consult Wingfield, the medical superintendent, and other psychiatrists before carrying out what might be a harmful experiment on a former medical officer of the institution.

Nancy had one more visit in the district – Liz Monclar's grave in St Xavier's churchyard. She thought of calling on Jilly but decided against this and had tea instead in a rundown café near the water-front.

When she returned to Rhys-Evans's office, he had Wingfield and one other staff member with him. Rhys-Evans did the talking.

'We have looked at the papers and listened to the tape relating to Elizabeth Monclar's death and the hospital records about her stay here. We have asked ourselves two main questions: Firstly, what would Dr Monclar have done faced with the risks to a patient of reliving the sort of mental trauma he had himself suffered? We feel he would have accepted the risk. Secondly, and this question follows from the first one? Would Dr Monclar be prepared to accept the sort of risks attached to this form of cathartic treatment? We believe his answer would be yes.'

Nancy hid her relief. She thanked the doctors and asked them to make whatever arrangements they pleased. Yet, as she walked through the grounds and that grim iron gate, she had her own misgivings about what amounted to a reconstruction of Liz's suicide in Monclar's mind.

She felt guilty herself.

chapter XXIV

A couple of days later, Nancy heard Rhys-Evans's voice on the phone just after she came on duty and she and Pat were changing shifts. She connected him with Monclar and, although she would dearly have liked to know what was said, she drew the line at eavesdropping.

Both doctors conversed for about ten minutes then, a few seconds after the line cleared, Monclar emerged from his consulting room and asked them to hand over his two remaining patients to the Clarkes. He beckoned Nancy into his consulting room and shut the door behind them. He sat her down on one of the chairs his patients used while he moved round behind his desk.

'Remember that day I took you to Borough-Hall, the mental hospital I worked in for two years?' She nodded. 'Remember the two women, Maud and Anna, who stopped me and asked about Liz, and you asked who Liz was?'

'Yes, Ted, I remember.'

'My twin sister.'

Nancy tried to sound surprised. 'Was she in the hospital?'

'Liz was a patient. She was schizophrenic like Maud and Anna. Only worse. Much worse. She committed suicide about three years ago in the hospital.'

'Was that while you were working there?'

'Yes.' Monclar rose and walked to the window to gaze out at the terraced houses behind their block. He spoke without turning to look at her, in a rough whisper. 'That was Rhys-Evans, the chief psychiatrist. You met him. They've found some drawings and writings Liz left, and a cassette with her voice on it. Maud and Anna either didn't know they were left in their things, or hid them. Now they want me to go and pick them up.'

'Are they sure they're Liz's?'

'No doubt. I gave Liz a small tape machine a month or two before she died and it's the same sort of cassette. Anyway, Rhys-Evans and others know her voice well.'

When he fell silent, Nancy said, 'Was this the boy and girl love story you told me the other week?'

'Yes. I should have told you the true story, months ago, but I couldn't.'

'That day you took me to Borough-Hall – you were trying to tell me then?'

'I was, but I was blocked. I've always been blocked about Liz ... when she was alive, and now when she's dead.'

'Isn't that a good reason for looking at what she has said and written?'

Monclar was now pacing back and forth in the small room, muttering that Rhys-Evans had left the decision to him whether he wanted to come to the hospital and study what they had found. Suddenly he stopped and looked at her. 'I don't know if I should go or not. I'm scared of what I'll see and hear.'

'What's there to be scared of now?'

'I can't explain ... but sometimes with schizophrenics like Liz you get pure truthfulness, pure emotion and it can bring every-thing back, and it can hurt.'

'But you tried to help Liz, you never did her any harm.'

'No, I loved her, and still do.'

'Then go, Ted.' She picked up his phone and handed it to him. For a moment he hesitated then put his index finger on the switch to clear the line while he looked at her.

'Nancy, darling, will you come with me?'

'I was going to suggest it,' she said, trying to keep her voice level and stop her heart from beating too hard. 'Now ring and tell him we'll go together.'

A few minutes after she had returned to her office, he called on the inside line to tell her he had arranged to go to Borough-Hall the following Friday morning. Nancy had no need to look at her diary for the date since she had already marked it there and on her computer.

It was 16 October. His birthday and Liz's. And the day she died three years ago. Why hadn't he mentioned it? Had he cancelled even the conscious memory of his own birthday after her death. Why? Maybe because his birthday reminded him of watching her kill herself. He seemed absolutely unaware of the anniversary, and this frightened her. Especially when she went back in her mind to the risks Rhys-Evans had cited in this form of psychiatric catharsis.

What if Monclar were as mentally fragile as his twin sister?

What if recapitulating the traumatic events of three years ago, listening to that dead voice and reading those poems pushed him over the edge?

Her worry showed. Pat had finished her work and was bustling about collecting her shopping and clothes to go off duty. 'Something's eating you, isn't it?'

'No, just tired.'

'And he's the same.' Pat pointed to Monclar's door. 'He looks as though he's been on the tiles all night or up to the eyeballs in Valium or something similar. What's up with you both? Lovelorn? Why don't you get your act together?'

'We're trying, Pat.'

Pat picked up her copy of the *Mail* which she bought every morning then stopped, struck by a thought. 'I hope you're not going to miss out all along the line,' she murmured.

'And what does that mean?'

'Well, you might have left the marital nest a bit too soon,' Pat said. 'Just as the male bird was going to feather it with beautiful gold plumage.' She flipped through her paper to an inside page. 'Get an eyeful of that.'

Nancy stared at the photograph and caption taking up almost half a page. Gascoyne was standing with half a dozen women, the jury of the Feminist Writers' Guild who had voted *Lifelines* their book of the year a few weeks after its publication. Holding up a copy of the book in one hand and a glass of champagne in the other,

Gascoyne was wearing what she knew to be his watch-the-birdie smile, something between a grin and a grimace. As the hero of the event, he did not look all that happy.

Two faces to his left and behind him Nancy caught sight of another familiar face, this one with a smile spilling over its sides. Anne Howells. She skimmed the extensive caption extolling the story and the writing and listing the amount of money it had earned and would earn from worldwide sales and rights.

When she had finished reading, Pat looked at her. 'Your Midas touch deserted you there, m'dear, didn't it?'

'With me, Pat, it's the reverse Midas touch – don't you know, I turn gold into dross or worse.'

Pat pointed to Anne Howells' face in the background. 'Isn't that the opera and centre-court ticket.'

'That's her.'

'Well, her tickets certainly came up, and now they've made it they can live happily ever after.' Pat picked up her shoulder bag, stuffed the paper into it, climbed into her coat and made for the door. 'Don't work him too hard,' she said, thumbing at Monclar's door, 'Leave him a bit of adrenaline for tonight.'

Poor Pat. Sex and money were the twin pillars of her personal utopia. She would never have raised a titter at the irony of Gascoyne making a fortune from a book conceived and begun by his wife, Nancy, alias Dorothy Armour, the romantic novelist. On the contrary, she would have pitied and condemned Nancy for an idiot who had drawn the winning number and given it away; she would have shouted false pretences, piracy, plagiarism and fought a running battle in Chancery. Poor Pat.

She turned Pat's advice inside out; instead of easing Monclar's burden she plied him with Mason's patients as well as his own to keep his hands and mind occupied and prevent him from thinking about his appointment at Borough-Hall.

But those three days to Friday seemed to her like a month of wet Sundays, and her mind envisaged every sort of evil that might flow from her insistence on confronting Monclar with that cassette and those papers.

On Thursday evening she even thought of ringing him to plead illness and allowing him to make the trip to Bermondsey alone. She ruled that out as cowardice, disloyalty to him and a form of betrayal, since she had planned the whole thing.

When he came to pick her up on Friday morning, she small-talked as they drove to try to appear unconcerned and put him at ease. But as they went through the gates he was so nervous, uptight, that she feared he might dent somebody's coachwork parking in the courtyard.

Rhys-Evans and Wingfield came to greet them and escort them to the chief psychiatrist's office where they were served coffee and biscuits. Monclar ate and drank nothing but kept his eyes on the large, buff envelope lying on Rhys-Evans's desk; they could see he was anxious to begin.

Rhys-Evans lied convincingly as he explained how they had come to possess the papers and cassette which might even have been hidden by Liz Monclar before she took her life. He did not believe Maud and Anna had wilfully concealed the material; they probably expected Liz to return and collect it one day. When he had finished speaking, Rhys-Evans pushed the package across his desk.

'Perhaps you'd like to look, Ted, and verify that it's something Liz wrote and drew and recorded.'

Nancy noticed Monclar's hands tremble slightly as he opened the envelope and pulled out the documents, the drawings, the loose leaves on which Liz had written her poems. He glanced at them.

'Yes, these were written by Liz,' he said.

Pulling out the small cassette, he looked closely at it, nodding. 'It's the type of thing I gave her,' he murmured.

Rhys-Evans had begun to cover his memo pad with a series of rings, joining them together as though wondering where they and he were heading. Finally he looked up. 'Ted, if you would like to choose somewhere quiet and study these papers and listen to the cassette you know your way around and you can pick your spot among the interview rooms.' He produced a small, hand-held tape recorder and slid this across the desk. 'You can use this to listen to the tape.'

Wingfield cut in. 'Perhaps Ted might want to take the material home and listen to it when he feels the moment's right.'

Monclar looked at both of them. Even as psychiatrists, neither of them understood how he felt at the sight of Liz's thin, spidery scribble or the ink smudges she invariably left on the paper; no one could feel the knot that was gathering and expanding in his chest, threatening to choke him. But maybe someone realized what he was suffering, the turmoil in his heart and mind. He felt Nancy's hand search for his own and press it. He heard his own voice, hollow and distant, say to those two neutral faces across the desk: 'The right moment has gone, the right moment to read my sister's words and listen to her voice was before she decided to die, when her thoughts meant something.' Nancy took the papers and cassette from his hand.

'Ted darling, they mean something now. Let's go and listen to them together.'

Rhys-Evans and Wingfield led the way to one of the interview rooms off the schizophrenic ward where Liz had lived for nearly five years on and off. White walls, tiled floor, a table and two chairs, a bench. Grey daylight filtered through frosted glass. Rhys-Evans handed Nancy the tape recorder and whispered, 'We're next door if you need us.'

If she needed them! What did they think, that Monclar might duplicate Liz's suicide, run for the highest window and jump?

If Monclar was conscious of the fact that this was one of the rooms where he and Liz had their final meeting, he did not show it. He had spread the papers on the table and was scanning them. Picking up the poems, he read them slowly, line by line, as though transfixed by her words. He read the poem about Timothy, the alley-cat, twice, his eyes filming over with tears as they moved over the lines. He tried to say something but merely shook his head and put down the poem.

Nancy sat beside him on the bench. She had clipped the cassette into the recorder and waited for him to signal that he had finished with the poems and drawings. She felt tense herself, for she had listened several times to the tape and was moved to tears by it. What effect might that dead voice and what it said have on her twin brother? When finally he pushed the papers away, she held up the tape recorder. 'Do you want to listen to this now?' she asked, and he nodded. She pressed the PLAY button. His hand sought hers and gripped it so tightly that she winced as the tape hissed then they heard Liz's voice, light and pitched high.

> Hallo Teddy, hallo my beloved brother, Teddy. My cell-mate before we were born, my soul-mate always, my sole and only mate ... by the time they find my voice here and you may hear it, I shall be gone whence travellers do return never, although parting from you is the deepest sorrow. As you can hear, I mix things up ... but sometimes I'm lucid and know ... and sometimes I'm lost in my own mind-speak ... but you know what I mean for you know what I am as well as I know myself ...

Liz's thin, tremulous voice sank to a whisper at times so that Nancy had to strain to catch the words. At the same time, she was observing Monclar, who had put an elbow on the table and was holding his head in his hand and making noises in his throat. When she asked if she should stop the tape he shook his head.

> One thing I'm always lucid about is my love for you. I love you, and I know no one could ever have loved me as you have loved me. You understood the cries from my heart and my mind and some of them were for you. For I could read my own anguish in your eyes and that hurt me more than I could tell you. [Long pause] How can I start to tell you what hell is like. Hell is where you are not ... it's where I go when I no longer see you or know you. Then life is hell, life is a knife turned in the heart, life is useless strife ... compared with that life, paradise is a black hole.

At this point, Liz's voice was a whisper and she began to mumble, repeat herself and utter nonsensical sounds and put together rhymes that meant nothing. For a full minute, the tape ran silent except for a slight hiss, as though Liz had lost the thread or forgotten to switch off. But after this lapse, her voice came through again:

Borough-Hall this bleak hole pushed me towards the black hole
and I asked myself what stopped me from throwing myself head-
first into it once and forever. You stopped me, Teddy my darling.
I clung to you as that half of myself that was alive. You know, I
never thought of myself as a whole being, just one half of us.
Even in my worst moments when I wanted to end everything,
your love kept me here. No one could have loved me as you have
loved me. I saw my own face in your face for so long that I drew
back from the black hole lest I drew you into it with me.

Teddy, you always said I was a poet and maybe I am. I was
thinking of you when I wrote this:

Time is as time was as time will be
Even when the world is not and we are naught,
I was here when the world was young,
When life's first whisper kindled the cold ash
And the sun warmed it into me.
I will be here when the glow dies
And the light turns again to dust.
Where will time be then?
Can I bid it stand still for me?
Will my voice be stilled,
Will there be light
Or eternal night?
Does love survive death?
If I could ask him who is flesh of my flesh ...
But I have this one dread:
What of Ted when I am dead?
Without him near I would not want to live,
Without me near would he survive?
If he said that dead I would be within him,
I would sacrifice my death for him.

Abruptly, Monclar reached over and grabbed the small tape
machine and switched it off. Then, as though to erase everything,
he hurled it against the wall and watched its plastic case break
apart. He was sobbing without restraint.

He turned to Nancy, put his arms round her, drew her into him and held her so tight against his heaving chest she thought he would break her ribs. She could feel his heart beating as his chest rose and fell. 'Forgive me, Liz,' he sobbed, repeating the three words over and over again.

Nancy held on until the sobbing and heaving gradually stopped.

Monclar pulled away to look at her, then said, 'Why didn't I see in time, why didn't I know, why didn't I understand?'

Nancy said nothing but found a handkerchief and handed it to him, and he wiped his eyes. 'Let's get out of this place,' he said, hoisting her to her feet and making for the door.

'What about these?' she asked, indicating the papers and the cassette.

He gathered the papers together and she retrieved the broken tape recorder and salvaged the cassette which she put in her bag.

At the door, instead of turning right and heading for the admin block and Rhys-Evans's office, Monclar hesitated then strode left along the corridor. Nancy ran after him wondering where he was going before it dawned on her. He was taking the same path that Liz had that day three years ago when she had struck him and escaped.

'Ted, stop!' she shouted.

But he paid no heed. He had reached the stairs leading to the third floor. There, he hesitated for a moment and she saw him climb them slowly, one by one. She followed, still calling to him to halt and come back. But on he went, through the door into the third-floor corridor.

When Nancy got there, he had already reached one of the windows. She tried to shout, 'Ted, don't!' but the words choked in her throat. She could only stand and watch as he levered the window open and thrust his head and half his body outside. She held her breath, praying he would not jump. For several moments he hung there looking down then slowly pulled back and stood by the window, still gazing at the spot where his sister had fallen. Suddenly, he banged the window shut so hard that the glass shivered in its frame.

He turned and noticed Nancy standing by the door holding on to the jamb. He walked rather unsteadily towards her and she could see that he had been reliving those moments of three years ago that had transformed his life; his eyes still mirrored his thoughts and emotions of those last tragic seconds of Liz's life. He had looked over the brink but drawn back in time.

She noticed his eyes and face change as he came close to her. He seized and hugged her. He whispered in her ear.

'Nancy, there's something I've always been meaning to tell you and I never could.'

'What was that?'

'I love you.'

She kissed him and he kissed her in return. She whispered in his ear. 'There, you've finally said it, and it wasn't difficult.'

'Because it's the truth and the truth is never difficult.'

'But Ted, you didn't need to – I mean, say it. I knew long before you did that you loved me. You didn't have to tell me.'

He pushed her away, gently, to look at her then kissed and hugged her before beckoning towards the stairs. 'We've finished here,' he said taking her hand and leading her downstairs and along to the admin building where they met and thanked Rhys-Evans and Wingfield. Evidently they realized what had happened, for they made no comment but walked to the car with Monclar and Nancy and said goodbye.

Monclar drove out of the hospital without a backward glance. Instead of turning west along the river towards the town and their practice, he pointed the car at the Thames, halting by the riverside between London Bridge and Tower Bridge.

For long moments Monclar gazed at the river lying under a mist which the autumn sun had not skimmed off even that late in the morning. When he spoke, he did not turn to look at her, and his voice only just carried to her ear.

'I've never told anybody what happened that day, and I even tried to black it out of my mind and couldn't,' he said, then continued. 'Liz you must realize was a paranoid schizophrenic who lived in her own delusional world seeing enemies and rivals and villains everywhere and projecting her aggression on to other people who, she then thought, threatened her.

'That morning she was all mixed up in her head. I tried to play along with her, to enter into her mental framework, but it was useless. I had become one of the enemies. She accused me of keeping her in the hospital, of stifling her talent, even of poisoning her. I could see the hate in her face, but I was not prepared for the way she attacked me with her fists then with a broom handle.

'Before I could stop her she had run upstairs and thrown herself out of that window on the third-floor corridor. It left me feeling that she hated me and had transformed that hatred for me into her suicide act.'

'But doesn't that type of schizophrenic believe they're being attacked when in fact they're doing the attacking?'

'Yes, and that's what Liz was doing. But I still couldn't get it out of my mind that she hated me.'

'Well, now you know she loved you, she loved you enough to sacrifice herself.'

Monclar nodded. For a while he stayed silent before saying, 'There was another thing that scared me – Liz and I were twins and there's a genetic factor in mental illness, especially schizophrenia. There's also a greater risk that the surviving twin will follow the example of the one who has committed suicide.'

Monclar was telling her why he had always recoiled from a deeper relationship with her. He was scared of schizoid and suicidal tendencies; he was also explaining why he had tested his nerve and his resolve by walking to the window from which Liz jumped and opening it.

'Hadn't we better get back to the practice?' he said, turning the ignition key and starting the engine.

She plucked at his sleeve. 'That way,' she said, pointing east down the river. 'I'm hungry and there's an olde-worlde restaurant on the dockside that does everything I like and don't make for myself – bubble and squeak, steak and kidney pie, ditto pudding, roast beef and Yorkshire pudding, Lancashire hotpot, cockaleekie soup, Irish stew, the lot.'

'How do you know about it?'

'I ate there the other day?'

'Oh! Then I'll ring and say we'll be late.'

'Stop worrying about the halt and the lame and the hacking coughs and the postnasal drips at Shepherd's Bush. I've told Pat to do an extra stint and hand over your patients to the Clarkes.'

'So you've fixed for us to have the afternoon off,' he said, grinning.

'Well, yes, when we've seen the flat.'

'What flat?'

'The flat I want you to see,' she said, and he realized she was teasing him with his own verbal ploy.

'This flat you want me to see – where and what is it?'

'Well, it's a part of our script that I took the liberty of writing myself.'

'And we play it out in this flat, is that it?'

'That's it. About the flat, it's a splendid flat with three bedrooms which should be enough, a big living room, a study, two bathrooms, late Victorian, brick-built, freehold. It overlooks Curtis Park and has a great view of the Thames bridges, the tower, there's a garden the size of a tennis court.'

'Sounds fine to me.'

'There's a snag.'

'There's always a snag. Is it a big snag?'

'No, not really. You see, he won't sell the flat without the medical practice.'

'What medical practice, for God's sake?'

'Dr Benson's practice – he's giving it up.'

'You mean old Richard Benson.'

'There's only one in Bermondsey – the one who set your broken leg when you fell out of the tree.'

'Well, I'm damned.' He turned to stare at her, wondering what next. 'I know that flat and the practice.'

'Oh, I know it's not much of a practice – a couple of thousand patients.' She turned to him. 'There's something else.'

'I thought there must be. What is it?'

'He'd like to sell it to a couple,' she said, embroidering a little.

'Well, aren't we a couple?'

'I think so.' She looked at him. 'It's a long way from the pinstriped reaches of Harley Street and the London Clinic.'

Monclar shot her a quizzical look, then burst out laughing.

'You seem to have fixed everything. Unless there's something you've fixed in secret and forgotten to tell me about.'

'No, darling, nothing. Anyway, I think we've had enough secrets for one day, don't you?'

Monclar nodded, then set the car in motion but headed upriver, away from the restaurant.

'It's the other way,' she commented.

He kept going.

'Did you put a deposit on the flat and the practice?' he asked.

When she shook her head, he said, 'Well, let's go and do that before old Benson finds himself another couple and sells them our place.'